KATHERINE GARBERA

USA Today bestselling author Katherine Garbera is a two-time Maggie winner who has written more than 60 books. A Florida native who grew up to travel the globe, Katherine now makes her home in the Midlands of the UK with her husband, two children and a very spoiled miniature dachshund. Visit her on the web at www.katherincgarbcra.com, connect with her on Facebook and follow her on Twitter @katheringarbera.

Eye Candy

KATHERINE GARBERA

Harper*Impulse* an imprint of
HarperCollins*Publishers* Ltd
1 London Bridge Street
London SE1 9GF

www.harpercollins.co.uk

A Paperback Original 2015

First published in Great Britain in ebook format by Harper*Impulse* 2015

A catalogue record for this book is
available from the British Library

ISBN: 9780008158088

Automatically produced by Atomik ePublisher from Easypress

Printed and bound in Great Britain

This one is for my sweet Rob for helping reaffirm my belief in true love and happily-ever-after.

Chapter 1

"Busted!" Garrett Mulligan said in a strong voice.

He liked the view from where he stood. Long legs encased in black hose with a seam running straight down the back. Left leg slightly bent as she shifted off balance and tried to jimmy open the ground-floor window. As a man he could stand here all night, especially as she bent forward and the hem of her tiny skirt rose, revealing the fact that she was wearing hose and not stockings. As a police officer he couldn't just let her break into his neighbor's brownstone.

It was early January, crisp and cool, as the snow from the last storm had already melted.

Instead of jumping she giggled. This party girl had had a little too much to drink tonight. Nothing he couldn't handle. Even with his busted foot and his suspension from the force he was still one of New York's finest.

"NYPD, miss, hands where I can see them," he said.

She giggled again.

"Breaking and entering is a serious matter," he said calmly, stepping forward and putting his hand on the small of her back to make her realize he wasn't going away. Her waist was tiny as his hand almost spanned her entire back. "Miss?"

"I'm not breaking the law. I live here," she said amongst her giggles.

"Hayley?"

"Yes, Officer Hottie."

"Step out into the light," he said.

He took two steps back and she did the same. She tipped her head to the side and smiled at him as she stopped in the circle of light provided by a street lamp.

She rolled her eyes and did a little pirouette. "Satisfied?"

"Not even close," he said, stepping closer to her and taking her hand, but he recognized her smile and now that she'd stopped giggling she sounded just like his neighbor. "I should be putting you in handcuffs and taking you down to the station."

She batted her eyelashes at him. "Is that really what you want to do?"

"It's what I should do," he said, but the images in his head were hot and naughty. Not at all what a cop on probation should be thinking of.

"Because I'm a bad girl?" she asked in a husky voice.

This playful, sexy version of his neighbor intrigued him. It was the balm he needed after spending the night with his family and once again declining to leave the NYPD.

Not even close to being really wicked, he thought. It was the smile that convinced him it was Hayley. Even behind her big glasses that smile had been a knockout and it still was.

"Why are you breaking into your own place?" he asked, crossing his arms over his chest.

"I lost my keys," she said, gesturing to her clutch handbag, which lay open on the ground with its contents spilling out.

He looked closer and saw that her bag was on a subway grate. Her keys were gone forever. "And why didn't you just call a friend?"

She started giggling again. Clearly she'd been out partying, but even so, bending over to retrieve her clutch shouldn't have been a problem.

"My skirt," she said, gesturing to it.

Her hand fluttered to the hem of the skirt, briefly touched it,

2

and then balled into a fist. He suspected she'd wanted to tug at the bottom of it. It was short. He took his time looking at her long legs and when he finally brought his gaze to her face, noticed her lips were parted as she stared at him.

"Ah, I see the problem..."

"Besides, who was I going to call at midnight?" she asked. She tucked her hair behind her ear and glanced up at the night sky.

"Me," he said.

"You? You're all into me right now, but yesterday you didn't even offer to hold one of my grocery bags when I was juggling them and my keys."

He hadn't even noticed her yesterday but he had been pre-occupied with the news that he'd be spending at least six more weeks in the ankle cast and on leave. "I'm noticing now."

"What's it say about you, Hottie, that you only notice me when I'm breaking the law?" she asked, that teasing note back in her voice.

"My name's Garrett—not Hottie," he said, ignoring her very accurate observation.

"I notice you ignored my question," she said with a little pout. "No matter. Now that you're here, would you help me out?"

"How?" he asked.

"Could you pick up my iPhone? I Googled how to break into an apartment. I think I might be able to make this work."

He shook his head. Bending down, he scooped up her purse and her phone. "No, I'm not going to help you break in. Besides you'd trigger the alarm and I don't think you want that."

"You're right. So what are we going to do? I can't hang out here all night."

She stood there in the moonlight in her "bad girl" clothes but her sweet girl-next-door attitude. And he was a cop even if he was on leave. He'd taken an oath to protect and serve.

He wanted to protect her and serve her.

Damn. He should walk away. She wasn't his problem.

But he knew he wouldn't. He'd never been able to resist a damsel in distress.

"You can sleep at my place and call a locksmith in the morning."

"Can't you break into my place for me?" she asked in that quizzical way of hers.

"Not with this bum foot," he said. "What is with you and breaking the law?"

"I'm changing," she said.

"Okay, change tomorrow. Let's go." Lord knew he'd become a master of pushing change off. He had mastered it with hours on the upper-body weight machines.

"I don't know if I should stay at your place," she said as he held his hand out to her.

"Why not? Don't you trust me to keep my hands to myself?" he asked.

She gave him a smoldering look from under her lashes. Her pixie haircut made her features seem almost ethereal. She was temptation incarnate and there was something in her eyes that said she knew it.

"No, I don't trust myself."

***

Honesty was something she'd never compromised on and it had gotten her into hot water before. But tonight it seemed she could handle anything. She glanced up at the stars littering the sky.

"I feel so…free," she said.

"You wouldn't feel that way behind bars," Garrett said.

She pouted at him. He was cute and sort of flirty, but then he'd remember himself and get all cop again.

"You already said you weren't taking me to jail," she reminded him.

"That's correct. Come on, bad girl. Let's get you off the street," he said, reaching for her elbow.

He was a leader, she thought. Even with his foot in a cast he took charge. He was steadier with an injured limb than she was in her heels. But most of that was down to confidence and she finally understood what Cici had been trying to say when she'd told her to own the outfit.

Garrett owned the street and everything around him. He moved like he knew his place in the world—even injured.

"You seem pretty steady given your injury…what happened by the way?"

"I was shot," he said.

"Were you scared?" she asked, and then realized that was probably a stupid question. "Of course you were, right?"

"No. I wasn't scared," he said, bringing her attention back to those electric-gray eyes of his. "I was pissed. They'd ambushed me and Hector. He was down and I was after the perp on foot when I got shot too."

"Femur?"

"Yeah, how'd you know that? No offense, but you don't seem on your A-Game right now."

She giggled again. "True. My grandpa was a surgeon. I just always knew the bones in the body. I must say I like the bones in your body."

"That's whatever trendy drink you had tonight talking," he reminded her gently.

"Maybe. But you are hot."

"Come on," he said.

His hand was warm against her skin as he lightly clasped her arm. He drew her closer and she was steady in the killer heels as she let him guide her next door to his brownstone.

Which reminded her of something she'd been puzzling over since he'd moved in. He was a cop and this was an upscale neighborhood. Granted a plain-clothes detective, but they didn't exactly make the big bucks needed to buy one of the brownstones on Manhattan's Upper West Side.

"Are you on the take?" she asked as he unlocked his door and stepped over the threshold.

"What?" he asked, glancing back at her like she'd just grown a second head.

She realized she'd spoken without thinking. Something she often did because she didn't have the filter that other people seemed to have that kept them from saying things so bluntly. "Sorry. It's just...never mind."

The foyer of his brownstone mirrored hers, with the stairs on the right instead of the left. His house smelled clean and welcoming like cinnamon and apples. And she had the paralyzing thought that she might have been flirting with a man in a relationship. But she'd never seen a woman leaving his place.

"Do you live alone?" she asked. He led the way into the living room and hit the light switch, revealing a blatantly masculine space with a huge brown leather sofa and a swivel recliner that was positioned in front of the flat-screen television. There were magazines on the heavy oak coffee table and she strained to see what they were. Surprised to see the *Smithsonian* magazine when she'd been expecting to see something like *Men's Health*.

"Yes, but back to your previous question...why did you ask if I was a dirty cop?" He leaned back against the doorjamb, crossing his arms over his chest.

She almost sighed out loud as the motion pulled the fabric of his black t-shirt taut against his chest. He certainly wasn't one of those donut-eating cops or if he was he worked out enough to compensate for it.

"These places are expensive," she said. "I'm renting from my dad on very generous terms."

"If you must know, I'm a trust-fund baby," he said.

She'd known her share of those and Garrett Mulligan didn't seem spoiled at all. "You don't strike me as one."

He rubbed his chin. "Much to my parents' chagrin. I've always trod a different path. My older brother is the perfect son."

"I'm an only child, so no chance of perfection in our family," she said, sounding bitter to herself. "So you're the rebel?"

"In a way. I'm not a lawbreaker like you," he said with a half-smile that made her melt inside.

"I guess you're just playing at being a bad boy."

That startled a laugh out of him and she realized there was a certain element of fun in letting go. She normally would have just let it go and retreated into herself, but tonight...well tonight she was the new Hayley.

"Careful! You might stir up more than you can handle," he said, taking three steps toward her.

She let her handbag fall to the floor and moved toward him with three hip-shaking steps. "I think I can handle you."

"Handle me?"

"Yes," she said, feeling brazen and bold. The world was her oyster tonight and she wasn't afraid to grab it with both hands. Actually...she raised her hands and put both of them on his chest, flexing her fingers to feel the firm muscles of his chest under her touch.

He was warm too, his body heat sinking into her fingertips. He felt like good dough that had been proofed and was ready to be kneaded. She shook her head. That was the old Hayley thinking something silly. The new Hayley...what would a bad girl do?

She glanced up at him because even in the ridiculous heels he was still much taller than she was. She saw he was watching her with that steady, even gaze he'd had on the street, but also a little bit of amusement.

He thought she was frivolous.

For a moment the shy girl inside of her withered a little and wanted to retreat, but she wasn't hiding any more. She leaned up and let her breasts brush against his chest as she wrapped one hand around his shoulder for balance before she canted her body forward.

"Is something funny, officer?" she asked in a deep husky voice, making sure her words were spoken right into his ear.

She felt him shudder and his hands came to her waist and he drew her off her feet more firmly into the cradle of his body, but then everything shifted and she felt them starting to fall.

He cursed and held her tight as he ensured she landed on him with her half on top of his chest and half on the floor. Hayley started laughing as she realized that maybe jumping from mousy to sexy was too much for her to accomplish in one night.

She glanced down at Garrett to find he was scowling.

"Are you hurt?"

"Just my pride," he said with a wry grin.

"Pride goeth before the fall?" she quipped.

"Definitely," he said. He grabbed her waist and pulled her more fully on top of him. She felt his jean-clad legs part and her silk-encased ones slid between them.

There was something almost erotic about the feel of the denim against her thighs and she shivered a little inside. She put her hands on his chest, but his hand on her waist moved up her back and he pushed his fingers into her newly cut hair, his hand shaping her head and drawing her down.

"What are you doing?" she asked on a breathless sort of sigh.

"Regaining the ground I lost," he said, moments before his lips met hers.

Hayley closed her eyes and then the timbre of the kiss changed as he angled his head and parted her lips with his. The warmth of his breath as it entered her mouth sent shivers of awareness down her spine. The smooth glide of his tongue over hers short-circuited her thoughts.

She stopped breathing.

Every nerve in her body was at attention. As his mouth moved over hers she felt the caresses of his thighs over hers. The movement of his hands over the back of her head as he massaged the muscles in her neck and she turned to putty.

She melted against him and over him. The kiss transformed her the same way the clothing had. He was awakening something

8

inside of her that she'd thought only existed in epic romance books and movies, but not in real life. Something she'd always longed for, but thought she'd never find. Something dangerous because though she was ready to change inside she hadn't yet.

She pulled back and looked down at him. His eyes were half-closed and a subtle flush had spread under his beard-stubbled cheeks. His lips were moist and swollen from kissing her. She lifted one hand and rubbed her finger over the stubble on his jaw, enjoying the slight abrasion against her skin.

He opened his eyes and she saw how beautiful they were up close. She would have said they were gray before, but at this angle she could see they were flecked with green and blue. She moved her hand from his jaw and traced the line of one eyebrow and then found a tiny scar at his hairline. She rubbed her finger over it.

"Ah, bad girl, you are killing me," he said, his voice was deep and sort of husky now. The words brushed over her senses like a blast of heat from a fireplace on a cold night. And this was a cold January night.

And his words were like a splash of water. He thought she was a bad girl. Bad girls didn't worry about where a man might have gotten a scar. Or think about how beautiful their eyes were... did they?

She didn't know.

"Officer Hottie, you know how to kiss," she said at last because it was the truth. She'd never been kissed like that before.

"I try," he said wryly.

He did more than that. But she knew she had to get up now. She had to get away from him and reassess what being a bad girl meant and how she was going to act. She used his chest as leverage to push herself up and her hips pressed down on his for a moment and she felt his erection.

He groaned and brought his hands to her hips, holding her in place as he rocked against her. She felt something deep inside of her clench and she rubbed herself against him.

9

"You're killing me," he said, using one hand on the back of her neck to draw her mouth back down to his.

The kiss this time was carnal and hot and she didn't have time to catalogue any of it. She just knew that he felt good underneath her and she was determined to not let him go. Not just yet.

Her breath caught in her throat. This was the kind of kiss she'd waited a lifetime for. She was practical, she reminded herself but the other part of her...the lost little girl deep inside knew it was kismet. That they were together for one reason and one reason alone.

It was destined.

Maybe after years of birthdays that she wanted to forget she was finally in a place where she could have one to remember. That felt right to her.

It seemed that Garrett Mulligan was her birthday present to herself and for once being herself had sort of worked out in her favor. Well being her new self, she thought, and then stopped thinking as his hands moved over her butt and his hips lifted and he rolled them both to their sides.

Chapter 2

Garrett wasn't a player despite the fact that he was single and dated around. Usually he liked to get to know a woman better before he jumped into a carnal kiss, but there was something about Hayley that made him forget his rules.

Hell, he couldn't even think beyond the taste of her lush, full mouth and the way her trim waist felt under his hands. He shifted his hips one more time and felt a feathering of sensation down his spine. Unless he was willing to do a lot more than kiss this bad girl, he better put some distance between them.

He rolled onto his back and away from her. Forcing himself to sit up.

"You must work out like a fiend to be able to sit up like that," she said.

She touched his abdomen and he chuckled. "Sit-ups and upper-body weight training are all I can do with my injured leg and foot."

"I thought you were shot in the knee," she said.

"I twisted my ankle in the pursuit after I was shot," he said. Images of that moment when Hector had gone down filtered through his mind, but he shoved them aside as he looked around his living room, grounding himself back in this moment.

"Whatever work out you're doing is definitely working for you," she said. She still lay on her back on the floor next to him, her

11

head tilted toward him and that dreamy smile on her face.

"Thanks, I try," he said sardonically.

"You're welcome. I believe in giving credit where it's due," she said. "So many people just try to tear you down."

She was serious. Something that didn't surprise him, really, because that was the image he'd had of his neighbor before tonight. But it was a bit jarring to see her sprawled out on his living-room floor looking like a centerfold from a racy magazine and to see her being so earnest.

He was giving himself major credit for rolling to his side and standing up instead of staying where he was and making love to her.

"Come on, bad girl, let's get you something comfortable to sleep in. It's getting late."

She looked over at him and giggled, then started laughing.

"What?"

"Sorry, I was just thinking I didn't turn into Old Hayley at midnight."

He shook his head as he offered her his hand. "Up you go."

She took it and he lifted her easily to her feet. She balanced herself with one small hand on his chest, looking up at him with that earnest expression of hers. He felt like she was searching for something, some depth inside of him.

He'd always felt kind of hollow inside when he wasn't at work, tracking down a criminal. She sighed and looked away.

Still hollow.

He didn't acknowledge the disappointment he felt, but it didn't stop him from feeling it. He led the way up the stairs to his bedroom. She followed behind him, stopping to look at the pictures on the wall in the hallway.

"Prints?" she asked.

"No. My investment portfolio from when I was thirteen," he admitted.

"Van Gogh?"

He shrugged. "I wanted some Lichtenstein, but my dad wouldn't

12

approve the purchase. My mom loves Van Gogh."

"She does? Are you close to her?" Hayley asked.

He had been when he'd been younger. She'd been the one to act as a barrier between him and his father when they'd been arguing. And he'd always liked the way she'd empathized with Van Gogh. It might have been a romanticized version of the artist brought on, no doubt, by her love of the Don Maclean song "Vincent", but in her voice Garrett had always heard a longing for something else.

"As close as you can be to your parents," he said at last.

"I'm not," she said at last.

"Not what?"

"Close to my parents. We are like oil and water—don't mix," she said.

"My dad and I are like that," he said, reaching inside his bedroom to flip the light switch on. "Want to see my etchings?"

She groaned. "That's a horrible pick-up line. If you really wanted to entice me then you should have offered your handcuffs."

He laughed and shook off the melancholy. "Come on, bad girl."

He opened the second drawer of his dresser, taking out a neatly folded black t-shirt and a pair of gym shorts, which he handed to her. "You can change in there."

She took the clothes from him as she walked across the room toward his bathroom.

He sat down on his bed and bent to rub at his calf muscle. Hayley was a pleasant distraction, but her presence didn't change the fact that he wasn't healing the way he should have if he was going to have any chance at getting back on the force. He was going to have to make a huge decision soon and it was one he'd hoped never to have to make.

The door opened and he shifted his gaze over to Hayley. She stood there in his t-shirt and nothing else. "Not quite the glam outfit I was wearing before, but how do I look? Still wicked?"

"Tired," he said.

"Tired? What about now?" she asked, making her lips pouty.

"Bad to the bone," he said. Feeling more tempted than he had in a long time. But his life was complicated enough right now without adding someone like Hayley to the mix. "You can take my bed for the night."

"No, I couldn't put you out any more than I already have," she said. "The couch will be fine."

He wasn't going to argue with her. He'd made the offer and she declined. He led the way out of his bedroom, very aware that she was following behind him as the scent of her perfume lingered in the air around them.

She dropped her clothes and purse on the recliner. He turned away as the hem of his shirt rose up the back of her thighs and went to the closet for a blanket. His mother was always coming by with little things for the house. So he was well stocked with everything.

He handed her the blanket.

"Thank you," she said. "For everything. You've been way nicer than you had to be, Officer Hottie."

"I live to serve and to protect," he said.

She reached for his hand and squeezed it. "Well, I can see why you are a part of New York's finest."

Except the direction of his thoughts showed him he wasn't. If he didn't get out of the living room right now he knew there was a very real chance that he'd be pulling her back into his arms and not letting her go until he was buried hilt-deep in her sexy little "bad" body.

"Good night, Hayley."

"Night, Garrett."

He turned abruptly on his heel and went upstairs for another sleepless night. But at least this time he was kept awake with the pleasant distraction of Hayley's body instead of his own fears about his future.

***

14

Hayley woke up early and with a start, falling off the couch onto the floor. She glanced around the room with the early-morning sunlight trickling in through the windows as she sat up. Last night...

Well, let's leave it at the fact that it hadn't ended at all the way she'd expected it to. She stood up and glanced at the skirt and top she'd worn out and knew there was no way she wanted to put them back on right now.

But then she had the niggling thought that a true bad girl would definitely wear them again. She just couldn't make herself don them right now. She grabbed her iPhone and dialed the locksmith, who assured her he'd be at her place in less than an hour, something she thought was a bit optimistic since he was coming from Queens.

Feeling a bit like a snoop, she wandered through Garrett's house until she found herself in the kitchen. She opened his fridge, finding stereotypical bachelor fare. A six pack of Coors, a couple of take-out containers, an open box of Arm & Hammer baking soda, which was living up to its reputation by keeping the fridge from smelling. He had two eggs and some milk and she opened his cabinets until she found the ingredients for a very basic muffin and a dark-chocolate bar.

"Busted again," Garrett rumbled from the doorway.

She glanced over her shoulder at him and groaned. He was shirtless and damn if those muscles she'd felt last night didn't look good this morning. He had a pair of jeans that rode low on his hips, revealing washboard abs and his hipbones. Really, she thought, who other than Ryan Gosling had a body like that in real life?

"For what?" she asked, trying to sound nonchalant and keep herself from jumping his bones.

"Stealing my food...that's a crime punishable by death in some parts of the world."

"Ah, Detective, I think you're rusty. I haven't taken anything.

Just assembled your meager food stuffs into something delicious," she said.

"What are you making?" he asked, coming closer. "Not an omelet."

"Can't sneak anything past you," she said. "Dark-chocolate-chunk muffins. Do you have a muffin tin? Otherwise it's going to be bars."

"You found my stash of chocolate?"

"Maybe you should have handcuffed me," she said with a wink. "It wasn't that hard to find," she admitted as he walked over to her, stopping when barely an inch of space remained between them.

He leaned forward and swiped his thumb over her bottom lip. "I think you stole some of my chocolate."

"I had...to taste...it," she said, her voice a mere whisper as he brought his thumb to his mouth and licked the spot of chocolate from it.

He was killing her. There were no other words to describe her slow descent from rational, normal woman to one so fevered that she was contemplating pushing him to the ground and falling on top of him and making breakfast out of his sexy body.

"Me too," he said. "Still feeling naughty this morning?"

"You have no idea," she said, but in the cold light of day she wasn't feeling ballsy.

She took a step back, but ran into the counter and as he advanced toward her she lifted up the spoon with the batter on it and he smiled at her, reaching forward and taking a swipe of the batter.

"I'm biting my tongue to keep from saying something sexist about barefoot women who can cook like a house on fire," he said, stooping down and brushing his hand against her leg as he opened the cabinet behind her.

She was in a fever thinking about the ease with which he touched her. It was as if he saw what he wanted and went for it. Why didn't she do the same?

She'd felt so empowered last night and she realized she wasn't going to let it end.

When he stood up she put her hand square in the middle of his chest and let her fingers spread open so that she could feel more of his hard, muscled chest under her touch.

She brushed her hand back and forth, the light dusting of hair on his skin tickling her palm. She noticed his eyes were half-closed and his mouth parted on a soft exhalation of breath. She leaned up and licked the corner of his mouth, where the tiniest smidge of batter remained.

It tasted good, but he was delicious. His lips parted as she flicked her tongue into his mouth, but before he could deepen the kiss she stepped back and winked at him.

"I think I need a little more sugar in the batter...not sweet enough."

"Something is definitely not sweet this morning," he said. "Tease."

"Tease?"

"Yup. I wanted to see if the bad girl was here to stay or if my mousy neighbor was back."

She stood up a little straighter and arched one eyebrow at him. "I'm not someone who pretends to change."

"Glad to hear it," he said, leaning in and taking the kiss she'd deprived him of just moments earlier.

It was carnal and hot and she clung to his naked shoulders as he gripped her waist and lifted her off her feet and turned so he leaned back against the counter. She wrapped her legs around his waist and plunged her tongue deep into his mouth until she no longer could taste anything other than Garrett.

He groaned and rubbed his hips against hers and she forced herself to lower her legs and step away. "Still think I might be mousy?"

"Hell no," he said. Before he walked out of the kitchen she forced herself to remember that she was playing a game with him.

It didn't matter that it felt real and scared her. This was just a game.

***

Garrett took a quick shower and came back into the kitchen to find five muffins sitting in the middle of his counter with a note. She'd obviously taken one for her trouble.

Thanks for rescuing me last night, Officer Hottie. See ya around.

His t-shirt was neatly folded next to it and he lifted it up and brought it to his face, assailed by the vanilla scent of Hayley's perfume. He groaned as he realized what he was doing. He was screwed up right now. Bored by his forced leave and the fact that his foot and leg wouldn't allow him to get back into shape.

He couldn't pull a Shia LaBeouf in *Disturbia* and solve a mystery looking out his back window, but as he took two muffins and the carton of milk with him to his back patio, he realized that he was very interested in what was going on next door.

Ah, hell, he thought.

He took a bite of the muffin and moaned at the delicious taste of it. She could cook; he'd give her that. And she'd certainly got his temperature rising outside of the kitchen as well.

His phone rang. He ignored it as the caller ID revealed that it was his brother, but Pete was persistent and Garrett didn't fancy an in-person visit from his sibling.

"What's up?"

"Hello to you too," Pete said. "Just a heads up that the head of security announced his retirement from the company today. Dad's already put your name forward to fill the slot."

Garrett cursed under his breath. "I politely declined his offer of employment last night."

Pete laughed. "The old man wants you back in the fold. He and Mom were really scared when Hector died. That could have been you, bro."

18

"But it wasn't. I can't just change who I am because Hector died. It would make his death stand for nothing," Garrett said, finally admitting out loud the thought that had been going through his mind for weeks now. He couldn't let Hector die in vain.

"I know that you can't change," Pete said. "Figured since I helped sabotage you last night at dinner I owed you a heads up on this."

"You did owe me. Why didn't you warn me last night?" Garrett asked.

"You're my little bro and I don't want to see you hurt," Pete said.

"Aww, didn't know you cared that much," Garrett said trying to keep it light because he didn't want to sound like a wuss and tell his brother that he loved him. But he and Pete had always been close.

"It's Mom's fault," Pete said.

"How do you figure?"

"She always told me to look out for you, just a habit now. And I can't protect you when you are out on the streets of New York, but in the company..."

"Forget it. Even if I wanted to trade my badge for a private-sector job, I wouldn't work for you or Dad," Garrett said. "No offense."

"None taken. How's the leg today?"

"Same as yesterday," Garrett said. "I'm meeting with the captain tomorrow to find out when I can go back to work, why?"

"Feel up to an outing?" Pete asked.

There was something in his tone that immediately let Garrett know that his brother was up to something. "Maybe. What'd you have in mind?"

"Crystal has a friend..."

"No thanks, I don't need to be set up," Garrett said.

"All you do is sit in the house and work out," Pete said.

He thought of Hayley and realized that maybe it wasn't the worst time for them to have met. "That's not true. The guys and I are playing poker tonight."

19

"Sitting around drinking with your buddies isn't the same as a date," Pete said.

Sometimes he took his role as the older brother a little too seriously.

"I met someone."

"Last night?"

"Yes."

"A prostitute?" Pete asked. "You left the restaurant after eleven."

"Not a hooker," Garrett said. Hayley might be playing at being a bad girl, but they both knew she really wasn't one. "My neighbor."

"Really?"

"She got locked out of her place and I helped her out."

"Sounds exciting," Pete said.

It was, Garrett thought, and he took another bite of the muffin and washed it down with a swallow from the gallon of milk before standing up. "She is. I've gotta go."

"Okay, if you change your mind, Crystal and I are going to candy-making class on next Friday at 7 at The Candied Apple."

"Don't hold your breath. That's not my scene."

"Mine either, but Crystal loves them so..."

"So you'll go. You're whipped," Garrett said.

"I am," Pete said. "I hope someday you find a woman who does the same to you."

Pete hung up and Garrett pocketed his phone. He knew he'd never let anyone have that much influence over his life. He did his own thing and that was as far as it went.

He stepped out onto his porch just in time to see Hayley walking up the street. She wore a pair of skintight jeans and a sleeveless top that hugged the curves of her breasts and her nipped-in waist.

He watched the sway of her hips and realized he wanted to see more of the bad girl he'd rescued last night, but he knew little about her. Being a detective he knew just how to go about finding out more about her. But getting involved with his neighbor wasn't a great idea.

When things ended he'd see her every day and that could get awkward. Maybe it was just the fact that he hadn't been out in a while that was responsible for his attraction toward her. He called his brother back and told him he'd meet Crystal's friend at the candy-making class.

Chapter 3

Entering her brownstone with the assistance of the locksmith was humbling. He just gave her a sympathetic look, but didn't make any other comments. She'd texted her co-owners, who were also her best friends to say she'd be late getting to the shop. Normally she got in at five.

Cici texted back to take the day off. Given all that had happened the day before she was tempted to just do it. Just take the day off. What would her dad say? He hadn't missed a day of work in a really long time.

Hayley entered her home and closed the door after paying the locksmith and stood there with her back against the heavy solid front door. Her house smelled of lavender and always reminded her of the week she and her parents had spent in Provence. She glanced at the console table and the picture of her mom.

She knew it was her imagination, but she saw censure in the expression. Edie had died three days after Hayley's eighteenth birthday and every birthday Hayley felt again like that eighteen-year-old. A girl-woman who wasn't sure who she wanted to be and who had never really fit the image of the woman her mother had wanted as a daughter.

She saw the envelope on the console table along with the fresh flowers and a gaily-wrapped present. It was big and she had no idea what he'd gotten her. She didn't see him all that often, maybe for dinner three times a year and at the board meetings for Dunham Dinners, their family company.

Her father, or one of his employees, had been here some-time between when she'd left to go out with her friends and this morning.

She'd never considered calling her workaholic father for assistance last night. In fact, she was pretty sure when she'd talked to him yesterday morning that he'd been on the West Coast.

"What'd you get me this year, Dad?" she asked the empty house.

When she was little she'd always gotten spoiled on her birthday and she had realized after her mom's death that her mom had been responsible for that. She had always thought it was her father who'd spoiled her.

She ignored the letter, which was one of many that her mother had written to her before her death. Edie had died of cancer, which had left her some time to plan for the events she wouldn't get to experience. And somehow she'd thought, they all had, that these letters would be a good idea.

But this morning, Hayley wasn't up to reading whatever her mom had to say about turning thirty. She wasn't sure when she'd be ready, but not today. Today she was still stepping out of the shadow that had been cast by her mom's death all those years ago.

Instead she lifted the birthday present from her father, which was a bit heavy, and carried it to the kitchen. She opened it. It was an espresso machine, which would probably require some serious reading of the instructions before she could figure out how to use it. She put it on the counter as she puttered around, eating the muffin she'd made over at Garrett's house.

She didn't feel any shame about last night. Why should she? Iona would laugh herself silly if she knew that Hayley had barely kissed Garrett and was calling that her "wild encounter".

And it was definitely her idea of a wild encounter.

She had a little regret. She pulled the slate chalkboard that she kept propped up next to her refrigerator on her Corian countertop and erased yesterday's message, which had said *Live Life To Its Fullest*.

She thought about it for a moment and then smiled as she wrote "Eat More Muffins", then she scratched it out and wrote "Kiss More Strangers".

She went upstairs for her shower and then decided that staying home wasn't what she wanted. She was too much of her father's daughter. It was a workday. She wasn't sick. She had to get dressed and go to work. Just once she wished she were the kind of woman who would play hookey, but she wasn't. She never had been.

She pulled out the tiny notepad that she'd been jotting down things in. It was her bucket list and she added "skipping work" to it.

Leaving her brownstone and stepping out onto the large sidewalk and its pretty tree-lined street, she glanced over at Garrett's place. Before walking to the end of the block and going into the small grocer.

"Running late today, Hayley?" Mrs. Kalatkis asked. She wore a colorful smock over her skinny jeans and long-sleeved purple thermal t-shirt. She had long inky-black hair, with streaks of silver going through it, which Hayley envied. She hoped when she started going grey that her hair would look as graceful.

"A little bit, Mrs. Kalatkis," Hayley said as she grabbed a bottled smoothie from the refrigerated cooler at the front of the store and the newspaper. The Kalatkis family had been on this corner since the 50s. Her father remembered them from when he first bought the brownstone in the 90s. They were always friendly to her.

"How was your birthday?" she asked. "We have a little gift for you. Stop by after work, okay?"

"I will, thank you. My birthday was good. I had a very nice time with my friends," she said. They'd gone to a nightclub that Iona's brother knew the owners of. It was the hottest new place: Olympus. She'd danced with a lot of different guys, but none of them had been as interesting as her hot cop neighbor.

24

"That's a good thing," Mrs. Kalatkis said. "Young people should enjoy life, not work so hard like you do."

"You were probably working hard at my age," Hayley said, tucking a strand of hair behind her ear and still feeling a little shocked by the shorter length. Her ears were actually a little bit cold this morning. She made a mental note to buy a hat.

"I knew how to play hard too," Mrs. Kálatkis said with a wink. "That's how I won Mr. Kalatkis."

Hayley smiled at the older woman as she paid and then left the shop. The foot traffic was heavier at ten than it would have been at four-thirty, when she was usually on her way to work. But she didn't mind it as she made her way through Central Park toward Fifth Avenue. The rent was high there, but it was all about location. And with the loan they'd gotten from her father's investment friends it had been doable.

Her mind was humming with ideas for new flavors to try at her shop. And when she turned onto Fifth Avenue she paused at the end of the block to admire her new sign. The Candied Apple had been her dream. She'd needed help bringing it to life and her father had assisted her with some backing. However, it had been Cici and Iona who'd really put in the hard work with her. They'd seen her little dream of having her own confectionary and added their own dreams of a stylish boutique and trendy place for people to hang out.

So The Candied Apple was a sort of mix between a trendy coffee shop and a really cool bar. They had mixed drinks and exotic chocolate-inspired dishes after five in their eating area at the back of the shop. During the day they were busy selling candy in their distinctive red-striped boxes with a green apple on top.

She felt a similar sense of excitement toward the shop as she did when she thought about Garrett. She remembered the feel of him underneath her last night. A twinge of regret went through her. She should have taken him up on his offer this morning. But one-night stands…well she'd had a few in her early twenties

25

and had given up on them.

He was still a stranger, but a part of her thought he might know her true self better than anyone else. Kissing him had been the closest she'd come to dropping her guard in years.

It was scary to be that vulnerable to a man she barely knew. But also thrilling. For the first time in a long time she felt truly alive. Like she didn't need to don her chef's whites and hide in the kitchen.

***

Cici and Iona were the best friends that Hayley had ever made. She imagined part of that was down to the fact that they'd all come together, not because they'd gone to the same school or grown up in the same town, but because they'd all been dated and dumped by the same guy—Damon O'Sullivan.

"Score!" Iona Summerlin said as she entered the room. She was tall and vibrant and full of life. Hayley often thought her first inkling that Damon was just toying with her should have been the fact that he'd broken up with Iona.

"Is that a sports metaphor?" Cici asked, coming in behind Iona. She had thick curly hair and wore stylish dark-rimmed glasses. Cici was a wiz at finance and without her guidance and help, Hayley was pretty sure that The Candied Apple would never have gotten off the ground.

"Not at all. I just got a confirmation text that we are going to be featured again in the All About Manhattan blog. That led to a boost in sales last time," Iona said.

"Why are they featuring us again?" Hayley asked.

"Those candy-making lessons you're giving. Valentine's Day is just around the corner and couples will want something fun to do," Iona said.

Hayley groaned. "I'd hoped that maybe no one would show up."

Cici gave her a sympathetic smile. "Those days are long gone.

There was a line in front of the shop when I walked up this morning."

"It was there when I arrived too. People need their chocolate fix when the weather turns grey," Iona agreed.

"That they do," Hayley said. She had been lost in thoughts of the previous night and Garrett and hadn't even bothered to pay attention to anything other than preparing her kitchen for the day's work.

She remembered the way his kiss had tasted. How it had been fiery and intense and she wanted to create a truffle that mirrored it. She started mixing ingredients together in her mind, trying and rejecting different spices until she thought she had the perfect—

"Hay, what's up with you today? You are staring at the counter like it holds the answers to the universe's mysteries."

"Nothing," she mumbled, reaching around Iona and grabbing Cici's quadrille notepad. She jotted down the ingredients so she didn't forget them.

"Ah, inspiration strikes," Cici said. "This one sounds spicy. Will that really taste good together?"

"It did last night," Hayley said, remembering the moment his tongue brushed over hers. Garrett had been all passion and control. She might have overdone the truffle a bit. He held something back from her.

Why did he do that?

She made a note in the margin, vaguely aware that her friends were watching her.

"Last night? You were with us," Cici said. "Did something happen after the cab dropped you off? He took you home, didn't he?"

"Yes," she said. She was being vague in no small part because she wanted to keep Garrett as hers. She wasn't entirely ready to share him with her friends.

"To which question?" Iona asked, sharp as a tack as usual. It was hard to get anything past Iona.

27

"Both," she admitted.

Iona's phone rang and she chewed her lip as she glanced at the caller ID and then back at Hayley. "I have to take this. Don't say anything until I get back."

She nodded. She wasn't about to start talking about Garrett or last night to anyone. Cici watched her but wasn't as aggressive as Iona, so when Hayley tore off the recipe she'd just jotted down and walked toward the kitchen Cici didn't stop her.

"You're going to have to spill it some time," Cici said as she gathered her notes together.

"I'm not ready yet. I need to process and I want to try this truffle."

"Go on, then. I have an exercise class in thirty minutes. Ugh! Why did I pick getting in shape as my thing for this year?" Cici asked.

"Because you are so wonderful at everything else," Hayley said with a wink as she walked away.

"Ha."

Alone in the kitchen she walked into the spice closet that was very well stocked. Before opening The Candied Apple she'd spent a year traveling around the world—the benefit of having lived at home with her father and saved every penny she'd made. She'd known from the moment that her mother had died nearly twelve years earlier that one day she would open her own candy shop.

Food was in her family's blood. Her father was the CEO of America's largest frozen food manufacturer. But she wanted to make her own mark. Not follow in his footsteps.

She gathered the jars of spices that she thought reminded her most of Garrett. This was really not a good idea. He was a guy. Just a guy, but since they were strangers and she'd kissed him, she felt safe in this little obsession.

She pulled out essence of orange since his aftershave had been a bit citrusy. Then some hot paprika from Spain and a dash of chili from South America. She brought them back with her to her workbench.

She reached for the large block of dark chocolate that she kept there. And her lips tingled as she remembered his kiss this morning—supposedly to taste the chocolate. She used her large knife to chop it up and then made a quick ganache. She divided the chocolate and added different amounts of the ingredients until she had a mix that was…well in her mind at least, Garrett.

She chilled the filling and then mixed up some chocolate to coat the outside of the truffle. She worked quickly, music filling her head. The low, slow beat of classic rock 'n' roll. That seemed to suit Garrett.

Damn.

She really needed to forget about him. And after she ate these truffles she would. He'd be her little birthday secret. Something that had been just for herself, to launch her on the new path for this coming year.

Cici came in and picked up one of the truffles, taking a bite and then moaning. "I love this. Mmm…it's so good. We have to add this to the store. What are we going to call it?"

"Midnight Passion," she said. Because that was what they'd had between them. And in the cold light of day it would be good for her to remember that instead of obsessing over a man that she wasn't going to see again…well not that way.

Iona returned and sampled it, agreeing it needed to be in the store as well. Hayley smiled to herself, thinking that last night had been fun for her ego and for her business. Not a bad way to start her thirties.

***

Garrett didn't have much call for a dining room, so when he'd moved into the brownstone he'd had it converted into a game room of sorts. There was a bar at the far end, a pool table in the middle and in the corner a six-person poker table. He would've invited Pete to join the game tonight but he didn't want his brother to hear the conversation.

Whenever a cop fired his weapon and killed a suspect they were pursuing the cop was automatically put on suspension until an internal investigation was carried out. Given that the perp had killed Hector Gonzalez, most of his peers on the force assumed Garrett was going to be cleared and be back to work as soon as his foot healed.

Hell, Garrett did too. He'd relived that night a million times and he knew there had been nothing else he could have done. The suspect had been advancing on him while his partner was bleeding out at his feet. In all his years as a cop he'd never been in that position before.

He'd kept calm, like he'd been trained to do, but in that moment he'd known with absolute certainty that if he didn't take him out, Garrett would have been lying facedown next to Gonzalez.

The doorbell rang and Garrett shoved the memories of that night out of his head and forced an easygoing grin as he went to answer it. He hobbled a little, thanks to his healing leg.

When he opened the door Ramirez and Maxwell were standing there.

"The trains from Queens were a nightmare. I need tequila and I need it now," Ramirez said, giving Garrett a bro-hug as he entered.

Maxwell did the same, both men making their way to the game room without directions. This game was monthly. They'd come together as rookies. All of them outsiders to the force at that time. There'd be an empty chair tonight. He didn't dwell on that as he saw Hoop coming up the street.

Hoop wasn't a cop anymore. He'd gone back to school and became the enemy…a public defender. But the guys still included him because…well they were all friends who'd seen each other at their best and at their worst.

"Dude, traffic was murder," Hoop said.

"I heard," Garrett said. "Tequila is being poured. I hope you

30

are ready to have your ass handed to you."

Hoop entered the brownstone and Garrett closed the door as they headed for the game room.

"I think all this R&R you've been under has addled your brain. I am the one who always wins," Hoop said.

"R&R? Your idea of a good time and mine are vastly different," Garrett said.

Ramirez handed him a shot of tequila and everyone settled around the table. Garrett felt like he was back to himself as the evening wore on, but the truth was the other guys were keeping it light and not really talking about anything important.

Never one to run from anything, especially his own darkest fear that maybe Internal Affairs had uncovered something he'd done wrong, he swallowed his fourth shot of the evening in a long gulp. "Anyone heard anything about my case?"

The conversation stopped and Hoop put his cards on the table. Ramirez stacked his together, reshuffled them and then stacked them up again and Maxwell just gave him a hard look.

"Nothing. The captain has been playing it close to his chest. IA was in his office for about forty minutes today but he wouldn't say why," Maxwell said. "I don't know if it had to do with you or not."

"Hell."

"I haven't heard anything," Hoop said. "I put a call in to a friend at the DA's office and she hadn't heard anything either."

That had to be good.

"Dammit, Mulligan, this is messed up. You were doing your job," Ramirez said.

Was he? That was it. Until he was cleared he couldn't have any peace. The closest he'd come to finding it had been last night when he'd kissed Hayley. But he knew that wasn't real either. He was in limbo.

Men in limbo could hook up but not feel anything real.

"I was hoping you'd heard something. I got an email this afternoon telling me to come in tomorrow."

31

"So that's good, right?" Ramirez asked.

Garrett's gut said that if the captain had good news he would have called and not emailed. "I don't know. That's why I asked you bozos."

"Bozos? That's harsh," Maxwell said. "Those two I can understand, but me? I'm solid."

He smiled and pretended to relax, but inside the knot that he'd been carrying since he'd fired his weapon just got a little tighter. His mother would say that worrying wasn't going to make the problem easier to solve, but he couldn't help it. He dealt in black and white. There could be no gray area when it came to his job or his life. And suddenly for the first time in a long time, he was afraid that he didn't know what was coming next.

His leg wasn't healing as quickly as the doctor had thought it would. The captain was being vague about the investigation into his actions and add his sexy neighbor to the mix and things just got more confusing.

Two months ago he would have slept with her, dated her for a few weeks and then moved on to someone else. That was his way. He kept it light because of the job. The badge. But if he no longer carried a badge…

Everything would change.

Without his permission. His world was going to be different, no matter what happened tomorrow.

He won two hands and lost four and at midnight, when the guys left, he figured he'd broke even. But that didn't matter. Cards and money came easy to him; it was the rest of his life that always seemed harder to figure out.

Chapter 4

The upper floor of The Candied Apple had been empty just three months earlier, but with Iona's urging, Hayley had set it up for candy-making classes. Hayley wasn't really looking forward to teaching it since she didn't really care for public speaking. But she was making herself do it.

She walked through the empty room that had ten stainless-steel tables set up facing the front of the room, where she'd be doing her demonstration. She wasn't wearing her chef's jacket and felt uncomfortable without it. The jacket was her armor and she wasn't that sure she wanted to face a crowd of people without it.

"Looking good," Iona said as she walked in.

Iona was a PR guru and looked like she belonged on the cover of a magazine or maybe up on the big screen instead of orchestrating campaigns for other people. She wore her strawberry-blonde hair stick-straight and let hang down to the middle of her back. Her eye make-up was dramatic, something Iona said she did for effect. But Hayley suspected she did it to hide her true self. She looked like a completely different woman with it on.

"Thanks. I was worried all of the equipment wouldn't arrive on time," Hayley said.

"I meant you, silly. How has it been today? Have you gotten used to your new look?" Iona asked, coming over to fluff Hayley's hair.

"Not really, sometimes I'd catch a glimpse of a woman in the mirror and then realize it was me," Hayley said. It was funny how a haircut and a little bit of lip-gloss could completely change a woman's life. "And a lot of guys flirted with me in the shop today and I...well, I sort of figured out how to flirt back."

"What was so hard about it?" Iona asked.

"I'm just not used to banter. Men usually ignore me, but that's definitely not happening anymore."

"Sounds interesting, how do you know it's 'definitely' not happening?" Iona asked. She moved around the room, adjusting the trays on the different tables and sorting through the cooking implements.

How was she sure? Garrett had been the one that she'd thought of all day as she'd flirted with strangers in her shop. She'd found the only way she could really do it was by picturing the men as him. "That hot cop that lives next door kissed me last night."

"Woo hoo," Iona said, walking back over to her. "That's what I wanted to hear."

"Oh, Iona, I don't know what to do. I was my brazen bad- girl best, but then this morning when I was leaving his place—"

"Whoa, you spent the night with Officer Hottie?"

"Yes," she said, then started to laugh.

"Um...what did I say about one-night stands?"

"It's not what you think...I lost my keys last night and got locked out of my place and he offered to let me sleep at his place until this morning," she said.

"So you didn't sleep with him?"

"No," she said sounding wistful, even to her own ears. "I didn't want to be too forward and I wasn't sure what to do."

"Surely you've kissed a guy before," Iona said. "Are you a virgin?"

"No, I'm not. But this was different. I mean I'm pretending—"

"You're not pretending. You're changing. Remember that and it will all fall into place."

She knew Iona was right. She felt the change within her and

wasn't about to tell Iona that she had a basket of The Candied Apple goodies she was planning to take over to Garrett's house after work tonight.

"It's not that easy. The last time I pretended to be someone I wasn't was when my mom was really sick," Hayley admitted.

Iona put her arm around her. "I'm sorry, sweetie. But you were a girl pretending to be grown-up."

"How do you know that?"

"Because we all are at that age. Looking back, I was so obnoxious when I was eighteen. I thought I knew it all," Iona said.

Hayley hadn't thought that. She'd thought that maybe if she changed enough her mom would get better. Even at eighteen she'd known that her behavior had nothing to do with her mother's health, but she'd thought if she tried hard enough maybe God would notice.

She sighed and shook off her melancholy mood. It was probably just that unread letter sitting at home that was bringing her down. She had something better waiting right next door.

Garrett.

"You still don't know as much as you think you do," Hayley said.

Iona winked at her as she moved over to one of the other tables. "So true, the main trick is to keep everyone else from noticing."

"How do I do that?"

"With confidence and bravado. Remember when we made you go into the board of directors of your father's company and ask for the loan?"

She nodded. But that was nothing like how Garrett made her feel. She'd had no problem telling the entire board that they would regret not investing in The Candied Apple because she had a confidence in the kitchen that was lacking elsewhere in her life.

"That was different. I'm very good at making candy."

"You are, but you are good at many other things as well. Kissing your hot-cop neighbor sounds like it is one of them."

"What if—"

"Don't. Don't second-guess yourself. You can either live your life or watch it pass you by."

"Are we speaking in cat-poster slogans now?"

"It's true even if a cute kitten said it," Iona said. Her phone twittered and she gave Hayley a hard stare before turning away to take the call.

Hayley knew that Iona was right. After all, she wanted to own her thirties in a way she hadn't been able to own her life in her twenties.

And…

She wanted to see Garrett again. He was the one person she'd been around in her new look who had actually made her feel comfortable in her own skin. She nibbled her lower lip as she forced herself to admit the real reason she wanted to see him again.

She wanted another chance to see if those kisses they'd shared were real. She'd never felt instant attraction before and she definitely wanted to experience it again.

***

After her conversation with Iona she had decided against packing up a basket of food for Garrett. Every time she pursued a man it didn't work out. She was going to just put him down in the category of fun. But when she got home late from the shop after staying all day to make the new truffle, she admitted to herself that she was sort of avoiding coming back here. It wasn't that she was afraid of seeing Garrett.

She wasn't.

Simply the fact that she'd spent the better part of her day thinking about him was reason enough to avoid him.

She had rotten taste in men. She knew this. She liked them for superficial reasons, so realistically she knew there was no place for the relationships to go.

The door to his brownstone opened while she stood on the

stoop to her own place and three men walked out, laughing and talking loudly. She shrank back into the shadows as Garrett joined them. He waved his friends off and then glanced over at her place.

She hesitated for a split second, inwardly groaning at herself for not using her common sense and then stepped into the light.

"Another late night?" she called.

"Yeah. Figured I should keep an eye out in case you needed me again," he said. Closing his door, he made his way carefully down the steps of his home and over to hers. He hadn't shaved today and there was a light dusting of stubble on his cheeks. She'd always thought she preferred a clean-shaven man, but there was something about that light stubble that said "bad boy". Rebel.

And it drew her like a moth to a flame.

"No need of a rescue tonight," she said.

"Dang."

She shook her head. "Want to come in for a drink?"

"Better make it coffee. I've been hitting the tequila pretty hard tonight and I've got an early-morning meeting with my captain."

"I've got decaf," she said. She finished unlocking her door and led the way into her house.

She heard him behind her as she put her keys in the bowl on the console table, where she'd left a lamp on. She met the eyes of her mother in the portrait that had been taken a year before she'd been diagnosed with cancer. To Hayley that picture was her mom at her best. Full of her power as a woman and determined that her daughter would be the best woman that Edie could make her.

She saw censure there again tonight.

Her mom hadn't approved of men with stubble.

Hayley led the way down the hall, not stopping until they were in her kitchen. She waved a hand at the espresso-maker her father had sent her.

"I haven't mastered this new machine yet, but it comes with all these little pods," she said, opening the box and pushing it over to him.

37

"My parents have a machine like this," he said. "I'll try this one."

He handed her the pod and their fingers brushed. Electric chills spread up her arm. She stared at him for what seemed like a long five seconds before he arched one eyebrow at her and she turned to make the coffee.

"You said you have a meeting with your captain? What's that about?" she asked.

She heard his footsteps on the hardwood floor and then the scraping of one of her stools as she assumed he drew it out to sit down.

"Probably he will tell me when I can return to work," Garrett said.

"That's good. Do you think it will be soon?" she asked.

"My leg still isn't one hundred percent," he said. "The bullet chipped a bit of the bone and my left leg is shorter now than my right."

She turned to look at him as the coffee brewed. He seemed so strong, so capable that she suspected he wouldn't let that bum leg of his be an obstacle to getting back on the force.

"You could wear a special shoe," she said.

He arched both eyebrows at her this time. "I could? Why would I do that?"

"To make them both the same length," she said, handing him his coffee and then making a cup of tea in the microwave for herself.

She offered him milk and sugar, both of which he declined.

"My buddies would rag on me," he said.

"Were those the guys I saw leaving your place?"

"Yeah. We play poker once a month. Last month…my partner was still a part of the group."

"I'm sorry."

"It's okay," he said, and then took a sip of his beverage. "Perfect. I think you've mastered the machine."

"I've always been good at pushing buttons."

"Well, you are certainly good at pushing mine," he said, putting his cup down and leaning on the counter toward her.

"Really? So far all I've done is…"

"Be yourself."

Herself.

She wished.

She was like one of those moms she saw in Saks with four kids and a million bags and each child was running in a different direction. Except that the four kids were just parts of herself and she had no idea how to tame any of them.

"That's sort of all any of us can do," she said at last.

"True enough," he admitted. "I'm struggling to figure out this convalescence. I'm so glad to be going in to see my captain tomorrow."

She took a delicate sip of her tea. She should have boiled the water on the stove instead of microwaving it.

"Then what will happen?"

"I'll put my uniform on again and go back to my life."

Back to his life?

Did that mean that he didn't know how to exist outside of his job?

Another workaholic, she thought. She seemed to find them even when they were disguised by a sexy, devil-may-care exterior.

Maybe it was the late hour or just the fact that he made her feel so out of control. Like she could say anything or do anything, but instead of being polite and letting that comment slide by she put her tea mug on the counter and leaned toward him.

"What do you mean by back to your life?"

***

She watched as he glanced around her kitchen, the overhead lights under the copper lampshades brought out a sort of blonde highlight in his brown hair. He cleared his throat.

"Kiss more strangers?" he asked.

39

"Um…what? I'm not sure that your life was about that," she said.

"No, that's what your chalkboard says. Is that your goal?"

"We were talking about you," she reminded him and hoped to hell she wasn't blushing, but could feel the heat in her cheeks and knew she was.

"We were. I guess I don't know what my life would be without going back on the force. I told you, I'm a shallow trust-fund kid. Asking you about kissing strangers seemed safer," he said.

Safer.

She knew exactly what he meant by that. She'd done the same thing with him all day. Referred to him as the hot cop or Officer Hottie. Anything to keep it from seeming like she might really be interested in this man who'd kissed her and, whether she admitted it out loud or not, changed her world.

"What are the chances you won't get back on the force?" she asked. She wasn't ready to talk about her chalkboard or whatever it was he made her feel. *Not yet.*

It had always been so much easier for her to listen than to talk about herself. She wondered if that had anything to do with how she felt about where she was in her life. Give her a hunk of chocolate and the ingredients for a decadent truffle and she was full of confidence.

Leaning back on the barstool, he crossed his arms over his chest. "I'd say about ten percent."

"Is that because your leg isn't fully healed?" she asked.

"Partially. Also Internal Affairs are conducting an investigation into the perp I shot and killed."

His words made the room seem heavier. She doubted she'd ever been in a room with anyone who'd killed another person before.

"Has that happened to you before?" she asked.

He shook his head. "This was the first time. I've fired at suspects who ran before and tasered a few, but this was the first time I was in a shoot-out."

He seemed lost. It was hard to tell exactly what was going on inside of his head, but she knew if she'd killed another person, even to save herself, that the memory of it would linger.

She wondered if going back on the force was a good idea, but then reminded herself he was an adult and could make his own decisions.

She reached out to him and he uncrossed his arms and took her hand. She squeezed it. She didn't know what to say.

Cops did a dangerous job. She knew that from articles she'd read in the paper and from the officers who came into her shop for candy and cocoa after their shift. She didn't want to think of Garrett in danger or dying.

"Do you want to talk about it?" she asked.

He looked at her. His grey eyes so full of emotion, some of it easy for her to identify—anger, fear, maybe self-doubt.

"No. Thanks," he said, firmly.

She took her hand back. Firmly put back in her place not as his friend but as the nextdoor neighbor who'd kissed him and tried to seduce him.

"I'm not…it's not you, Hayley," he said. "I've had too much to drink and I feel angry when I think about what happened. I don't think it's a good idea to talk about it."

He was wise even when he'd had too many, she thought. "Too bad you didn't lose your keys, then you could spend the night here."

"Honey, when I spend the night here it will be because you asked me too, not because I had too much to drink."

She sighed. "I want to believe that."

"Why can't you?" he asked.

"Because I have horrible instincts when it comes to men."

"I find that hard to believe," he said. "I'm not lying to you."

She wasn't sure she could trust him or herself. She wanted him to be this fantasy guy she'd always dreamed of. Someone who wouldn't lie to her, was a red-hot lover in bed, and put her happiness first.

She had to drop her guard. Like Iona said, she had to be confident in her actions. In her new persona. And the new Hayley didn't have bad taste in men.

Garrett was a cop and funny and sweet and sexy. She could go on all day.

That was when it hit her that it really didn't matter if he wasn't a great guy. She was already starting to fall for him.

"Okay. So are you seeing anyone?" she asked.

"No, I'm not. Unless you count a sweet birthday gal who stayed at my place last night."

"I'm not sure if we count her or not," Hayley said.

Getting up, he came around the counter. He put his hands on her shoulders and leaned in, kissing her in a sweet way that felt like goodbye.

"Let me know when you decide," he said and then walked down the hall and out of her home.

Chapter 5

Garrett felt out of place at the station. It didn't matter that he'd always felt more at home there than anywhere else. He no longer was a part of the brotherhood. No matter how much he tried to pretend he was. He felt it in his bones.

Until Internal Affairs finished their investigation and he was back in uniform, he would continue to feel like an outsider. Sort of the way he had the other night at poker. He had that feeling that everyone else was still the same, but he knew that he'd changed in a way that wouldn't allow him to go back to who he was before.

Would he even want to?

How did a man go back to living as he had before he'd killed another man? Maybe if he figured that out he'd be able to move on. To get past whatever it was that woke him in the middle of the night—not just his sexy neighbor—that restless feeling in his gut that made him go to his home gym and work out until he was exhausted.

But he was stubborn and giving up something that had been a major part of his soul for as long as he could remember wasn't going to be easy. The station was buzzing with activity and cops – friends – called out as he walked back straight, his gait as easy and casual as a man with a slight limp could be.

A lot of the guys had worked with him and Hector for a long

43

time.

Brothers. The ones he'd chosen. These were his people—or were they? No one was too sure when he'd be cleared to come back to work.

But today it felt different. When he got to the captain's office the door was open and the captain sat behind his desk. He stood up as Garrett approached, which made him pretty sure this wasn't going to be a good meeting.

Captain Malone had been on the force almost twenty years and had thick grey hair that he wore in a military buzz cut. He had a hard face—one that had seen atrocities and injustice, but his eyes said he still believed in fighting the good fight.

Fuck me.

Garrett felt like he was slipping a little. Maybe he shouldn't have come to the station straight from an hour's session at the gym. He was edgy and maybe that was because the last time he'd been in the station had been right after Gonzalez had died. When he'd sat at his desk filling in statement forms and dealing with grief, guilt, and a little too much anger.

"Mulligan, good to see you," he said, shaking Garrett's hand. "How's the leg?"

"Getting there, Sir. I'm confident that once I'm back on the street it will be up to snuff," Garrett said.

The captain nodded and then leaned back in his chair, crossing his arms over his chest. Garret knew that look and it wasn't good news.

"I.A. cleared you," Malone said without any preamble. "Their investigation of witnesses and reviewing your statement brought them to the conclusion that if you hadn't fired with lethal intent you'd have ended up in the morgue next to Gonzalez."

That knot of tension that had been in the pit of his stomach since he'd realized the suspect was dead finally loosened. In his mind he'd known there had been no other course of action. But having the official report made him feel better.

"Great. So when can I come back to work?"

"As soon as the doctor clears you. I read the report from the physiotherapist," Malone said, drawing a folder closer to him and flipping it open.

"I'm stronger now than I've ever been," Garrett said.

"I can see that. You are one of the few guys I've seen who is actually bigger after convalescence than he was before the accident."

"I had a lot of time on my hands, Cap. And nothing to do but wait for this damned leg of mine to heal. I was going a bit stir crazy in my house."

"Can't say I blame you, kid. The doctors are concerned about the strength of your leg. It's clear they've done everything they can from their side. How's it feel?"

Garrett thought about the answer for a long time. He wanted to lie to the captain. Just say it was great, but what happened if he was chasing a perp again, like he had been with Gonzalez, and his leg gave way? What if he let down his partner?

"It's getting there," he said at last. "I am running on the treadmill for about thirty minutes a day. But I still have some fatigue issues with it and I haven't tried running on the street yet."

"Fair enough. I appreciate the honesty," Malone said. "I know you are anxious to get back to work, how would you feel about riding a desk for the next six months until the P.T. feels like you are checked out for field work?"

He'd hate it. He didn't want to sit in an office all day. Being a cop to him meant being out on the streets. Protecting the city and the community he loved.

"I'd hate it."

"I know the feeling, Garrett, but this might be your only option. I can't put you on the street unless you pass medical," Malone said.

"Fair enough. I'll do the desk thing for a few months," Garrett said, but he knew that he wasn't going to be satisfied and feel like he was himself again until he was back on the streets.

Malone laughed and shook his head. "Fine. Three months. I

was thinking of assigning you to cold cases. They need someone with your kind of drive and investigative skills now that O'Neil is retiring."

Cold cases. That was intriguing. Something he hadn't considered he'd be able to do before this.

"I like the sound of that, Cap."

"I thought you would. I don't want to lose one of my best," Malone said.

Garrett nodded. "When would I start?"

"Monday. I understand you have a doctor's appointment tomorrow. As long as he gives you the all-clear you're good to go," Malone said.

"Great. Back in blue," he said and meant it. But he had a few remaining doubts about his actions on the night and how he'd feel facing down the barrel of a gun again. He wanted to believe that nothing had changed and he was still the man he'd been, but something niggling in his gut made him doubt it.

"Yes. Back where you belong," the captain said. "We've missed you around here."

"I've missed it too," he said. "I was going crazy staring into my own backyard."

"I bet. Nothing interesting in my neighborhood," the captain said.

He was about to agree, but then remembered Hayley. There was definitely something interesting there now.

Garrett got up and left the captain's office. Walked through the precinct realizing that nothing had changed. He still felt removed from the hive of activity. Like he wasn't part of the fraternity any more.

Would he ever really feel like he was a part of it again?

***

Hayley couldn't ignore the summons from her father. He'd sent

46

her a text that morning that he was back in town and would like to see her for cocktails at seven. She was nervous, as only a meeting with her dad could make her, and she skipped over her new wardrobe for one of the plain tweed skirts she usually wore in winter.

Except when she put on the skirt, turtle neck, and blazer and looked at herself in the mirror she really didn't look like she'd expected. She took off the tweed skirt, which went to her mid-calf, and put on one of her new plaid mini skirts instead. She swapped the blazer for her leather fitted jacket and when she looked in the full-length mirror again she felt more like herself.

She applied some make-up and put on a pair of boots with a decent heel before heading out the door. She took a cab to Rockefeller Center and the elevator up to the thirtieth floor, where she found him waiting for her.

He smiled when he saw her and gave her a hug and a kiss on the cheek. "Hello, my dear, you're looking pretty tonight. I like the haircut."

"Thanks, Dad," she said. She'd been a little nervous, wondering what he'd think, but her father had always been too busy with work to really worry over the details of her life the way her mother always had.

"I hope you don't mind, but I booked us a table for dinner as well as drinks. I realize we hadn't had a chance to celebrate your birthday yet."

"That's great. I don't have any plans tonight," she admitted. "I have a meeting with the board of directors next week that I'm sort of preparing for."

She never wanted him to think that she wasn't concentrating on her business and doing her best to make it a success.

"I can't wait to hear your presentation. The board has been very happy with the decision to invest in The Candied Apple. I'm really proud of you," he said, leading the way to the bar, where he ordered two Manhattans.

She found a tall table with standing room and waited for her father to bring the drinks over. His approval made her feel good, but it was always a hollow victory. The one parent whose approval she had always craved was forever beyond her.

Her dad joined her, handing her cocktail glass to her. "Happy late birthday," he said.

She lifted her glass and took a sip. Manhattans always reminded her of her parents. It had been their drink. And as soon as she was old enough her father had ordered her one. It was a Dunham family tradition. And one she savored. She only drank Manhattans with him.

"Dad..."

"Yes?" he asked.

"Do you think Mom would be pleased with the way I turned out?"

He set his glass on the table and gave her that serious look. His eyes were the same hazel color as hers, so it was a little unnerving at times to look into them. "Yes. I do. She was very proud of you when she was alive."

Did he mean that? Or was this simply one more thing that he was out of touch with in her life?

"Why do you say that?" she asked. She couldn't imagine her mom being proud of her. All she could remember were lectures on dressing better and standing up straight.

"We used to talk on the phone every night while I was travelling and she'd tell me everything you were doing. She was proud of the way that you took your own path instead of just following her example."

"She said that?" Hayley asked. It was hard to reconcile his words with the mom she remembered. Of course, as an adult she realized her parents would have been different when she wasn't around, but she doubted her mom had a complete personality make-over.

"Well, not in so many words," he said with a rueful grin. "But I could hear it in her tone."

48

Hayley had heard that tone as well and she hadn't gotten the same message. Her father probably was coloring his memories by the fact that her mom was gone.

"Did you read her letter yet?" he asked. "I had my assistant bring it over with your birthday present."

"I haven't read the letter," she explained. "Thank you for the espresso maker. I've already used it."

"You're welcome, my dear," he said.

She asked about the West Coast and he told her about his trip to Los Angeles, where the Dunham Dinners test kitchens were. "I'd love to get you to develop some desserts for us to use in a frozen range."

She nodded. He was always asking her to do that. But she'd never really wanted to be a part of the family business. And then she realized that she'd been running from it and from him.

Why?

Maybe she didn't approve of her family any more than her mother had. She did sometimes feel that the cooking she did was superior to the stuff her father's company produced. She was more like her mom than she realized.

"Let's talk about that idea further," she said. "Maybe we could tie it in with The Candied Apple, maybe make it a featured limited-run dessert line."

He nodded. "That's a good idea. We can discuss it over dinner."

They were seated a few minutes later and spent the entire meal discussing the frozen-dessert idea. Her father was excited. And Hayley felt a little bad that she'd waited so long to agree to it.

She had always felt so businesslike and mature in her twenties and, granted, she was only days into her thirties, but already she seemed to be making better choices...

Maybe even the decision to kiss Garrett?

Where had that come from?

"Do you need a ride home?" he asked.

"No, I'm going to walk. Thanks, Dad."

49

Garrett lingered in the back of her mind as she and her father said goodbye. His driver was waiting to take him to his home on Long Island and she stood in the taxi line for a few minutes not really wanting to go home but unsure of where else to go.

"Hayley?"

She glanced over her shoulder to see Garrett and another man standing there.

***

Garrett had been out with Hoop celebrating being cleared of charges. His lawyer friend had been the only one available on short notice to celebrate. The other guys were in rotation and working tonight.

"Evening, Garrett," she said, walking over to him. She looked cute in her mini-skirt and leather jacket.

"This is Jason Hooper," Garret said.

Hoop held out his hand and Hayley took it. But instead of shaking it Hoop brought it to his mouth and kissed the back of it.

Hayley smiled as she pulled her hand back and Garrett elbowed his friend in the side.

"What?" Hoop asked.

"Nothing," Garrett said.

"I think he objected to you kissing my hand," Hayley said.

He did. He thought it interesting that the woman who'd walked away from him and kept putting up barriers had noticed.

"Indeed. Hoop has to head home for an early court appearance tomorrow, but would you like to join me for drinks?"

She took a deep breath and looked up at the night sky. "I would. I can't stay out too late—I have to be at the shop at five."

"Five. Damn, woman that's earlier than my court start," Hoop said. "Maybe—"

"No. Go home and prepare like a good lawyer," Garrett said.

His friend laughed and leaned over to kiss Hayley on the cheek.

50

"It was very interesting meeting you. Hope to see you again."

Hoop walked away and Garrett just watched his friend leave. Then he glanced back at Hayley, noticing that she was watching him carefully.

"How do you know a lawyer? Is he your attorney?"

He took her hand and led her back into Rockefeller Center toward the bank of elevators.

"Where are we going?"

"I was thinking 65 at the Rainbow Room. They've got a nice view and we can sit and chat."

"Sounds so respectable."

"It is. You can't be a bad girl every second of the day," he said.

"Tell me about it."

He hit the elevator button and soon they were seated in some round, comfortable chairs near the window. He'd had to tip the maître d' to ensure it, but it was worth it. She ordered a Bailey's neat and he ordered Kahlua and coffee.

The conflicted feelings he'd had all day were starting to ebb now that he was sitting across from Hayley. He figured it was down to the fact that she was a sexy woman that he wanted to get to know better.

She was a puzzle, much like the cases he'd worked on the force and just the distraction he needed. Despite the fact that he was cleared by Internal Affairs, he still wasn't back to where he had been before the incident.

Would he ever be?

A part of him wasn't sure.

"So you asked if Hoop was my attorney," Garrett said after their drinks arrived. "He's not. Just a friend who happens to be a lawyer."

"One of your trust-fund friends?" she asked.

"Nope. We were rookies together. He didn't like being a cop, so he went back to school and became a lawyer."

"That's interesting. I wonder what made him do that," Hayley said.

Was she interested in his friend? He realized it didn't matter. Hell, yes it did. He'd kissed her. He wanted her. And no other man was going to—

What?

They were neighbors and sort of acquaintances, nothing more. But the way he felt, he knew he wanted it to be more. Maybe it was the fact that he'd gotten good news today and he felt like he was going to have his life back. His real life.

As soon as he put the uniform back on and got back out there, he'd face his fears and move on. Until then it felt like doubt was going to keep riding him like a monkey on his back.

"It is. You'd have to ask him."

She nodded. "So what happened at the station today? Did you get good news?"

"Yeah. Internal Affairs cleared me of any wrongdoing in the shooting. The investigation concluded that if I hadn't shot with lethal intent I'd be dead."

She reached across the table and squeezed his hand. "I'm so glad you are here."

He looked into her pretty hazel eyes. He was glad too. He hadn't been sure earlier today where he was going and, to be perfectly honest, he still wasn't entirely sure what the future held, but he knew he wanted to be right here at this moment.

"I'm glad you're here as well. What were you doing here tonight?"

She pulled her hand back and took a sip of her drink. "Birthday dinner with my dad."

She was hiding something. She revealed little true pieces of herself and then retreated.

"Sounds nice. Does he live here? Or was he visiting?" Garrett asked.

"He has an apartment in the city, but lives on Long Island... in the Hamptons. He likes to work from his home office there when he's on the East Coast."

"Your family makes frozen foods, right? Is that how you got involved in the candy shop?" he asked. He wanted to know more about her. He knew she kissed him like the bad girl she'd been pretending to be, but what else was going on in that pretty little head of hers.

She shook her head. "Yes to the frozen foods. My father's family were one of the first to jump on the bandwagon of making and freezing dinners back in the 50s and they've changed with the times to stay popular even today."

"They do make a pretty good meatloaf dinner," Garrett said. When he and Gonzalez had been on stakeouts they'd usually relied on frozen meals while they'd been in the apartment the city rented for them.

"I will make you that same recipe at home and it's even better."

"You want to cook for me?" he asked.

"Maybe if you're lucky." She tipped her head to the side as she flirted with him.

He felt a zing down his spine and he leaned forward to be closer to her.

"How do I get lucky?" he asked.

She smiled. "If I have to explain it, then I don't think you will."

He laughed out loud and shook his head. He wasn't sure about this woman, but every second he spent with her made him want to see her again.

He leaned over the table and kissed her. Just a quick, passionate kiss that he knew took her by surprise. She shifted back in her chair and put her hand up.

"I can't do this."

"Do what?"

"Kiss you. Date you. I'm...I just can't," she said and got up and left the restaurant.

He watched her leave, wondering what he'd done wrong. It had been a light kiss to match the mood. But he'd certainly sent her running.

Chapter 6

The class space was on the second floor and afforded them a good view of her shop. She felt a little thrill when she heard Marti, one of her employees, explaining how the way they blended the chocolate with different spices created a unique taste experience.

Hayley's dream was slowly coming true. And she was doing it on her own terms with the help of her good friends Cici and Iona. She noticed couples walking into the shop. Some of them stopped at the candy bar for her signature drink "the candied apple". It was a martini-based confection that she'd altered using an apple gastrique and spun sugar apple garnishes.

A party of four entered and she looked at the laughing couples, hoping that someday—

Whoa.

Wait a minute.

Hadn't Garrett said he wasn't seeing anyone? Why did she even care? She'd walked away from him more than a week ago and hadn't looked back. She'd been afraid and now...

"Oh, my God."

"What?" Iona asked. "Did you spill hot sugar on yourself? I warned you to be careful."

"No. It's Officer Hottie. He's here. He's...with a woman. Figures."

"Dirty rat," Iona said.

"Really? Are you Bugsy Malone?"

She shrugged. "My mom had a strict no-cursing rule and my brothers and I had no choice but to respect it."

She shook her head. She wanted to laugh, but inside she just sort of shuttered and a part of her died. The daring woman who'd been reborn on her birthday.

And it was then that she realized something profound. She couldn't change for her friends or for a man. She had to change for herself.

"You're right, Io, he is a dirty rat. Can you cover the greetings for a few minutes? I just want to go and check some things in the kitchen."

"You got it. Take your time," Iona said.

Time, Hayley thought as she went into the only closed-off space upstairs. A small pantry that was used to house dry goods needed for the classes and a big industrial-sized sink. She put her hands on the basin of the sink and leaned forward, looking at herself in the mirror.

She felt unsettled...irritated maybe? The emotion swamping her was new and foreign.

Jealousy.

Anger.

Envy.

She shook her head and looked again at her face. How more pronounced her small nose and cheekbones seemed now that her hair was cut so short. She wasn't going to be played by Officer Hottie – objectifying him helped her a little – or anyone else. She'd made a decision on her birthday to change her life and cowering in the stock room wasn't what she'd had in mind.

***

Nina O'Neill was charming and pretty, so it definitely wasn't her

55

fault that he wasn't interested. But all through dinner as he sat next to her he couldn't help thinking about Hayley and the kiss they'd shared. His leg was a persistent ache and the day had been long—filled with lots of workouts of his upper body and a very depressing conversation with his captain about his potential return to the force.

Agreeing to a blind date had to be his dumbest idea yet. Proof that he was useless unless he was on the beat protecting people. He knew he functioned better when he could get out of his own head. Which was why he'd agreed to doing this favor for his brother.

But Crystal's friend didn't seem to really need a date with her. She'd spent the entire evening talking about herself and about the ring that Pete had bought for Crystal. It was interesting and he knew he was irritable, probably because all evening long he'd been comparing Nina to Hayley.

That's right, he was obsessing over his neighbor, who in all likelihood he'd probably not see unless he waited by his front door and "accidently" ran into her. He'd contemplated it while he'd been doing reps with his weights earlier. Hence him being out with Nina.

Dinner at a chic uptown bistro hadn't been bad. He'd had a steak cooked just the way he liked it—rare. His brother and he had even managed to sneak into the cigar room for a smoke before the ladies had arrived.

"I have been dying to try this place," Nina said as they got out of the cab in front of The Candied Apple. The outside was all glass and wrought iron with a large green apple over the door. The glasswork was similar to the artist Chihuly. Garrett paid the cabbie and then held the door open for Nina. His brother and Crystal were in a separate cab since they'd gone home to let their dog Baskins out. Nina's thick brown hair fell in waves around her shoulders and Garrett couldn't help thinking that it was too long. She should have a cute little pixie cut like Hayley.

They made their way through the crowded shop to the bar set

up at the bottom of the stairs. Nina stepped up and ordered two of the house specialty cocktail while he glanced around the place. Even off duty he couldn't help scanning a room and checking it out. He'd always been like that.

He noticed the shelves full of all sorts of confectionary, the employee behind the counter, who was explaining the fine art of chocolate-making to a customer. The buzz of conversations whirled around him. He didn't see a threat and then shook his head. Good thing, given his bum leg.

"Don't you agree?" she asked him. She was nervous and kept glancing at her hands when she spoke. He didn't blame her. It was clear they were both out of their comfort zone doing a favor for a friend – or in his case a brother – rather than actually being on a date they wanted to be on.

"I'm sorry, I wasn't paying attention," he admitted as he got his wallet out to pay for the cocktails Nina had ordered. He had to get Hayley out of his head. It was easy to blame the timing of meeting her. But he knew that there was something about her.

"I said I have been dying to try one of these since *On Trend* named this as one of their top five most-intriguing cocktails. Haven't you?"

"Uh…yeah," he said. He knew it would be pointless to remind her that until six weeks ago he'd been working on the streets, more concerned with catching drug dealers than what cocktail was hot, new and trendy. "I am totally not *On Trend's* reader."

"I know. I was trying to make conversation. You could try a little harder," Nina said.

"What?" he asked. He was doing his level best to be present, but he had a lot on his mind. He was concerned about his job, his brother wanted him to jump ship and return to the family fold and then there were his frequent dreams about Hayley.

"To act like you're interested in me. Crystal said that Pete and your family are worried about you. That's why I agreed to come, but you've hardly said two words and frankly I'm out of conversational gambits."

Her words humbled him and made him realize that whenever he did things with his family he tended to start out with attitude. "You're right. I can be a real bastard at times. I shouldn't have agreed to come out tonight."

"It's okay," she said, putting her hand on his arm and for the first time he noticed she had really pretty blue eyes. Her nails were short and had a plain buff-colored polish on them. "You're injured and not sure what's happening with your job. I'd be a total bitch if I couldn't go into my office every day."

"What is it you do again?" he asked.

She shook her head and dropped her hand. "I'm a vet. I have a clinic on the Upper East Side. That's how I met Crystal and Pete. They brought Baskins in to see me. I told you all about it on the cab ride over."

He sighed. "I'd ask for a do-over but..."

"You're not really interested," she finished for him. "Why did you come out tonight?"

"Pete asked me," he said. No use telling Nina that he'd been bored and about to go stir crazy by himself.

"Fair enough," she said, lifting her glass toward him. "To family and the things we do for them."

At another time he might have really hit it off with Nina, he thought, lifting his glass and tapping the rim to hers. "To friends."

The first sip of the drink was an eye-opener. There was an intense explosion of apple and caramel on the palette and then the sensation of warmth as he swallowed. He took another sip as the aftertaste of sour apple lingered.

Pete and Crystal arrived and they ordered another round of cocktails. Garrett leaned back against the wall next to the high bar table, where they were waiting for the class. He was afforded a nice view of the loft area and as he glanced up he caught a glimpse of those long curvy legs he'd first noticed two nights ago.

Then shook his head. Now he was seeing Hayley's legs. He

put his martini glass on the table. He needed to stop drinking and tomorrow start looking for something productive to do with his days.

He noticed everyone at the table was looking at him. Damn. He'd missed something else.

"Sorry."

"Bro, you're embarrassing me," Pete said. "Nina said she'd rather eat candy than make it."

"Never tried making it," Garrett said. "But I'm sort of leaning toward just eating as well. And how am I embarrassing you?"

"Not paying attention. Crystal and I hardly ever get to see you," Pete said. "You could at least pretend to be interested in being here."

"You saw me for dinner not that long ago," Garrett pointed out.

Crystal rolled her eyes before getting to her feet. "I'm going to the ladies' room."

"I'll come with you," Nina said.

Pete's gaze followed his fiancée and for the first time Garrett noticed that his brother didn't seem as in love with Crystal as he once had been. Trouble in paradise? But he wasn't about to interfere. Clearly if this night was any indication, he wasn't on his A Game when it came to women right now.

"What's up?" he asked Pete.

"Could you try a little harder?" Pete asked, rubbing his hand through his hair and taking another deep swallow of the cocktail.

"I am. She's perfectly charming, but not exactly my type," Garrett said. That was the truth. Nina was a lovely woman, but for where he was in his life – not sure what was going on at work – she wasn't the right person for him. Why couldn't he get Hayley out of his mind, then?

"What is your type?" Pete asked. "You've never been one to get serious about a woman."

"My job isn't exactly the kind of one that encourages long relationships and I don't know what my type is. Nina seems a little reluctant to get involved too. But enough about that, what's up with you and Crystal?"

"Nothing. She says we don't go on enough dates or have social couples as friends. I was hoping you and Nina would hit it off so I wouldn't have to keep going out with her friends and their husbands. I'm just not that into gold or fantasy football."

His brother did look stressed. Garrett wondered if it was the upcoming wedding, which was only six months away, or maybe the retirement of the head of security at the office. "I will try harder, but me and Nina aren't going to be a thing."

"It's okay. You can't choose who you fall for," Pete said, clapping him on the shoulder.

The women came back and they headed up the stairs to be greeted by a redhead with cream-colored skin, but as she was talking Garrett glanced past her and noticed the one woman who'd been on his mind all evening lurking in the doorway.

Hayley.

***

The bowl of chocolate ganache sat on the workbench between the four of them. Garrett's distractions were all gone and he'd become the star pupil of the class. Hayley smiled and flirted, but he could tell it was an act. None of the charming innocence of the woman he'd met and kissed a few nights ago was there.

"This group certainly seems to be doing well. The next part is where your hands get dirty," Hayley said as she came over to their table. She'd given him the cold shoulder all evening, but he couldn't fault her teaching methods or her attitude with the others at their table.

"I don't mind getting messy," Garrett said. He wanted to say something – anything – to shake her and see her react to him. But he guessed showing up at her cooking class with a date wasn't a good idea.

To be fair, he had no idea she taught candy-making. Or that he'd be so fascinated by it.

His brother chuckled. "That's the truth. When we were kids his nickname was—"

Garrett elbowed his brother in the gut. Childhood nicknames should stay firmly hidden in childhood. "Never mind that. Hayley, this is Nina, she's my brother's vet."

Nina gave him an amused look and he knew he was acting like... well like a man who was in the throes of a crush. He groaned. But the truth was he wanted Hayley to know this wasn't a date.

"Nice to meet you, Nina," Hayley said, holding her hand out to the other woman. "I've been thinking of getting a dog recently. Maybe I could pick your brain later?"

"I'd love to talk animals with you. I also host an adoption clinic once a month. That might be a good place to start," Nina said, handing Hayley her card.

Hayley pocketed it. "I will."

"How do you know Garrett?" Nina asked.

"I'm his neighbor."

"The one who lost her keys?" Pete asked.

Garrett groaned again. He knew his older brother could tell that he was attracted to Hayley...hell, a blind man probably could pick up on the clues since he kept fawning all over her.

"Why, yes, I am," Hayley said. "What did he tell you about that?"

Garrett was ready to elbow his brother again, but Pete just shrugged. "He just mentioned that you'd needed his help. Since his injury Garrett has been desperate to save someone."

"Desperate?" Garrett asked. His brother couldn't help needling him and this night was really turning into one from hell. "I haven't been desperate. It's just that protecting the community is my calling."

Now he sounded like a big lame-o.

Hayley smothered a smile and arched an eyebrow at him.

"Well my 'calling' involves chocolate and making it for others,"

61

Hayley said.

"Hi there. I'm Pete's fiancée. Garrett definitely needed to get out of that house and go somewhere other than the gym," Crystal chimed in. "Don't you agree?"

"I wouldn't say all those hours in the gym were wasted," Hayley said, winking at him. "It's time for you all to use those melon-ballers and start making your truffles."

She demonstrated one for the group and then, after they all tried it, she moved on to another table. Garrett stared after her. He noticed that she was just as friendly with the next group. Was she doing it to prove something to him?

What? They weren't dating. As she'd said, they were neighbors. In fact, she'd made it very clear that she didn't want to date him.

Of course, that just made him want her more. Nothing spurred him on like a challenge.

"So that's the lady you rescued?" Pete said, a note of interest in his voice. His brother had melted chocolate on his hands and was holding the melon-baller loosely in his left hand. Pete was never going to be a master chocolatier.

"I just said she was," Garrett retorted, concentrating on making the truffles. He was going to have to work twice as hard to make up for Pete's lack of skill.

"She's cute," Nina said. "And really talented. That article I mentioned earlier had a profile about her. Her father is the frozen-food king Arthur Dunham of Dunham Dinners."

Everyone had heard of Dunham Dinners. They were probably the most famous frozen-ready meals in the country. Interesting that she was making candy instead of trying to take over the reins of her father's empire, but that had been something she didn't want to discuss. She kept a lot of herself hidden away.

"I wonder why she doesn't work for him. Did the article say?" Garrett asked. Why hadn't he thought to read her profile? Probably because she'd walked away and he was busy trying to get back on the force…well, back to his old job on the force.

"She had a cute quote in the article that said she likes sweet things. But I guess you'd have to ask her," Nina said.

Crystal looped her arm through his. "I bet you're glad I made Pete invite you along."

He looked at the woman who was going to be his sister-in-law and for the first time realized that she saw him as family. Pete and Nina were both using forks to roll the balls of chocolate through different toppings. Crystal drew him away from the table.

"I am. Maybe I have been a little too closed off."

"Maybe? We all know you needed time to recover from the injury and from Hector's death," Crystal said. "But we miss you. You're my crazy soon-to-be brother-in-law, I like that."

He swallowed. He wasn't ready to talk about any of that. Not with Crystal or his brother or anyone. Even the little bit he'd revealed to Hayley seemed like too much. He needed to figure it all out for himself first.

Despite the fact that Internal Affairs had cleared him, he hadn't cleared himself.

"Thanks, Crystal."

"It was my intent to do a little matchmaking and find you a woman to distract you. But seems you didn't need my help after all."

He nodded. The truth was, he had needed Crystal's help. He hadn't realized this was Hayley's store or what she did. Crystal went back to their group and Garrett noticed that Hayley had disappeared behind the door at the front of the room.

He followed her into the room, startling her as she was coming back out with a box of cocoa powder. She stumbled into him and he wrapped his arms around her, steadying her.

"I'm always catching you," he said under his breath as he stared down into her eyes. There were lots of emotions swirling through them, but none that he could identify. She felt so good in his arms. He wanted to keep her here. Hold onto her because when he did he felt grounded.

"You're always surprising me," she admitted at last. She had on an apron that had The Candied Apple logo on it and their slogan "Take One Bite". "I didn't expect to see you here tonight."

"Me neither," he admitted. But he was so glad they'd run into each other again.

"So, you're on a date?" she asked a tad too casually.

He shook his head. "No, I'm not. I'm out with my brother, his fiancée, and their vet."

"That sounds like a date."

"Well, in that case, you've been on it too, because I haven't been able to think of anything but you all night."

She frowned slightly, studying him. He'd looked at enough perps to know she was searching for the truth in his words. He wasn't a fancy talker like Hoop or his brother Pete. He shot from the hip and saw the world in two shades, black and white.

But somehow Hayley seemed to fall in the middle of that. She wasn't all good or all bad. She was human.

Just like he was. It was a good thing to remember.

But he'd always wanted to be better.

The kind of cop that garnered respect for the badge and lived his life up to a certain standard. And he always had until he'd killed Paco.

A drug dealer who'd left him no choice and left his world shattered.

He was broken, but there was something about Hayley that sort of fixed him.

He looked into her eyes again.

What else could he say?

Words had never been his strong suit and when he saw doubt in her eyes, he lowered his mouth to hers and showed her with his kiss that he meant everything he'd said. He hoped she got the message because this was the only weapon available to him.

Chapter 7

He tasted like coffee, martinis, and temptation. It wasn't enough that she knew he wasn't for her. He was dating. On a double date with his brother. That meant off limits. Except he smelled good.

Too damned good.

That scent reminded her of the wildness that came in the wind just before a rainstorm. She should run except she didn't do that any more.

She was a bad girl. The kind of woman who wrote things like "kiss a man in public" on her bucket list. Okay that wasn't daring at all. But she'd never been the type of woman who'd inspired a man to a public display of affection before. And she wanted to be.

Some sort of femme fatale.

One that didn't have to worry about consequences. She wanted to be that kind of woman.

Bad girls could just revel in the feel of his tongue rubbing over hers. The way his hands slid down her back, pausing to squeeze her waist before settling on her hips.

He held her loosely, but there was no doubt in her mind that she was trapped. Not by him. Not physically. But by her own desires and her own needs.

Needs that she'd never considered before. She'd never thought of herself as a sexual being, but all of that had changed after one night in this man's house. Well one night and one drink.

For the first time in her adult life a guy was kissing her and it was all she could do not to move away from him. Not to run screaming in the opposite direction because she wanted to melt at his feet.

Wanted to grab him by that slim tie he was wearing and pull him deeper into the storage closet, close the door, and not emerge until she'd learned all his secrets.

But she couldn't. She was at work.

She might be playing at being a bad girl, but she'd always known that there were consequences. And she wasn't about to let a man compromise that.

Someone cleared their throat and Garrett didn't jerk away or allow her to. He rubbed his lips over hers one more time, slowly lifting his mouth from hers and turning to look over his shoulder at Cici, who was standing there.

Hayley felt herself turning a deep shade of red...she had to be, her face was on fire. But she just lifted one eyebrow at Cici.

"Did you need me?"

Cici nodded. "I think everyone is done with their truffles. I need some more boxes for them."

Hayley had them in her hand. She reached over Garrett's shoulder and handed them to Cici. And Cici, being the good friend she was, just nodded her thanks and turned around to leave.

Oh. My. God.

She was going to die of embarrassment. Melt into the floor like chocolate over a bain-marie until there was nothing left.

"You should get back to your date."

"Hayley—"

"This isn't the right time, Garrett. You can't leave your date and I don't really want to face her having kissed you. I like her. That's not cool. At least not in my book."

"I agree. But we were never really—"

"Go and finish it."

Instead of stepping back, he tightened his fingers on her hips and leaned in. His aftershave was spicy, masculine, and addictive. She loved the smell of it.

"I'm not used to being told what to do."

"You have to have been at some point," she said. Looking into his very serious eyes. She'd read the account of the shooting that had led to his suspension. She knew that cops had to answer to their superiors.

"At work. Not in my personal life."

"I'm not trying to take control," she said. "But I have a class to teach and you have a woman who came on a blind date who doesn't need another reason to think men are jerks."

He nodded. "I already apologized to her."

"Good. Now go. If you are as serious as that kiss suggested why don't you meet me here in the morning for coffee? You can keep me company while I get the shop prepared for the day."

"What time?" he asked.

"Five a.m." This had to be one of her dumbest ideas except avoiding him hadn't worked. She hadn't stopped thinking about him or the night she'd spent at his house. It had been two weeks since her birthday and she was no closer to figuring out what she wanted…that wasn't true.

She was slowly coming into her own once again on the business front. Pursuing that idea her father had, but personally—that was where she always struggled. And somehow that struggle seemed tied to Garrett.

"I'll meet you at your front door and we can come here together."

"Deal," she said.

He pivoted and walked away and all she could do was watch him go. That same chaotic cocktail of excitement and fear mixed in the pit of her stomach. She'd wanted change.

Craved change and a chance to prove to herself that it was okay to start living again. But he almost felt like too much.

She went back into the classroom and managed to avoid

67

looking at Garrett and his party while acting as if nothing had happened. Luckily she'd been making candy for longer than she could remember and truffles had long been her specialty. She'd made them for her father when he used to travel so he'd have a little taste of home with him.

She finished up the class and everyone trickled out, including Garrett, and Hayley busied herself cleaning up the classroom.

"What the hell was that?" Cici asked coming up to her.

"Um…he's my neighbor."

"That's taking friendly pretty far. Dish. I need to know what's going on," Cici said.

"Not yet," Iona said as she walked in. "I want to hear this. Did something happen with the sleepover guy?"

"Is he the sleepover guy?" Cici asked. "She was making out with one of the students in the pantry tonight."

"Really?" Iona asked.

Hayley wished a hole would open in the floor and swallow her up. She was the boring friend. The one who randomly jotted down candy recipes while Cici and Iona talked about their exciting sexcapades. She wasn't the one who did anything that anyone found interesting. Until now.

"It was Garrett, my neighbor. The one at whose place I spent the night. You both want to know about the same guy," Hayley admitted to her friends. "I'm still as confused now as I was earlier, Iona."

"What's going on?" Cici asked.

Hayley explained who Garrett was, catching Cici up on everything that had happened. Kissing him was becoming a habit. One she didn't want to break, but she saw something in him. Something that said he was lost and looking for a distraction.

And she wasn't.

She had finally decided to stop living under the weight of guilt and expectation that had been tied to her mom. She wanted her thirties to be the time when she came into her own. And as sexy as Garrett was, he didn't seem like the right man for her.

Maybe it was time to stop letting the old definitions of who she was dictate her life. She had changed her clothes and cut her hair—now it was time to change her world. And she was going to start with getting to know Garrett much better.

***

Garrett wandered through his empty house just after midnight. He'd always been a night owl who'd gotten his late-night fix working stake-outs. Not any more. He knew he couldn't go back out on the streets with his leg the way it was.

The doctor had been pretty clear that his leg would get to seventy per percent of where it had been. At best.

At best.

That was the dumbest phrase he'd heard in a long time. It gave a person a certain sense of hope, but then dashed it again. A cop who couldn't run full out after a perp shouldn't be on the street. He should be behind a desk.

But he wasn't going to be satisfied with that. He wasn't sure he was still the cop he'd been before the shoot-out. He needed to know what it was like to face down a perp with a gun. Would he freeze? Would he just fire without thinking?

He needed to know that he could still handle himself in that situation. But until he got the strength back in his leg that wasn't going to happen.

He paced into his living room and glanced at the sofa, remembering Hayley there. He sat down on the cushions, imagining he could still smell her vanilla perfume.

God, he needed to make a decision about his future. He was thirty-five and for the first time in his life he didn't know what was going to come next.

He didn't want to work for his family's company. Nothing that Pete or his parents said would change his mind on that front. And working at the station but being a desk cop didn't appeal. It just didn't suit him to stay inside all day.

He needed to figure out something else to do. But right now all he wanted to "do" was Hayley. He had an image in his head of her wearing nothing but that apron she'd had on tonight and those spiky boots.

Sexual frustration was messing with his head and turning him into a slightly obsessed man. Kissing her at the class tonight…well, he didn't regret it exactly, but he knew that he should have waited.

He had that feeling that there was nothing left to lose so he was acting like there were no consequences for any of his actions.

As penance for being probably the worst date that Nina had ever been on, Garrett had volunteered to work a four-hour shift on the following Saturday at her animal-rescue shelter. He was looking forward to it if he were honest. He'd have something to do besides work out and re-think the past.

Being brought down by a bum leg was like a living hell for a man of action. He heard a noise in the back yard and got up. He reached in his waistband for his weapon but it wasn't there. He was suspended, so they'd taken it from him. He grabbed the baseball bat he kept in the corner before pushing aside the blinds to glance onto his tiny patio.

Hayley stood there. She had a bottle of rum in one hand and her cell phone in the other.

He put the bat down and opened the French door. "Locked out again?"

"Nope. Thought we could chat."

"We have plans for breakfast tomorrow," he reminded her, but he'd stepped back so she could come inside. She wore a gray mini-skirt and a faded t-shirt and had a very determined look on her face.

"We do. But I couldn't sleep and I saw your light was on," she said, which wasn't really much of an explanation. She walked down the short hallway and into his kitchen. What was she doing here?

"How did you get into my back yard?" he asked, glancing over at the fence. It was six foot high and wooden. He'd known young punks who could scale them, but Hayley wasn't the type.

"I used a step ladder. When I was younger my best friend and I used to live next door to each other. I became really good at climbing fences. I guess it's a skill for life."

"I'd love to see that on a resume," he said, following her.

"Luckily I work for myself, so no resume needed," she said. "What about you?"

"What about me?" he asked. "I don't need a resume either."

She shook her head. "I meant, are you going to work for yourself if you can't go back on the force?" she asked as she took two juice glasses and poured a couple of fingers of rum into each of them. "Do you want a drink?"

"Yes. Want Coke with that?" he asked. He wasn't much of a straight-up rum person.

She nodded and he retrieved two cans from the fridge. They both added the Coke to their glasses and took a sip. Garrett leaned back against the counter and stared at her.

There was a hint of vulnerability in the set of her mouth and he realized that she wanted something from him, but was unsure of how to ask for it.

She'd been so bold last night and even earlier when she'd put him in his place. But now she was different.

"What's up? Not that I mind you dropping by, but it seems like something is bothering you."

"I just realized that I don't know you at all," she said carefully, looking down into her glass for a minute before lifting her head and meeting his gaze straight on.

"So? That's what tomorrow is for," he said, taking another swallow of his drink. He was looking forward to seeing more of her on her own turf. In fact, he'd pretty much seen her here in his place. He sort of liked it.

She took a sip and then glanced around his kitchen. "You're

71

right. I was being…old Hayley."

"Old Hayley?" he asked. That was an odd way of referring to herself.

"Pre-birthday make-over. I was a bit of a worrier."

"But now you're not?" he asked, reaching for the rum and topping up both of their glasses.

"That's the goal. But, to be honest, old habits are hard to break."

"Tell me about it. When I heard you in the back yard I reached for my weapon, only to remember I'm not a cop anymore."

"Don't you know that?" she asked.

"Yeah. That's the dumb part. Every minute of the day since I woke up in the hospital I have been reminded of what is missing in my life. Yet when I heard a noise suddenly my instincts were like let's do this." It was easy to talk to her. In fact easier than it had been to discuss this with Pete or Hoop or anyone else.

She tipped her head to the side and studied him. He wanted to stand up straighter. To preen a little and let her see that he was still solid and worth her attention. But he wasn't so sure anymore.

"That's kind of why I'm here. I'm making some plans for my future. My business is taking off and finally I'm proud of the life I've made. And you're sort of…"

"Sort of what?" he asked.

He didn't like the sound of this.

"Lost."

***

Lost.

Well fuck. That was the last thing he wanted anyone to view him as. It didn't really matter to him if that was the truth. He was used to being the protector. The hero. Not lost.

"Well, you're wrong," he said, sounding defensive to his own ears. Hell, how had she seen what he'd been so adept at hiding from everyone, especially himself?

72

"Really? Because I've been wandering through life since I turned twenty-one and I'm pretty familiar with what lost looks like, Garrett. I thought maybe you could use a friend."

"I don't want to be your friend," he said, putting his glass on the counter and advancing toward her. She held her glass with two hands right in the middle of her chest, but otherwise didn't move.

"You need a friend. Someone who you didn't know in your old world."

He stopped and shoved his hand through his hair. His old life. He didn't want to admit that he wasn't going back to the world he'd left. He would move on when he was ready to move on. He didn't want it to be because of some punk that had forced him into an action he had been reluctant to take.

"And you want to be friends?" he asked carefully. Because friends was the last thing he wanted to be with her. He wanted her naked and writhing under him. He wanted her mouth crushed against his, her curvy body pressed up against him. Damn. He was getting hard just thinking about her.

"Well, I did until you told me we couldn't be friends," she said.

"Sorry, but I don't think of you as a friend."

He saw that his words hurt her. But she was complicating his life. He didn't need the added distraction of his attraction for her. Hell.

He usually had a lot more finesse when it came to his dealings with women. Why did she rattle him so much?

"I just meant…it's hard to think of you as a friend when all I can think about is how you felt pressed against me when we fell together."

She took a rather big swallow of her drink and then put it on the counter. "If that's true, why haven't you followed up on it? I haven't exactly been giving you the no-trespassing signs."

"Well, you sort of walked away from me at Rockefeller Center and when I kissed you tonight—"

"Fair enough. But still, there was no reason for you to come to

73

my shop with a date. It's been two weeks. You could have stopped by my place if you were interested. Unless you're a coward."

Coward.

He felt every muscle in his body tighten. It was bad enough his leg still wasn't at capacity, but to hear her call his behavior on the line like that pushed him past the limits of his self control.

"Coward?"

She arched both eyebrows at him. "Just calling it like I see it. You knew where I lived."

He closed the gap between their bodies. And brought their faces closer together until he felt the warmth of her breath against his lips with each of her exhalations, which were getting shallower and shallower. The tips of her breasts brushed against his chest like a whip over his already aroused senses.

Suddenly he did feel cowardly. He'd been sitting at home by himself trying to prove he needed no one, but he definitely needed Hayley.

He needed the soft curves that were pressed against him right now. And he sure as hell needed her mouth. He licked her lower lip and then groaned before he took the kiss he'd been denying he wanted.

Her tongue rubbed over his and shivers went down his spine as his blood seemed to run heavier in his veins. His cock hardened and he canted his hips forward, rubbing the ridge of it against the center of her body.

She moaned and shifted on her tiptoes, the glass she still held in her hands bumped his chest and he reached between them to take it from her. He lifted his head from hers and put the glass on the counter next to her.

He rested his hands back on the counter behind her on either side of her hips.

"Interesting," he said.

"What is?" she asked.

"That you kiss better than I remembered," he said. His mind

had been telling him there was no way that the intimate moments they'd shared had been real. That it was only his confinement in his home that made the kiss seem so incendiary. Like they were both going up in flames. But the proof was right here almost in his arms.

"Uh, that doesn't sound like much of a compliment."

"Trust me, it is," he said, lifting his hand and toying with a strand of her short hair. He tucked it behind her ear and noticed that she had a scar behind it.

"What's this?" he asked.

"That is something that happened to me when I was young and dumb."

Dumb didn't fit with his image of Hayley, but they'd all done things in their teens that they regretted. Or at least he had. Though, to be fair, he'd been a little stupid, but it had put him on the path to being a cop. Something he definitely didn't regret.

He leaned around to get better look. He'd seen a lot of injuries and if he had to guess, he'd say it was from glass. "Car accident?"

"No. I was sneaking back into our house and fell into a table that had been moved. There was a large vase on it and it fell with me," she said. She shifted away from him.

He let her go.

"Why were you sneaking in?" he asked. "I thought you were a good girl who was turning bad. That sounds kind of rebellious to me."

She shook her head and then gave him a hard stare. "Do you really want to know this? We can't be casual acquaintances if I tell you about my scars."

Scars. Plural. She had more than one. Well, most people did. He had scars on the inside as well as the ones on the outside of his body. But there was something in her eyes that intrigued him. It might be stupid. He'd already said she was the wrong woman for him right now. He reached for her hand and threaded their fingers together. "Maybe I was wrong when I said we weren't

75

friends. I want to know more."

She sighed. "My mom and I fought a lot. She wanted me to be her little miniature and that was stifling. So from the time I turned fifteen I sort of asked myself what would Mom do and then did the exact opposite."

He rubbed his thumb over her knuckles. He'd be lying if he didn't admit to being turned on by her comments. He knew there was more to her than a good girl trying to change her life.

"You must have made some peace with her," Garrett said. "You have been living a pretty good life."

"I didn't. She died before I wised up," Hayley said. She took her hand from his and walked away.

He should let her go. He wasn't in a position to fix anyone right now. He had to get himself back to his old form. Except that he couldn't simply let her walk away. Fixing her might be the distraction he needed from the mess his life was in.

Chapter 8

Garrett didn't really know what to say to Hayley. He followed her into his living room and found she had sat down on the couch and was holding her glass against her chest again.

It was late at night and, like his father used to say, that was when the demon of regret came to call. Garrett suspected that was why he'd been up and wandering around his house. But he understood her regrets...death was a cheat especially when it touched the lives of those closest to someone.

He regretted his partner's death. That he'd been a little annoyed that Hector had talked a lot and texted him memes of celebrities doing dumb things. But after Hector had died he found he missed those very things.

"I'm sorry about your mom," he said at last. The silence in the room felt oppressive and he knew that was because of the pall cast by her unresolved issues.

"Thanks. She got really sick when I was seventeen—cancer. And I wasn't ready for it. Not that I ever would have been," Hayley said, turning to look at him. "She wanted to tell me a bunch of things because she knew her chances of surviving weren't that great, but I didn't. I thought she was doing it to make me become her little clone."

She shook her head and Garrett's heart ached. With that one

confession they weren't strangers who had the hots for each other anymore. They had shared too much to be anything less than friends. He looked at her different.

He sat down next to her, put his arm on the back of the couch, and drew her into the curve of his body. "When did you realize she wasn't trying to play you?"

"When her hair fell out. You had to know my mom. She had been a beauty queen and was always perfectly put together. I freaked. I mean really freaked. My dad stopped travelling and for the first time since I'd been a little kid we were all together," she said.

"Why for the first time?" Garrett asked.

He had a really nice voice, she thought. The kind she could listen to for hours and he seemed genuinely interested. It had been a long time – okay, it was the first time ever – that she had talked about her mom. Most of her friends already knew about the cancer and that her mom had died.

She tried to remember that she had decided getting to know him better was a bad idea. Except, if that was the case, why was she here? Why wasn't she in her own big lonely brownstone instead of sitting on this couch with the hottest guy she'd ever met?

"Hayley?"

She shook her head and put down her drink glass. Alcohol wasn't a good idea for her. She made dumb choices when she drank and they always seemed like they'd work out, but never really had.

Not even Garrett.

"Um...sorry. My dad traveled a lot for business, so usually he was gone and I attended a boarding school so I wasn't there. But that summer we were. And suddenly Mom didn't care that I wasn't perfect and I tried a little harder to be what she wanted. We spent a lot of time at our summer cottage and walked on the beach every day. Mom all covered up...I was starting to mature... well, as much as a seventeen-going-on-eighteen-year-old girl could, but it wasn't soon enough.

"She died three days after my eighteenth birthday."

Hayley turned away and wiped a tear from the corner of her eye. "You'd think after all this time I'd be used to her being gone, but some days…it hits me harder."

"I know what you mean."

She looked at him. "How? I thought your parents were still alive."

"They are. I meant missing someone who's gone. My partner died the night I got this injury. We still had plans, you know?"

She shook her head. "Because of the cancer Mom and I had tied up everything. She wrote a bunch of letters for me to open on each of my birthdays and had time to tell me everything. Nothing left to talk about." Except that she hadn't realized at eighteen there were still a lot of questions she wanted to ask. Like how it felt to fall in love. How had her mom known her dad was the one?

These were dumb questions, she thought, but honestly, those were things she wanted to know.

"Did you open your letter from her the night we met?"

"No."

"Why not?"

She rubbed the back of her neck. She'd just said she wasn't a spoiled child anymore and she really wanted to believe that was true, but she hadn't read the letter because each time she read one she was forced back to that moment when her mom died. Forced back to the girl-woman she'd been. And this year she wanted to keep moving forward.

"I just didn't want to remember."

He lifted his glass toward her. "To not remembering."

She picked hers up and took a sip, but her head was already buzzing and she knew that it was too late to induce good sense. "Have you figured out how to do that yet?"

He gave her a rueful grin and shook his head. "Exercise helps and flirting with a pretty woman, but beyond that, no. Nothing else I've done can dull the memories of that moment."

"I wake up sometimes thinking that I need to call her and tell her about my day," Hayley admitted. "Crazy right? It's been twelve years... when will I forget?"

"Maybe you're not supposed to forget," he said. "Maybe some people leave such a powerful imprint on our hearts that we will always carry them inside of us."

Maybe it was the alcohol or maybe it was the intensity in his gaze, but Garrett was making a lot of sense for a man she thought was too confused by his future to get serious. She put her glass down again and turned to look at him.

***

Garrett had been trying to tell himself that Hayley was like every other woman he'd ever encountered and, truth to tell, she might be, but he was different. The incident had changed him. Seeing his partner die, killing a suspect, it had left scars on him that he wasn't bouncing back from.

The injury to his leg was easier to focus on. He could pretend that once his leg was healed he'd be able to carry on like before. But a part of him was beginning to realize that wasn't going to happen. The captain had been noncommittal, but it didn't take a genius to figure out that a cop who had a bum leg was a liability.

For the first time he wasn't sure of his future. One damned second had changed everything. The decision of Paco Rivera to run when they'd pulled him over had shattered the life that Garrett had naïvely believed would always be his.

"That was surprisingly deep for this hour of the night," she said, tucking a strand of hair behind her ear.

Her ears were small and delicate. He noticed the nice-sized diamond studs in each ear earlier. Was he really obsessing over her ears? He must be...

Obsessed.

He knew it.

It wasn't just the changes inside of him. There was something about Hayley that made him want to be a better man. A stronger man. Not physically. Frankly, he was so pumped up right now that there wasn't really anywhere for him to go. But emotionally.

He needed to be on his A-Game because from the first moment they'd met, he'd known she was different. She kept him on his toes and, if he were honest, slightly off balance at the same time.

"That's how I roll," he said. Keeping it light was his usual way of dealing with women. Being a cop was dangerous, damn, he knew that better than most.

"Really? I saw you more as 'me man, you woman,'" she said.

"I'm not a caveman. You've seen me cleaned up," he said. He knew how to dress nice and could even pull out all the stops on a date.

She arched one eyebrow at him and gave him a sardonic look. "I have. I saw you flirting with me while your date—"

"We talked about that," he said. Nina had even forgiven him why couldn't Hayley. "I've apologized for it and *you* came here tonight."

"That's right, I did come here tonight," she said almost pensively.

"Why did you?" he asked. It seemed like after midnight was the time when most people lost their inhibitions. He had seen it more than once during his time on the force and experienced it for himself as well. After midnight the consequences of deeds didn't seem as strong.

"I thought I'd already said, I was lonely and curious," she admitted.

"Curious about what?" he asked, moving closer to her. She smelled of chocolate and vanilla and something else that was uniquely Hayley. A scent he couldn't get enough of. He put his arm along the back of the couch and reached out to touch her ear.

As he traced his finger over the shell of it and then fondled the diamond stud, she shivered and looked up at him, a slight flush on her face. Her lips parted and her breath seemed to come

81

more quickly.

He knew why she was here. The words that she wouldn't say. She'd come here tonight to prove something to herself. Or maybe to him. To make him her boy toy and he was more than willing to be that. But a part of him wanted more.

Obsession?

It was there in the back of his mind and he was conflicted. Well, as much as a horny thirty-something man could be. He wanted her. He could be her man for the night for a few weeks, but he wanted more. He knew he wasn't truly in a position to offer her anything more than sex, though, and that sort of pissed him off.

"Why are you looking at me like that?" she asked.

"How am I looking at you?" he countered.

She chewed on her bottom lip. "I can't really describe it. It's like…well, like you want me, but you're angry about it."

He pushed to his feet, giving a wry laugh of derision. She'd put her finger on it. "I know that I'm not the right type of guy for you."

He heard her shifting on the sofa cushions behind him. "How do you know that?"

"Because of the way you act around me. You always seem to be on the edge of your own control. Almost as if you are daring yourself to be here with me."

"What do you want me to say? You came to my class, you flirted with me. I'm here tonight because I want to know if there is anything more than that between us. You make me want to be that woman I was pretending to be on my birthday," she said.

He shoved his hands through his hair and turned, losing his balance a little as he forgot to adjust for his bum leg. Fuck it, he thought. Every time he thought he was moving forward he fell on his ass. And usually she was there to witness it.

"Don't pretend with me," he said, at last, as he steadied himself. He put his hands on his hips, trying to find a good position for his leg. Her words had made him realize that he'd been pretending for too long. Pretending his life hadn't changed that day he'd shot Paco. Pretending that working out was going to give him the full recovery he needed. Pretending that he wanted only one night with Hayley, when from the first time he'd touched her he'd known he would need a lot more.

But if he'd learned anything during his time trapped in the house recovering, it was that the future had its own plans. And whether he wanted one night or a hundred nights with her wasn't up to him. Or, to be honest, even up to Hayley. Life played out on its own schedule and Garrett realized all he could do was adjust to it.

And to a man with balance problems that was scary.

"I am trying. It's a lot harder than you know to leave behind all the old fears," she said. "That chef's jacket and my baggy jeans were so comfortable. And my new wardrobe is fun and flirty, but I'm not sure I am. I want to be...I'm rambling, I'm sorry."

"It's okay. I'm pretty sure that you aren't as unhappy about leaving your comfort zone as you think," he said.

"Why?" she asked.

"You wouldn't be here with me tonight if that were the case."

***

He stood there like he owned the world, but he'd already revealed to her that he was as broken as she was. It was funny how they both did such a good job of hiding that from everyone, and if she were being honest, with herself. But tonight she didn't have to hide it.

She'd talked about things with him that she'd kept tucked deep inside for too long. She wondered why that was. Why Garrett? Why not another man? But for some reason she was drawn to him.

Okay, his tight-fitting jeans and totally ripped arms were a big part of it. But she was afraid to let herself just be attracted to him. She didn't want to be one of those women who had a long list of ex-lovers. It didn't fit with the image she held of herself

– the image of a woman who was smart about her choice in men.

Except that she ached to kiss him again. Those few stolen moments in the pantry at The Candied Apple weren't enough. She felt hollow and empty and had come over here tonight to finish what they'd started on her birthday.

It wasn't just the alcohol that was making her brazen, it was her own desire to not get to the end of her life and find it full of regrets. The kind of should-haves and would-haves that made the choices she did make seem safe and boring.

And if she were being perfectly honest, she had to admit that her mom had died at thirty-eight. A part of Hayley wanted to make all of these years really count. And now that she'd—

"Woman, what you are thinking?"

"Just trying to justify being in lust with you."

He threw his head back and laughed.

She stared at him for a moment. Was he laughing at her? Then she realized that what she'd said was very funny. Emotions and desires couldn't be tamed or justified. She wanted him. She'd been trying to put all sorts of labels on it. To tell herself that it was okay for it to be lust because he was lost and that was all he could handle.

But she'd lied. Garrett Mulligan could handle anything life threw at him. Even flirting with one woman while on a date with another one. He had a confidence that even a severe injury and a life-altering decision couldn't really shake--and she wanted that.

She wanted to figure out how he bounced back with that damned swagger of his. She needed some swagger of her own. She needed to somehow figure out how she could own her life the way he owned his. She needed…him.

She pushed to her feet and closed the distance between them. With each step she took she shed the doubts and fears that had dogged her since she'd turned eighteen and realized that she was on her own. Sure, her dad loved her, but he worked. He was always on the road.

And she'd emulated him to some extent, working hard to start her own business. To create her own identity she'd never really admitted that she needed her mom's approval of the woman she was. She frowned.

That was the problem with drinking. It made her thoughts a lot harder to control. So instead of concentrating on the hot guy standing there, so close now that she could feel his body heat, she was bombarded with regrets. She shook her head, hard. She wanted this night for herself. No plans or hidden agendas. Just what Iona called pure sexual release.

She put her hand on Garrett's chest and looked up into his eyes. He always watched her carefully. She guessed that was part of him being a cop and observing everything. But she didn't want him to see her clearly. She wanted to pretend that she still had all those barriers to protect herself.

But she knew that it didn't matter how she cut her hair or changed her make-up, they were still barriers. And she needed them. She went up on tiptoe because he was taller than she was and she liked that. He just stood there, let her set the pace, and she liked that too.

Damn.

There was too much about Garrett that she liked. But then from the moment they'd met she known that. She leaned forward and her lips felt dry. How could that be? Just a moment ago they were fine. Now they sort of tingled and she wanted to lick them, but didn't want to look weird or awkward.

She closed her eyes and the scent of his aftershave filled her senses. She felt his heat, his warmth, inhaled the scent that she was beginning to associate only with Garrett and knew that she wasn't going to back down. It didn't matter if he could see past the barriers she had frantically been putting in place. The need for him was stronger than her urge to protect herself.

He wouldn't hurt her. Not physically—but emotionally? She had to be very careful that she remembered who she truly was and the kind of man—

His lips brushed over hers. A soft and gentle touch that startled her. She opened her eyes.

"I'm all for building anticipation, but damn, woman, I thought I'd die if I didn't kiss you."

She was glad he'd done it because she had been getting so lost in herself. And wouldn't it be better to be lost in Garrett? She kissed him then. Not the tentative embrace that she'd been driving herself toward but a full-on kiss.

His mouth opened against hers, his lips were so soft. His taste just right and as she braced herself against his chest, she turned her head and deepened the kiss. Thrust her tongue into his mouth. He sucked hers deeper and everything feminine inside of her responded. Everything conflicted and confused silenced itself as her body took over and her mind was blissfully silent.

Chapter 9

There was something about kissing Hayley that made him feel like he was alive – truly alive – and not in the comatose state he'd existed in for the last six weeks. He needed this. Needed her. He stopped wondering why she was different as the kiss deepened and his body demanded that he make her his.

He put his hands on her hips and drew her closer to him. She didn't move her hand, so it was caught between their bodies. His erection nestled into the notch at the top of her thighs and her breasts were cushioned against his chest. She moaned and the sound washed over him. He reached up to take her wrist in his hand and pulled her arm from between them. Put his hands back on her ass. God, she had a sweet ass. It filled both of his hands as he pulled her even closer to him, rubbing himself against her.

Her legs parted and she shifted against him, bringing him into deeper contact with her. She lifted one leg and wrapped her thigh around him. He hardened so quickly he thought he'd cum in his jeans—something he hadn't done since he'd been a teenager. He ripped his mouth from hers and took a deep breath, but that didn't help.

The scent of her surrounded him and with each inhalation that smell was being imprinted on him. On his very being.

Her lips were wet and swollen from his kisses and parted. Each exhalation of her breath brushed over his own mouth and made him realize how much he wanted to taste again. He needed to have her tongue in his mouth as his hands roamed up and over her back. He brought his mouth down on hers as she pushed her hands up under his t-shirt and up his back. He shuddered and fought for control as she scraped her nails up and then down his back.

She shifted her shoulders and the tips of her breasts rubbed over his chest as he thrust his tongue deeper into her mouth, sucked hard on her tongue. He was losing control and in a minute he'd have her pants off and be inside of her.

All the finesse he'd acquired with women had faded. There was just a primal need to mate with her. To make her his and never let her go. He was more than his base instincts, he reminded himself, but his body disagreed.

He pushed her t-shirt up and fumbled for the clasp of her bra. He undid it and as soon as the fabric pulled away from her body he lifted his mouth from hers and looked down at her. Taking the hem of her t-shirt in his hands he ripped it up and over her head. Tossed it on the floor. She shrugged out of her bra and he took a single step backward, keeping his hands on her hips to look down at her.

Her skin was creamy and white, like the smoothest silk in the world. Her breasts were full and heaving with each breath she took. Her tiny pink nipples hard and pointed. He rubbed his thumb over one of them, watching as it tightened a little bit more. She shuddered, reaching for him again.

"I'm not sure about this," she said, but her hands held him tightly and as she looked up at him, her hazel eyes more brown–almost cinnamon in the light–it seemed she was sure.

"I am."

He'd learned from a very young age that if he wanted something or someone he had to go after it. And there was no doubt in his mind that he wanted Hayley.

Had wanted her since he'd first glimpsed her in the moonlight trying to break into her own place.

He lowered his head once again, not breaking eye contact with her, and kissed her. He meant for the embrace to start sweet, but the moment her lips touched his, a fire started and roared throughout his body.

Adrenaline pumped through him and he forgot for a moment that he wasn't the man he used to be. He lifted her off her feet, intending to carry her somewhere he could get her clothes off, but he made it only one step before his leg buckled and he felt himself starting to go down.

He turned, so the wall between the kitchen and the living room caught his fall. She pulled her mouth from his.

"Are you okay?"

Hell!

No, he wasn't okay. He was turned-on – hot as hell – and all of a sudden his damn leg was reminding him of his reality. He hadn't been with a woman since the injury. His leg was a mess of scar tissue and still-red, angry scabs.

"Yeah, sorry about that."

"Where were you trying to take me?" she asked, linking her hand with his.

He looked down into her face and some small corner of his heart that he'd never realized was important suddenly felt flooded with Hayley. There was no other way to describe it.

"The kitchen counter. I figured it's the right height."

She peeked around his shoulder into the kitchen and then stepped away from him, giving him the once-over.

"It might be."

She walked slowly away from him. Her hips swaying provocatively with each step as she glanced back over her shoulder at him. "Are you going to come and help me find out?"

Hell yes!

But he needed a moment to make sure his leg was working. Probably all the blood rushing to his groin was to blame. But he wouldn't trade his bum leg for anything. This moment with Hayley had shown him what had been missing in his previous sexual encounters—as satisfying as they had been. There hadn't been a connection that went beyond scratching an itch.

And Hayley, who had point-blank told him she was changing into a bad girl, had shown him she was a good woman. A "forever" kind of woman. A part of him worried about that because he was a cop and his life was dangerous. He wasn't a "forever" kind of man.

But tonight he just had to be her man. Just be Garrett. He hadn't felt like he was enough for anyone since the night Hector had died. Hayley had given him a gift without even intending to and he would do everything he could to repay that.

***

Hayley stood next to the butcher-block countertop in the middle of Garrett's kitchen. The kitchen had always been the one place she'd felt at home. Much more so than the bedroom, where the guys she'd dated had always seemed to have an expectation of her that she couldn't measure up to.

But with Garrett, all that posturing and pretending had ended when he'd stumbled. She'd stopped looking at him as some sort of sex god and realized he was human. It changed the way she looked at him and some of the uncertainty she had about him had drifted away.

He walked toward her with a smooth stride that reminded her of a tiger circling its prey. She reminded herself that she'd invited this particular tiger to play with her. She braced her hands on the counter behind her and gave him her best come- hither look.

She admitted to herself that this was exciting. And she hardly felt like she was pretending to be someone else tonight. She felt like Hayley.

He stepped up to her and put his hands on her waist, squeezing it between his hands and then slowly letting them drift down her thighs, splayed his fingers, and rubbed them slowly, sensuously up toward her hips from her knee. Shivers spread out from his touch, going straight to the center of her throbbing womanhood.

She shifted next to him, the restless need growing inside of her, and he moved even closer between her legs, sliding his hands around behind her and drawing her closer to him until she felt the roughness of his jeans against her skin.

If he weren't standing there, giving her something to hold onto she would have fallen down.

He swept his hands up and down her back. His caresses were smooth and sure, but his skin was rough. There were callouses across the ridge of his palm and they abraded her skin as he touched her.

She shifted under his hands, enjoying that sweet abrasion. The movement caused her nipples to brush against his chest. He was hot to the touch.

"Back where this whole thing started," he said.

"Seems right, doesn't it?" She ran her finger down his chest. There was a light dusting of hair there and she followed the path that it made swirling over the pads of his pectorals and watching as his flat, brown nipples tightened. She skimmed her finger lower as the path of hair narrowed and disappeared into the top of his jeans.

She teased him by tracing that point where flesh met fabric. Then coming back to circle his belly button with her finger.

He heard his breath catch as she slowly reached for the button at the top of his jeans and undid it.

Then it was her turn to gasp as he slipped his hands up under her skirt, putting one arm around her hips, sliding his fingers into her underwear as he drew her panties down her legs and tossed them on the floor.

He pushed her skirt to her waist, undid the zipper on his jeans, and then stepped forward between her legs. She reached for him again. Slipping her hand into the opening of his jeans.

He wasn't wearing underwear and she wrapped her hand around him. Sliding her touch up and down, she reached lower to skim her fingers over his balls and then cupped them.

Rolling them in her hand as he stood there with his eyes closed. She guessed he liked that. She had read about this in a magazine, but hadn't had a guy to try it on. She tightened her fingers carefully and then circled his shaft again, moving her hand up toward the tip and swiping her finger over the head.

He pulled her closer to him with his hands on her hips, cupping her butt and feathering his finger along her crack. She shivered and almost lost her grip on him as his mouth slammed down on hers. His finger kept moving up and down and though she'd never thought of that type of caress as something that would turn her on, it did.

She was wet and ready for him. She tugged lightly on his cock, bringing him closer to her opening, but he pulled his hips back and lifted his head. His lips were wet from kissing her and his eyes half-closed. His breath sawed in and out of his lungs and she noticed a slight flush to his skin.

She shivered as he took one hand off her butt to palm her breast. He pinched her nipple between his thumb and forefinger and leaned over her, forcing her back.

But he brought his arm up behind her, holding her with his hand at the back of her neck and his arm supporting her along her spine. He lowered his mouth and delicately took her nipple between his teeth, flicking his tongue over it until she moaned.

She'd never been a moaner—before this.

She reached again for his cock, but he bit her nipple and she forgot everything except the way she felt. Her arms fell to her sides and then to the back of his head as he started to suckle her nipple.

She felt his fingers between her legs, his palm rubbing over the hair that covered her feminine secrets and then he parted her—his finger rubbing over her clit in just the right way. She lifted her hips, wanting more of his touch as the sensations grew stronger.

Desperate she shifted against him and grabbed his cock, stroking her hand up and down it, trying to draw him closer to her. As nice as his hand and mouth were she wanted him inside of her.

But then her orgasm burst over her and she sat there shivering in his arms.

***

He was barely able to keep himself from coming when she did. She was hot and sexy. And though he wanted to claim her, to make her his, he knew that she might never be.

Looking down at her flushed body, seeing how her lips had swollen from his kisses, enflamed him. He turned her in his arms, so that she faced the countertop and then leaned over her, pressing against her back. He kissed her nape and nibbled a path from her neck down her shoulder.

Blood was rushing through him. He couldn't think of anything except how pretty her skin looked. She had a small birthmark in the middle of her back, just under her left shoulder, and he brushed a kiss over it.

No tattoo in the middle of her back or anything else marred the smooth surface of her skin. He thought of what she'd said and hadn't said. How she'd worked hard to make her business a success and never taken the time to figure out what she wanted as a woman.

He was flattered and humbled that she was here with him now, that she'd chosen him to be the man she went on this journey with.

Hell, it might be the increased level of hormones in his body, but he felt something more for Hayley than he wanted to admit.

He wished that he could say this was just sex. She was just some hot chick that he was banging.

But she wasn't.

She hadn't been since he busted her trying to break into her own place. She'd been so cute and so unintentionally sexy. Two things that had turned him on and, to be honest, he hadn't been turned off since.

"That first night when you bent over, I imagined you like this."

"Did you?" she asked, shaking her hips and rubbing them against his groin.

He groaned.

"What did you imagine?" she asked.

"This," he said.

Drawing his hands up and down her back, slowly cupping her butt and then leaning over to rub his cock against the opening there. He wasn't going to take her that way, but he liked the way she felt against him.

She shivered a little and her hips moved against him.

"I just like the feel of you, Hayley," he said. "Your back is so smooth."

He ran his finger down it and found a small scar in the indentation right at the small of her back and he leaned down to kiss it.

She shivered in his arms; the smell of sex and Hayley surrounded him as she reached behind her back for his cock. He pulled his hips back.

"Don't."

She glanced over her shoulder at him, her eyes intent. "I want you."

"I know and I'm hanging on to my control by a thread."

"Don't," she said, repeating his command. "I'm ready for you."

She gazed at him and all of the control he'd been fighting to command was gone.

"Are you on the pill?" he asked. It was something that had been ingrained in him for a long time. He wasn't about to take chances with an unplanned pregnancy.

"Yes."

"Thank God."

She gave a nervous little laugh and he shifted around her again. Cupped her breasts with his hands as he drew back his hips and found her opening. And thrust forward, driving himself deeply into her. Her body was tight, fitting him so perfectly, as he drew back and thrust again and again.

She moved against him, pushing her hips up and back into each of his thrusts. He felt the feathering of sensation down his back and knew his orgasm wasn't far away, but he wanted her to come again.

Wanted to feel her body tightening around his cock before he lost it. He slipped one hand down her body to fondle her clit as he lowered his mouth to the back of her neck and bit her lightly.

She called out his name and started to move more urgently against him as he began to pump deeper and harder into her. She tightened around him, making tiny moaning sounds that helped to drive him over the edge.

He drove into her one more time and felt his body empty. He continued to pump into her three more times until he was spent. He collapsed against her back. He leaned over her. Careful not to crush her under his weight.

He pulled out of her and turned her in his arms, cradled her close to his chest, afraid to look in her eyes. Afraid to let her look into his. He didn't want her to see the truth there.

The fact that while he was as lost as she'd said he was, he might have been found in her arms. In her body.

She'd shown him something deep within his soul that he'd thought he'd never find. She rested her head against his chest, lying right over his heart. Surely she could hear the racing of his heart.

He wrapped his arms around her, held her tightly to him until he realized that he didn't want to let her go.

He had to.

He knew it and stepped back.

She looked up at him, a little unsure, and he wanted to curse. He hadn't meant for any of this to happen. He lifted her up onto the counter and then turned, feeling that pull in his knee. He dampened a dishtowel and tenderly washed between her legs. He felt himself stirring again, but wanted to think.

Needed to think and not just make this about sex.

Though it easily could be.

He walked away from Hayley. He would clean up and then come back and regroup. Figure out how they moved on from here.

Because he knew that one night wasn't going to be enough for him.

He had no way of knowing if it would be for her. She had admitted to wanting to change her life. She was trying to be a bad girl not the girl of his dreams.

Chapter 10

Somehow, Hayley had convinced herself that by changing her hair and clothing she'd changed inside as well. But as she waited for him to return to the kitchen, naked and lying on his butcher-block counter, she knew she hadn't.

Yes, the experience of sex had been profound, leaving her shattered. She'd had no idea her body could feel like that. But inside her heart she also ached.

That kind of sex should have been soul sex. It should have been with a man she'd committed herself to. Not a boy toy. Not a guy she knew she had no intention of ever seeing again.

She rolled onto her side, hugging her stomach, and looking for answers where there weren't any.

The sad truth was that the woman she thought she wanted to be...well, that girl didn't exist and it was beyond time for her to admit it.

"Damn."

She glanced up and saw Garrett standing in the doorway. He'd pulled on his jeans and had zipped them, but left the top button undone. He held a damp washcloth in one hand and the other was held loosely against his chest.

"What?"

"Regret. I had hoped..."

"Not regret," she said. She wasn't going to feel guilty about this experience. Garrett was the kind of lover she'd always dreamed of finding, but had never expected to.

She just wasn't the type of woman a man carried into his kitchen and made love to on his counter. Well...she hadn't been.

She sat up and looked at him. His hair was a little longer than it should be. She took it as an indication that he wasn't as sure of his future as he should be.

She crooked her finger and he slowly walked toward her. She'd decided to take this night for herself and she wasn't about to let it go now. She wanted every hour until dawn and then she would deal with the repercussions of this night.

She *had* changed.

Damn.

She hadn't realized that it wasn't just clothes and make-up. From the night that she'd locked herself out of her brownstone she'd been slowly becoming a new woman.

Maybe it was just by thinking she was bold that she actually was becoming bold. Or maybe it was Garrett. With his well-built chest, smoldering eyes, and kisses that made her melt.

"Yes?" he asked as he stepped between her legs and put his hands on her thighs.

"I want..."

But the words escaped. What did she want? She wouldn't have been able to imagine what he'd done to her earlier and she wanted more of that. More of him. As much as he'd give her and then she wanted a little bit more.

She wanted to own him the way he seemed to own her body. But she'd never really been a sexual being. Maybe in her mind and fantasies, but in real life she was sedate. Proper.

"Yes?"

"You," she said. There it was. "I want to be the kind of woman you want all night."

"You already are."

"I don't feel like it. What happened between us...it felt like a fluke. Like it didn't really happen."

He gave her a slow, sexy smile and she felt something melt inside of her. Not a sexual melting but more of a thaw of her heart. She hadn't even realized she'd been hiding it in ice before this moment.

But she knew now she had been. Afraid to feel or let anyone close to her.

He stroked his fingers on her inner thighs. She parted them a little as she reached out and grabbed onto his whipcord-lean waist. His skin was hot to the touch and smooth. Almost soft but like a layer of silk over tempered steel. His muscles were firm and hard, well developed.

"I love the way you feel," she admitted.

"Me too, baby," he said. Then glanced up at her. "Do you mind if I call you that?"

She shook her head. No man ever had before. She wasn't the type—but maybe she was the type. Or at least with Garrett she was the type.

She wanted to think that she could experience this sexual intensity with another man, but a part of her knew she couldn't. That this was something that came from the two of them. Something that couldn't be replicated.

Precisely why she should be running for the hills instead of drawing him closer to her, rubbing her center against his hardening erection and sliding her hands up his chest.

She wrapped her arms around his neck and drew them together until her breasts were cushioned against him. Until she could tangle her fingers in the long hair at the back of his neck. Until his mouth found hers and she stopped thinking.

Sensation washed over her and she realized that with Garrett she experienced all the senses much the same way she did when she was in the candy kitchen experiencing new flavors for the very first time.

He made her feel alive.

She bit his bottom lip because she didn't want to feel this alive. This type of awakening was uncomfortable.

He sucked her lower lip and put his hands on her butt, drawing her even closer to him, grinding against her. She shuddered and realized that there was no going back to sleep now.

Not that she'd really want to. This was the change she'd craved. The one that she'd hoped to find on her birthday. She'd thought over the last few weeks that she had been moving forward, but as his hands moved over her body she knew she'd been lying to herself.

***

Garrett skimmed his hands down the sides of her body. Her skin was so soft and smooth. His body was covered in scars, both from his job and from the way he'd lived his life. He lowered his mouth to her shoulder and bit lightly at the spot at the base of her neck.

He wanted to leave his mark on her. Wanted her to remember him, long after he became her salacious one-night stand. She'd told him that she had bad taste in men. And the man he used to be would have jumped to prove to her she didn't.

But that man had a future and this one wasn't sure. He pushed the thoughts aside and concentrated on her skin.

She smelled better than any other lover he'd ever had. She was vanilla, cinnamon, and chocolate. Hayley was a potent aphrodisiac. One he didn't try to resist.

He just gave in and slowly devoured her. Caressing her back with long, sweeping motions while he found her mouth with his, liking the feel of her swollen lips under his.

He thrust his tongue slowly, languidly into her mouth. The hurry of the first time was gone and now he could enjoy this woman he hadn't been sure would ever be his.

His.

That had to stop.

100

He had to stop worrying about life when it was here, in this moment, unfolding in front of him. She was alive and so was he.

That's right, he was fucking alive. He hadn't died that day when Hector had. He'd lived and it was about time he stopped waiting for life to start again.

He put his hands on her waist and lifted her, drew her forward until she was at the edge of the butcher-block counter and then he lifted his mouth from hers. Stared into her eyes, wanting her to know that he'd changed. That the messed-up man who'd made love to her earlier was gone.

He drew his finger down the center-line of her body. Right past her breasts to her belly button. She had a small stud pierced there and he circled it with his finger. He liked the contrast between her smooth skin and the abrasion from the stud.

She shifted in his arms. Her hands coming to the waistband of his jeans as she pushed his zipper down.

He felt the cool air rushing in on his naked skin and then her fingers as she wrapped them around his cock. Stroking up and down his length. He hardened under her touch as she leaned forward and put her other hand on the back of his neck, drawing him forward until she could whisper into his ear. She whispered dark, sexual words that drove him to the edge. And the laid- back feeling disappeared as he knew he had to have her. Had to be inside her again.

He fumbled in his back pocket for a condom; he'd put another there when he'd gone to the bathroom. He didn't know where this night was going to end. But he knew himself well enough to know that until she walked out the door he wanted to spend every second in her. His arms wrapped around her and his cock buried deep inside of her.

She was his.

His.

He circled her belly button with his finger and then slid his hand lower, brushing over her feminine secrets and slowly parting her until he found her clit.

She moaned his name. She was getting turned on. Really turned on. He knew that sound now. Almost as well as he knew the way her body felt when he slipped inside of her.

The memories of it made him harden and he felt a drop of pre-cum at the tip of his cock.

She caught it, rubbed it with her finger and then looked him straight in the eye as she brought her finger to her mouth and licked it.

He almost came on the spot. He needed the condom on. Now. He brought it up to his mouth, intending to tear the packet with his teeth because he didn't want to stop touching her. Couldn't stop touching her.

He let his finger drift lower, circling the entrance to her body as she took the packet from him. She opened it and then he shifted so she could put the condom on him. She was careful and bit her lower lip as she positioned it on the head of his cock.

"I've never done this before."

"If horny guys can do it, I think you can," he said, his voice low and raspy to his own ears.

She laughed. He could tell it was unexpected by the way she glanced up at him as she did it. "What about horny girls?"

"I only care about you," he said.

And he did. That was a startling truth. He'd told himself he wanted to be with her as she tried to figure out who she was. That he'd be her bad boy and teach her in some way to be a bad girl. But that wasn't true any longer. She mattered to him.

She rolled the condom down the length of his cock and then cupped his balls before stroking her hand back up his length.

He positioned his hips until the tip of him was right at the entrance of her body. And this time, when he acknowledged that Hayley mattered, seemed like a first time for them. He slowly slid forward until he was buried all the way in her body.

She wrapped her legs around his hips and her arms around his shoulders as she moved against him. He grabbed her butt with both hands and tried to go slow, but, honestly, with Hayley all of his old tricks didn't work. When he was inside of her all that he wanted was completion and for her to come longer and harder than she had with any other man.

Her moans made it harder for him to have any control and he felt the beginnings of his orgasm and knew he was going to come. He slammed his mouth down on hers and felt her suck his tongue deep into her mouth, just as her body started to tighten around his and he emptied himself. Thrusting again and again until he felt drained. She slumped forward and he braced his hands on the counter next to her.

She rested her head against his chest and held him, with her hands moving slowly up and down his back.

He felt alive. Scary alive.

The kind of alive he'd only ever felt when he'd been undercover and about to bring down a criminal. This wasn't supposed to happen with a woman.

"Twice in one night. I guess I can check that off my bucket list," she said in her breathless little voice.

"Sex is on your bucket list?" he asked, it was distracting. The panic he felt when he thought of how much he needed her ebbed a little.

"I haven't had a lot of it, so yes."

He'd had a lot of lovers. And now they all sort of blended together. They weren't Hayley and that seemed to be the only thing that mattered.

He wanted to lift her effortlessly off the counter, but wasn't too sure his knee would allow it. "Wrap your arms and legs around me."

She did and he gently stepped backward, lifting her until she could slide down his body and put her feet on the floor.

"Sorry I can't carry you," he said.

"It's alright. I think I'd feel weird if you did," she admitted.

"Come upstairs with me," he said.

She nodded.

He linked their hands together and led her up the stairs to his bedroom. Walked through the darkened room to the adjoining bathroom, where he'd left the light on. He put her on her feet next to the big garden tub that he'd been taking advantage of since his injury.

"What is this?"

"Something on my bucket list," he said. Which was a complete lie since he didn't have a bucket list. He'd always just lived. But with Hayley he was different.

"And that is?"

"A bubble bath with my lover," he said. But in his mind he knew it was a bath with Hayley. No other woman would do.

"Me too," she said, with that shy smile that made his heart beat a little heavier.

There was emotion but also expectation in her gaze and he wanted to be man enough to deliver everything she wanted. Wanted to be...but was unsure if he was.

***

After the bath Garrett dried her and led her to his bedroom. She hadn't intended to spend the night when she'd come over here. She'd just needed to know if they had a relationship or not. She hadn't expected the bare emotional sharing she'd ended up doing—or the sex.

His room was a mirror of hers with a large bay window facing the street. He had a leather loveseat there along with two bookshelves on either side of it. It was a cozy little reading area.

She wanted to know what it was he read there, but didn't ask. She wasn't the bold woman who'd hopped the fence between their yards and come over here with a bottle of rum and too much bravado.

Her body was a little achy in places that it had never been

before. And as she curled up next to him with the sound of Sports Center in the background, she felt like this was someplace she wanted to stay.

Damn. He was so comfortable. She seemed to fit perfectly into the curve of his shoulder. His arm around her back and for the first time in a really long time, she almost felt safe. Not that she was in danger or had to worry about anything. But he made her feel like this could be where she belonged.

Garrett was her transition into the next phase of her life. Not her forever man. She knew that. There were too many things about him that were unpredictable and about his life that made her unsure if she could fit into it.

"I know I invited you to come to work with me today," she said before she let herself get too comfortable and drift off to sleep. "But I understand if you'd rather not. Do you want me to leave?"

He muted the TV and shifted onto his elbow so he could look down at her. He had a slight bit of stubble and she had to resist the urge to reach out and rub her fingers over it.

"No. I wanted to go in with you so I could see you in action."

"It's not that exciting," she admitted. Aware that she was back-pedaling a little bit. As much as she enjoyed being with Garrett now, she knew in the morning all the usual worries and doubts would swamp her.

Maybe it would be better to just walk away tonight. Make this a one-night stand. That wasn't on her bucket list, but she thought maybe it should be. A night of sexual fun with no consequences.

But there were consequences. Already she felt something more for Garrett than she ever had for another man. And there was no denying it.

"I think it will be a lot of fun," he said.

"Why?"

"I'll be with you."

Chapter 11

Her alarm went off at 4:30 and he groaned as he rolled over and pulled her closer to him. But she wedged her arm between them, rolling to her side and standing up.

"What's the hurry?" he asked. Damn, he hated mornings, especially when he was in bed with someone as warm and cuddly as Hayley. Though, to be honest, she wasn't exactly cuddling up with him right now.

"I have to be at the shop by five to start making my products for the day."

He groaned.

"The Candied Apple is important to you," he said as she grabbed a t-shirt from the open closet shelf and pulled it on.

"Yes, it is. Are you coming with me this morning or are you no longer interested?"

"Damn. Morning comes quick for you doesn't it?"

She shrugged. He wasn't sure if it was regret or just rethinking going on in her head. She seemed to want to retreat from him and from herself this morning.

"I'll go with you. Let me get dressed."

When he stood up, his knee twinged and he realized that he was going to have to do a lot more than a long soak in the tub with a woman to recover from Hayley.

He padded naked to the closet, grabbed a pair of boxers from the shelf and then pulled on his jeans and a button-down oxford-style shirt. When he came back out of the closet she was nowhere to be seen.

He hurried into the bathroom, brushed his teeth and combed his hair before going downstairs to find Hayley standing in the foyer.

"I have to change too."

"Okay. I'm ready."

"Um...want to just meet out front in five?"

He pulled her into his arms and kissed her since he'd been sort of hoping to do that since she woke up. "Sure. I'll bring the coffee."

"I know I'm...thanks."

"You're welcome."

She walked out the door and he went to make them both a cup of coffee. She was complicated. The more he got to know her, the less he realized he knew about her. Each layer he pulled back just revealed more layers, each more complex than the one before. And if he were a different man or maybe at a different place in his life he'd just walk away.

But she fascinated him.

He remembered the tears in her eyes as she talked about her mom. About losing her...in way those wounds were as fresh for Hayley as his grief over losing Hector.

He knew he was reluctant to let himself care for anyone right now, but somehow she was making it impossible for him not to care.

He poured the coffee into two commuter mugs that bore the emblem of his family's sporting-goods chain, locked up, and went to wait for her.

She came out of her front door with her hair still wet, wearing a pair of faded jeans, biker boots, and a cashmere sweater.

He handed her the coffee as she slung a large leather bag over her shoulder. She took a long sip and then smiled at him for the first time that morning. Her hazel eyes seemed shy and the woman herself unsure. Not at all what he'd come to expect from her.

But then laying his soul bare to her hadn't been easy either. She was the only one to have seen his scars and to have seen his true weakness.

"I needed that. First thing to know is I'm cranky in the morning," she said, leading the way briskly up the block.

"You don't say?"

Mr. Kalatkis was putting out some fresh produce in the bins in front of his shop as they passed. He called out good morning and gave Garrett a wink when Hayley wasn't looking.

He winked back.

But whatever Mr. Kalatkis was thinking, this was way more complicated than that.

"So why do you start so early if you hate mornings?" he asked as they walked through the light early-morning pedestrian traffic.

"My mom was a stickler for getting up and getting to work. Before she got sick she used to wake up at five and from the moment she got out of bed she didn't stop until she had her Manhattan cocktail at seven. She was a dynamo."

What was it like to never know your parent as an adult, he wondered? She was basing what she thought a woman should be on an image formed in her teenaged years.

"You have her fierceness," he said.

"You think? I doubt it. I'm just stubborn and don't want to admit that she was stronger than I am."

They crossed the street and then entered the alleyway that lead to the back entrance of The Candied Apple. She punched a code in and let them into the building. The kitchen was on the first floor.

"Are you here to work?" she asked. Some of her crankiness was leaving her. Once they'd entered her shop she seemed to breath deeper and relax.

"I think you saw my efforts last night. It might be better if I just watch."

"You can chop chocolate from the block," she said. "No real skills necessary."

As she worked, he saw the nervous-cranky woman fall away and a Hayley that he'd only caught a glimpse of before appeared. She was sure as she moved around the kitchen. Funny as she shared anecdotes from when she'd first started cooking and the classes she'd taken in Paris. He realized for the first time that she was at home here. This was the place where she didn't have to pretend to be someone else. And it showed in her every movement.

"Try this," she said, bringing him over a spoon with a bit of chocolate on the end of it.

He opened his mouth and she fed him. The taste exploded on his tongue. The soft chocolate tasted both sweet and spicy and reminded him of nothing as much as kissing Hayley.

And he realized this new layer was something else he'd have to figure out. None of the pieces seemed to be adding up to the whole woman. But his gut said he was getting much closer to finding her.

What was he going to do with her once he found her? He was a man who was lost and unsure of what his future held. So why was having her in his life so damned important?

***

"Get ready to dish," Iona said as she entered the kitchen at ten past nine. "Cici told me more about the kiss she witnessed between you and Hot Cop."

"Hot Cop?" Garrett asked. "Is that what you call me?"

"Butter my biscuits," Iona said. "He's here?"

"I'm here," Garrett said.

Maybe it was the lack of sleep she'd had the night before, but she started laughing and couldn't stop. Iona looked so shocked and Garrett slightly amused, but also nervous. And she didn't blame him. It would have been easier to meet her father than her best friends.

"Iona Sommerlin, meet Garrett Mulligan, Garrett this is Iona. She's a marketing genius and one of my business partners in The Candied Apple."

"Nice to meet you," he said, holding out his hand, which was covered in chocolate dusting powder.

"I'm withholding judgment until I get the scoop on last night. Cici didn't want to gossip," Iona said to Hayley. "It took me three martinis and a promise she could stay at my parents' summer house before she'd even admit that she'd caught you making out in the pantry...that's not the Hayley I know."

She looked at Iona. Seeing past the flawless make-up and fashionable outfit that cost a small fortune. Iona was concerned. "I thought you suggested I change."

"I did. But you can't change too fast...will you give us a moment?" she asked Garrett.

"Yes. I have to call and verify my physical therapy appointment," Garrett said. "I'll see you later, Hayley?"

"Yes."

He gave her a quick kiss that felt like he was proving something to Iona and then he walked out the back door to the alley. She watched him leave, realizing that all morning she'd been pretending that last night had been normal for her. And now that Iona was here, she wasn't going to be able to do that anymore.

"Okay, what is going on?"

"Um...I have no idea where to start. Ever since my birthday, when he helped me out, I have been wondering if the kiss was a fluke."

"You know it wasn't. You kissed him a couple of times. I'm guessing something more happened last night?"

"Yes. It was...I don't know, Iona. I mean I can tell that he's not really in a position to start a relationship, so it's sort of one step forward and two back. But every time I'm with him all the doubts I have just seem to disappear."

110

She looked down at the marble workbench and the chocolate she was working with. It was so much easier to deal with this then to try to figure out what she wanted from Garrett. Because, honestly, she had no idea.

"Sleeping with him was...well I have no regrets. I'm not kidding when I say I didn't expect him to be so..." She didn't know how to put it into words. How he'd rocked her perception of herself and made her realize that she was the sensual being she'd always wanted to be.

"Okay," Iona said.

"Glad you approve," she said sardonically.

"I'm not sure I do. But I can see that you're caught in his trap."

"That's just it," she said, glancing up at her friend. "It doesn't feel like a trap. He's funny, and messed up. And strong and scarred. He's all the things I've ever thought I wanted in a guy and all these places that I'm sure I could fix."

Iona crossed her arms over her chest.

"You can't fix him. You're still not sure who you are."

She hated it when Iona was right. Especially when Iona was right about something that Hayley was happily pretending didn't matter.

"Just let me have this," she said. "It might be a mistake. I'm not sure it isn't. But for right now it feels good and I haven't felt this connected to a guy ever."

"Okay," Iona said. "I'm here if you need to talk or gush about him or worry."

"Thank you," she said, realizing that true friendship was one of the best things that she had. "Since you sent my help packing, put on an apron and get dusting."

"Ugh. I'm really better with a marketing plan."

"Save the queen-of-the-universe routine, Io. I've seen you stuffing truffles in a box at three a.m. so we could open this place," Hayley said. Her friend would do anything to make the business successful and since she was the exact same way, they'd

111

always seen eye to eye.

"Doesn't mean I like it. Where's your assistant?" Iona asked.

"I gave her the morning off. She covered for me on the day after my birthday," Hayley said. Her friend glanced down at her manicure, but then sighed.

"Another night involving Hot Cop. He's messing with your business, girl. Make sure you don't do anything crazy. You've always been so focused on work."

"So has my dad," Hayley said. "And I don't want to be a workaholic when I'm in my sixties with no real connection to my kid...I want kids and a family and this. I intend to have it all."

"With Hot Cop?" Iona asked.

She tried to picture a future with Garrett, but right now all she could see was him taking her in his kitchen last night. Beyond right now, she just couldn't see the two of them. "I don't know. But he's showing me things I didn't know I wanted in my life."

"Sex?" Iona asked.

"Good sex," Hayley said. She'd had plenty of the blah variety and now she knew that sexual attraction was an important element for her future Mr. Right. She had no idea if he would be Garrett, but admitted to herself that she was sort of building that Mr. Perfect around his image.

And that was dangerous.

Iona was right in that she needed to figure herself out before she attempted to try to fix anyone else. She thought of the letter from her mom that was sitting at home on her nightstand. Still unopened—unread. She hadn't wanted to see what her mom thought she'd have in this year.

Her mom had been careful to be vague about what she'd have. She always wished that Hayley had a good man in her life and she always counted her father as that man, but the euphoric feeling in her stomach made her want to believe that Garrett could be the one her mom had hoped she would find.

Hayley had realized about halfway through the day that she had no way to get in touch with Garrett and after two more days had passed he'd left a note in her mailbox saying he had something personal going on and would contact her when he was through it.

He was trying to get back to work on the force, so she got it. But since she'd slept with him she was feeling more vulnerable than she wished she was. Had she gone too far? Shown him too much of herself?

She suspected it had something to do with the physical therapy he was going through for his knee. Or maybe some sort of rigorous retraining to be reinstated on the force.

To be perfectly frank, she didn't care. She thought that the intensity of their night together had scared him. God knew, it had frightened her. Since she'd received his note she'd been a candy-making fool. Working from five in the morning until late each night.

She shook her head, cranky because her period was due to start any day and Iona had lined up a full day's worth of press for her to do to promote The Candied Apple for Valentine's Day. She arrived at the radio station where she was going to be doing an interview twenty minutes early simply because she'd needed the distraction of riding the subway and then walking to a place she'd never been before.

And it had worked for the twenty minutes she'd been trying to get the map app on her smart phone to work. But now that she was waiting in the green room with a bottle of water and listening to the morning deejay while waiting for her interview to start, she was getting angry again.

She got that sex didn't mean love. Even though she was dumb enough to start to let herself feel something more than lust. What she didn't get was how she could have been so wrong about Garrett.

She'd seen him a lot before she'd slept with him. In fact, it had been damned hard to avoid him. So what the hell happened?

She tucked a strand of hair behind her ear. In the three weeks since her birthday it had started to grow a bit. Still not really long, but the pixie cut wasn't as extreme as it had been when she'd first had it done.

Now she felt like this shorter hair was a part of her. The production assistant came to get her to go into the interview and explained how radio interviews worked. She gave the assistant a box of truffles and had one for the deejay as well.

She took her seat across a big table from the deejay, who pushed his earphones off and greeted her.

"Hey there. I'm Thom."

"Hayley," she said, shaking his hand. The booth was all high tech and did nothing to calm her nerves. "These are for you."

"My wife is going to be excited when I bring this home. She's dying to drop in for one of your candy-making classes. Your chocolates are her favorite."

Hayley blushed a little. "Thank you. I'll leave a card with you so you can come down and try a lesson for free."

"Thanks. Did your PR person explain that this segment is one where people call in and try to guess what you do?" he asked.

"Yes. And your PA gave me some additional pointers," Hayley said. Feeling aggravated again. This wasn't the type of thing she was good at. But Iona had been firm in that Hayley was the public face of The Candied Apple and she had no choice but to do this. At least it wasn't television.

A note through her door. It wasn't exactly what she'd been expecting, but it worked. No explanation for days' worth of silence other than his return to work had been delayed. She got it.

She understood how his job was his life—hell, hers was the same and right now he was trying to figure out what his new path would be.

She had cautioned herself to go slow, but being Hayley that meant she'd rebelled against the warning. She'd never been able to take advice, even from herself.

A tall woman with reddish-brown hair walked into the room and smiled at her as she took a seat next to Thom. "Mona does the news. After she's done, then we will have your interview."

Hayley nodded at the other woman. The big headphones she had on made her feel weird.

She listened with half an ear to the news until she heard that local cop Garrett Mulligan was being sued by the family of Paco Rivera for wrongful death. Even though he'd been cleared by law enforcement in the death.

Her hands shook as she realized that Garrett hadn't told her what was going on. Given the man she'd come to know, she guessed he'd done it to protect her. She got through the interview at the station and immediately texted the shop to say she would be taking the rest of the afternoon off.

She went back to the tree-lined street, where she knew she'd find Garrett and knocked on his door. There was no answer and she feared he might not be home. She dug in her big purse for her notepad. She jotted down her cell-phone number and the words "call me".

"Um...hello," a man said.

He was very familiar-looking and she thought she might have met him with Garrett before.

"Hello."

"Pete Mulligan," he said, holding out his hand. "Garrett's brother. We met at the candy-making class."

"Nice to see you again," she said.

He had a key in one hand and it didn't take a genius to figure out that Garrett wasn't here.

"Will you give Garrett this?" she asked, holding out the note.

Pete took it. It was hard to look at him without seeing Garrett. They both had the same dark-chocolate eyes and square jaw. Where Garrett's hair was a dark brown, though, Pete's was dirty blonde. He reached into his pocket and pulled out an envelope.

"He asked me to give you this," Pete said.

She took the envelope, dying to open it. "Thank you."

There was nothing else to say to Pete and she felt awkward just standing there, so she left, walking over to her brownstone and going inside. She put the envelope on the console table in the entry way right next to the one from her mother.

She had two notes to open and both of them filled her with excitement and dread.

Chapter 12

Garrett didn't like hiding out. It went against the grain, but he also didn't want to attract any attention to himself or to Hayley. The civil suit hadn't been unexpected, but both Garrett and the captain had thought that given the fact that Paco had killed Hector perhaps his family wouldn't go after Garrett.

So he'd left his brownstone and had been staying with Pete for the last few days. Not exchanging phone numbers with Hayley hadn't been a smart move. At first he'd wanted to talk to her. But then as he realized how ugly this court case could get, he'd thought of it has a blessing in disguise. He didn't want any of this to touch her.

"What are you doing?" Pete asked as he entered his apartment in Central Park West. Pete and Crystal had moved in together after they'd gotten engaged. His brother's apartment used to be very masculine with lots of modern art and sleek design elements. Pete liked everything neat and tidy.

But now the place was an odd mix of Pete's modern stuff and Crystal's antiques. His future sister-in-law owned a very upscale antique shop in the Village.

"Reading a book that Hoop recommended," Garrett said.

"Anything you can use?" Pete asked.

"Not yet. But I'm meeting with the attorney later today, so

we will see."

Pete walked over to the couch where Garrett was sitting and put his leather duffle bag on the table and handed him a note. "I gave her yours as well."

His brother's cell phone rang and Pete glanced at the screen. "It's Crystal. I'll take it in the kitchen. Can I bring you anything?"

He shook his head and opened the note from Hayley. Just her number and the words "call me".

He held the paper loosely between his thumb and forefinger.

What was he going to say?

He wondered if she'd heard the news yet? It wasn't exactly headline stuff since there wasn't a real scandal around the incident. He'd been within his rights to defend his life.

He pushed himself up to his feet, picked up his duffle bag and walked out of the living room into the guest room he'd been using. He tossed the bag on the bed and then paced over to the window. This room had a view of the alley and the building across from it.

It was a sunny February day and the light from the sun trickled down between the buildings. He rubbed his hand over his chest and thought about what to do next. If he ignored her note… she'd probably be pissed at him.

But if he called her, the goodbye note he'd written wouldn't matter.

He had always put others before himself. Always sought to protect his family, friends, his community. How could he call her now?

How could he not?

He took his phone from his pocket and dialed her number. It rang three times before she answered it.

"Hello?"

"It's Garrett."

"I just heard the news. How are you?"

"I guess you didn't read my letter," he said.

He heard rustling on the other end of the line. "No. I put it

118

next to the one from my mom."

That couldn't be a good thing.

"I'm sorry. I didn't have your number and I didn't want to call you at work."

That sounded lame even to his own ears. He wanted to be able to tell her that he was more unsure of his future than ever. The civil suit just made the doubts that had been plaguing him since the incident that much stronger.

"It's okay. I get it. What can I do to help?" she asked.

"Are you sure you want to get involved?" he countered.

There was a silence on the line that felt protracted and he knew he'd said the wrong thing to her.

"Did the night we spent together mean anything to you?" she asked at last.

More than he wanted her to know.

He debated how to proceed quickly. The truth was he needed her. He wanted someone by his side who wasn't related to him. He wanted the friend that Hayley was becoming. But he also didn't want any of this to touch her or her life.

"Yes. But this is a complication I have no contingency plan for. And I don't think it's fair—

"Who said life was supposed to be fair?" she asked. "My mom said that to me once. And at the time it wasn't what I wanted to hear from her, but it makes sense. Things happen. Never in the way we want them to and in their own time. If life was fair I would have met you when you were back on the squad, but I'm guessing you wouldn't have noticed me then."

"I would have," he said, but he got what she was saying. Life was random. He didn't need more proof than he'd already had. Things happened and all anyone could do was react to it and move on.

"Whatever. You didn't before you were laid up."

She was right.

"To make up for being a really bad blind date, I volunteered to help Nina out with her rescue-pet adoption session. I'm going down to her vet clinic this afternoon from four till six. Would you like to join me?" he asked.

"I would," she said. "I was planning to go anyway and maybe see if owning a pet is right for me. It will give me a chance to see another side of you."

He hoped she'd like what she saw. The last month had left him with a badly damaged image of himself. But he was slowly rebuilding that image. The captain had offered him a shot at cold cases, something Garrett hadn't ever thought he'd be working on. But more than that, Hayley offered him a chance to be more than a cop and more than a man. She offered him a chance at a relationship and he hadn't realized until he hung up the phone with her how much he needed that.

***

Hayley got changed into a pair of jeans, a long tunic sweater, and her Ugg boots. She put on a stylish winter hat and her coat before catching a cab to the vet clinic, where she was supposed to meet Garrett. She was thirty-five minutes early.

A bad habit of hers.

She hated to be late, but being just on time was tricky. So she was almost always at least twenty minutes early to everything. She went into the clinic and saw the pretty vet, who had been Garrett's blind date. She was standing over a pet pen that held two smallish dogs. Hayley was the first to admit she had no real understanding of breeds, but to her untrained eye one of them looked like a poodle mix.

"Hello, Nina. I'm Hayley Dunham. Not sure you remember me. I hope you can use another volunteer this afternoon," Hayley said.

"We can always use another warm body. I remember you from the candy-making class. I love your shop and have been practicing the techniques I learned that night."

"I'm glad to hear it. So what can I do?"

"I've got more dogs in the kennels in the back that have to be brought out here. I don't take appointments on the first Wednesday of the month. Instead I try to get these rescue dogs into good homes. How are you with pets?"

"I'm good at loving them," Hayley said honestly. "But know nothing about commands or anything like that."

"Perfect. Why don't you take care of these two while Mia and I get the rest of the animals up front?"

"No problem," she said.

"Did Garrett invite you down here today?" Nina asked as Mia went into the other room.

"Yes. Is it awkward?"

"Not at all."

Hayley looked at the two little dogs in the pen. Both of them were looking up at her with their tails wagging. She'd seen pens like this before at the pet store. She sometimes went to the one near her father's house before visiting him. Just to look at the dogs and hug them. It was hard to go home and not feel...well sad.

She reached down and petted both of the dogs. They licked her hand and danced around. She looked at the tags around their necks and saw that the poodle was called Daphne and the other breed, which really looked like a puppy, was called Sandy.

Mia and Nina brought in more dogs, filling up the pens. The front door to the clinic opened and Garrett and his brother Pete came in. Pete smiled at her and went to help Nina in the back, while Garrett walked over to her.

"Hi." She stood up and linked her fingers together to keep from reaching out and touching him. She felt awkward. He had a good reason for the distance he'd put between them over the last few days, but it was still tense seeing him again.

"Hi," he said.

He wore a pair of faded jeans and a thick, wool sweater that had two buttons open at the neck. He had on a pair of thick, dark Ray-Ban Wayfarer sunglasses and a New York Mets baseball

121

cap. He pulled the glasses off and placed them on the bill of his baseball cap.

"What are we supposed to do?" he asked.

She took a deep breath. Nothing personal. That was good. Really it was.

"I'm not sure. I've just been petting the dogs and keeping them calm. Mia has been placing bowls of water in each pen. Maybe she needs help with that," Hayley said.

The little dog that she'd been petting went up on her back legs like a meerkat and stared up at her. She didn't make a sound, though some of the other dogs were whining and barking. She smiled at the little dog—Sandy.

"Do you know what breed this is?" she asked Mia when she came back.

"Miniature dachshund," Mia said. "Garrett, can you help with the larger dogs?"

"Sure thing," he said, following Mia toward the pens on the other side of the room.

Hayley couldn't help herself—she reached for the little dog and scooped her up. As soon as she held the dog, she scrambled up her shoulder and curled herself around Hayley's neck.

"She likes you," Mia said.

"I like her too."

"Volunteers can become new pet-parents," Nina said as she walked back into the room.

Hayley wasn't sure she wanted to adopt a dog, but as the afternoon wore on and she talked with the families who came in to look at the dogs, she couldn't help watching Sandy. Daphne had already found a lovely new owner and Hayley found herself hoping the other little dog was still available at the end of the day.

Garrett was really good with both the dogs and the people who came in to look at them. Seeing him talking to the families gave her a little insight into the kind of cop he must be. She was impressed by him. He was calm when the animals got a little rowdy and though she saw him wince a couple of times, he didn't hesitate to crouch down to be on the same level as some of the kids who came in to look at the dogs.

That vague, faceless image of the kind of man she wanted to settle down with now had a new quality. He had to be good with pets. She looked down at Sandy, who had curled into herself in a corner and looked so small.

"Nina, I'd like to claim Sandy for myself," Hayley said. "Is that okay?"

"My goal is to get all of the dogs into good homes, so I hope you don't mind but I'll need to ask you a few questions," Nina said.

Hayley smiled at the vet. "I'd be worried if you didn't. I have had dogs before and had been waiting until I got The Candied Apple off the ground before getting another one. I will have a bed for her in my office, where she can stay with me during the day. It's not in my kitchen, but in the shop part of the store."

"Sounds like you have thought this through," Nina said.

"I have," Hayley said

"Yes," Nina said. "I'll have Mia start the paperwork."

She knew that falling for Garrett was dangerous. More so as she finished filling out the paperwork and caught him watching her.

She wanted his attention. Not just as a lover, but also as a man and she wasn't sure she was ready to share her life with someone.

***

When his session was over and more volunteers came in, Garrett went to find Hayley. He found her in the hallway leading to the examination rooms holding the small dog she'd been playing with earlier.

"Couldn't resist?" Garrett asked, walking over to her.

"No. This is Sandy."

He rubbed the little dog's head and she turned and licked his hand. "Have you had a dog before?"

"Yes. I've been waiting for the right dog for me," she said.

"I'm glad. Do you want a hand getting the dog and all this stuff home?" he asked.

"Are you sure you should go back to our street?" she countered. "I haven't seen any press, but I assume that's why you weren't there today."

"I think we'll be fine. Pete said he didn't see anyone either. I wasn't sure what would happen when the story broke," he said.

"Then I'd love the company," Hayley said.

Garrett was glad. He felt like he might have driven a wedge between them over the last few days. And he didn't want that. He gathered up the dog bed and food and a large amount of toys that Hayley had purchased from the vet.

"Some of these toys are bigger than she is," he pointed out.

"Nina mentioned that Sandy would like them," Hayley said. "I took a cab here, but I planned to walk home with her."

"Okay."

"Can your knee handle that? I saw you wincing a few times earlier."

Broken.

Every time he started to forget there was a reminder. "I'm fine."

"Okay. I wasn't implying you weren't. Just trying to be kind."

Kind. It was something that he felt got lost a lot in everyday life, but he appreciated her actions.

"Thank you. I'm actually getting a lot better. The knee is healing and almost back to normal. It's the shortness of the tendon that is causing the real worry. But my doctor thinks that once I'm used to it, it won't be a problem either."

"I'm glad to hear it. When you went silent I was wondering if you'd had bad news about your return to work."

She stopped by the coat rack and put Sandy on the floor, keeping hold of her leash as she reached for her coat. Garrett took it from her and held it up for her. She slipped her arms in the sleeves before buttoning it up. She took the knit hat from her pocket

124

and pulled it on as well.

Garrett donned his jacket and then led the way out of the vet clinic. It was dark and chilly as they made their way back toward Central Park West and their homes. The path through the park was lit and silence built between them.

Hayley didn't know what to say to him. She felt like they'd hashed out nothing, but was unsure where they would go from here. "I wish we'd had more time to talk after our night together."

He stopped walking and pulled her out of the foot traffic into the lighted area in front of a shop. Sandy sniffed around at their feet.

"Me too," he said. "My life feels like it's a bigger mess now than it was a few days ago, but I want a chance to get to know you. When we get back to your place…can we order in dinner and talk?"

"Yes," she said. "I have to work in the morning…"

"I won't stay late," he said. He put his hand on the wall behind her, leaning in. "The letter I had Pete bring you—it was meant to be a goodbye. But I'm not ready for that yet."

"Good. Me either. I'm not making promises of forever or anything," she said, quickly.

He remembered that she was changing her life too. He nodded. "Fair enough."

They walked the rest of the way, talking about the city and the changes they'd both seen in the time they'd lived here. Garrett was aware that she was keeping the topics light. The little dog stopped once or twice to sniff as they were walking and he thought it was cute the way that Hayley held her each time they crossed the street.

As they got closer to the block where they lived, Garrett started to scan the people on the sidewalk. He knew that once word got out that he was one of the Mulligan Sports Nation heirs that the press would probably swarm around him. His attorney was doing his best to minimize the effect of the law suit, but they all knew that there was only so much that could be done.

When they passed the corner shop Mr. Kalatkis waved them over. Sandy was excited by all the scents of the shop and strained at the leash to get under the vegetable table.

"Garrett, there were some people in here earlier asking about you," Mr. Kalatkis said. "We told them you were a good client and always made us feel safer. But Tony said he thought he saw a news van parked by your place."

Just what he was hoping to avoid.

"Thanks, Mr. Kalatkis."

"It's okay," Mr. Kalatkis said. "Tony has the van stocked up to make a delivery to your place, if you need a distraction to get in."

Garrett was touched. The Kalatkis family had always made him feel part of this little community and now they were rallying around him again. "Thank you. But it's probably better if you don't get involved."

"Why? You're a part of our family now, Garrett, and we protect our own," Mr. Kalatkis said.

Hayley nodded. "Thank you, Mr. Kalatkis. What's your plan?"

Garrett looked over at her. "Unless you want to talk to the press or go back to staying with your brother."

He was used to being the one to look out for everyone else. He wasn't too sure he liked having the tables turned on him. Yet at the same time it made him feel better about his current situation and anything that enabled him to go home with Hayley was a plan he definitely wanted to be a part of.

Chapter 13

Hayley had to admit that since meeting Garrett her life was much more interesting. She felt more alive, as if she was shaking off all of the old expectations of who she should be. She hardly ever felt like she knew what was going to happen from day to day.

Her thirties were starting out to be as exciting as she'd hoped, but not in the way she'd anticipated. She figured she'd have some fun dating different men and really experiencing life before she found Mr. Right. Instead she was with this crazy, complicated man.

Garrett wore Mr. Kalatkis's coat and had pulled his baseball cap down a little, and walked next to her with a very careful stride. There was no sign of his subtle limp as they made their way down the street. The reporters were all clustered near his front door and since the plan was for Tony to deliver to her place and sort of block the sidewalk while Garrett came into her house she thought they might pull it off.

"I feel like Trixie Belden."

"Who?"

"Heroine of my favorite book series when I was growing up. She solved mysteries and snuck around keeping the bad guys from finding her while she foiled their plans."

"I feel more like the Scooby Gang."

She laughed. "Maybe we should have dressed you like Shaggy."

"I guess if I stopped shaving that might work, get myself a beatnik soul patch and let my hair grow."

"I don't think we have that much time," she said as he watched Tony pull his truck up on the sidewalk, blocking the view of the street.

"True," he said, they walked quickly to her place and she had already given Garrett the key, so he let himself in and she followed him, making sure no one was paying attention to them. And they weren't.

Garrett was greeted by Sandy. Tony knocked on her door and handed her a box of groceries and she wrote him a check for them.

"Thanks, Tony."

"No problem. We have to look out for each other," he said.

"I agree."

"You okay?"

"Yes. Seems Mrs. Kalatkis included dinner in here. Want to join me?"

"Sure," he said. "In fact I'll cook." She gave him a look from under her lashes. "What are you going to cook?"

"Frittata. I noticed you have eggs and cheese."

"Frittata?

"Okay, I'm not exactly sure that you have any culinary skills," she said, taking a seat at her breakfast bar while he started gathering together the elements he needed to cook.

"Fair enough," he said, breaking the eggs into a bowl and whipping them with a fair amount of skill. "Tell me about your day."

"Why?"

"Because if I think about mine I might say things I regret."

"It's okay to say them to me," she said. "I know you're going through a lot of stuff right now."

"That's sweet of you, but I really don't want to."

Just that little reminder that they weren't really a couple. She took a deep breath and looked down at her hands. Her day? It was like every other one since he'd come into her life. She thought about him way too much, obsessed over the unopened letter from her deceased mother, and made truffles and candy. Seemed like talking about the candy might be safest.

"We're getting ready for V-day at the shop."

"V-day?"

"Valentine's Day...it's one of our biggest money-makers and this year we ordered some special boxes and have put together a 'love mix' of truffles."

He looked up from his egg mixture. "What is in the love mix?"

"We're still debating it. Cici wants our top sellers, since that's where the most profit would seem to lie. Iona said we should be putting our most exotic flavors together so that couples will experience something exciting."

He added some Parmesan cheese, which he grated, Parma ham, which he diced, and some fresh parsley from her window box to his mixture and poured it into a frying pan before looking up at her.

"Sounds like some solid plans. What are your thoughts?"

She stretched her arms over her head before leaning forward on her elbows. "I don't know. Maybe a mix of both of those. But how do I come up with an exotic truffle? Everyone defines it differently. We can't say 'try this, it's exotic' and meet the mark every time."

He kept an eye on his frying pan and leaned back against the counter, his long legs stretched out in front of him.

"What do you think is exotic?"

She thought about it. The problem was she thought he was exotic. He was different and exciting. Something that she'd never experienced before. "Flavor-wise I like the mix of chili with a nice sweet chocolate. It's always been my favorite. But not everyone can handle the heat."

"I can."

He was flirting and after he'd brushed her aside when she'd tried to get him to talk about his day she wasn't sure that she wanted to flirt back.

But her mind was overruled by her heart and body. They didn't care about deep emotional sharing. They wanted...she wanted him. She wanted to just experience this exotic time with Garrett until the next phase. Which she freely admitted might be goodbye.

But maybe she was pushing too hard, trying to find something because she'd decided she was ready to find Mr. Right. It didn't make Garrett her man. Was she using him to fill a gap? Or was this real?

It was hard to believe it could be real when they couldn't really connect. And she knew it wasn't fair to judge him harshly, but the truth was he didn't want to let her in and in the past she would have been happy letting him keep her at arm's length. But she wasn't anymore.

Maybe this was what real change was all about.

***

Eating with Hayley made him feel a sense of normalcy he hadn't experienced since his childhood and he knew that a lot of it stemmed from the fact that he'd deliberately chosen fraternity over family. The brotherhood of cops was where he felt most comfortable, but sitting on her couch and listening to her talk about the time she'd spent in Paris learning the art of candy was strangely satisfying.

As the warmth of that satisfaction spread throughout him he felt a spear of guilt. Hector had a wife and two small children. For weeks now, Garret had been ignoring the fact that he was alive and well and Hector wasn't here. That the single cop should live while the married father of two died didn't seem right.

But then nothing about that night seemed right, he thought, glancing out her back window to the yard, which seemed much like his. It was the yard of a single person. A few pieces of patio furniture covered for winter, but Hector's tiny little yard in Queens had a swing set and a tricycle. He hadn't even had a chance to

130

teach his son to ride a regular bike.

Hell.

He should go out there and let the press get at him. Guilt weighed heavy on him. And not just the stuff from killing a suspect he was supposed to arrest. Intermingled in all that guilt was grief.

Grief for things that could never be the same again.

"You okay?"

What? He glanced over at her and noticed she'd put her wine glass down and sat forward a little.

"You seem lost in your thoughts," she said. "Do you want to talk about it?"

Hell.

No, he didn't want to talk about it. He wanted this evening to continue to be an interlude away from his real life. And he knew that was no way to start a relationship. That real men didn't date women and pretend that their lives weren't a mess. Did they?

"I'm sorry. I was actually thinking about something you said earlier." Liar. But he ignored the jeering voice inside his head. "That love has different flavors for all of us."

"What were you thinking?" she asked.

To him it seemed she might know he'd been lying when he said it, but he was sticking to this. "That love is highly personal. Retailers have been bombarding us with images of love since January the first, but the truth is each of us defines love and our lovers in a different way."

"That's deep for a week night," she said, with a wink. "I agree with you. In a way, that was my argument about having that 'love' box. Each of us thinks of love, feels it in a different way. For me love will never be the home I grew up in," she admitted.

Her mom. He would hate to lose either of his parents, but to know they were going to die... Would it be better for Hector's sons if he'd had time to write them letters to open on each birthday? They'd still grow up with him. They'd still feel his presence missing from their lives daily.

131

"What does love mean?"

She shrugged. "I hate to say this because everyone seems to have it all figured out, but I'm not sure what love is. I love my parents, but we're sort of brought up to do that. So what if that's not real? I think I better lay off the wine," she said.

But he knew that she'd gotten deeper than she wanted to. He should respect that, the way she'd respected his need to not talk about the big, obvious elephant outside their door. But he couldn't. He wanted to be a hero for someone. Anyone.

Hayley.

"That's not true. I see signs of how much you care in this house, in your friends, in that shop of yours that you pour all of your heart into. You might not be able to define love, but it is all around you."

She tilted her head to the side and leaned against the back of the couch. "I wish."

"I know. Are you okay?" he asked. "Did you read that letter from your mom?"

"No," she said. "Not yet. I'm fine. Just feeling a little blue tonight."

He was too. "I might be bringing you down. The case and all the stuff going on in my life. Not exactly ideal boyfriend material."

She eyed him with that dark-gray gaze, making him feel like she could see all the way to his wounded soul. "You're better than anyone else."

That warmed the empty parts of him. He put his beer on the table, shifting around so that he faced her. "I have something that will cheer you up."

"Really? Or is it something that will cheer you up?" she asked.

"I think it will work for both of us."

"Okay, I'm game. What is it?"

He stood up and held his hand out to her. "Want to learn how to pick a lock?"

"What? I thought you were going to suggest sex," she said.

132

He wanted her. Hell, it was impossible for him to be in the same room as her and not want her. But tonight he felt too raw and exposed. So, no sex with Hayley.

"Don't you want to learn? I mean you did Google it."

She gave him one of those half-smiles of hers which he was coming to realize masked her real emotions. "Okay. But I should tell you that once I learn I might not be able to give up a life of crime easily."

"Luckily I'll be right next door to keep you in line," he said.

"Like having my own personal cop," she said.

"Exactly. Grab your coat and do you have that stepladder handy? I don't think I'll be able to get over the fence any other way."

She got her coat and the stepladder and twenty minutes later they were standing at his back door and he showed her how to pick the lock.

She was a quick student and funny. She made him laugh as she jotted down notes so she'd be able to remember every step. And he realized that despite the fact he'd thought that not having sex would be safer, it hadn't been. She was still getting to him, touching those wounded parts of his soul and reminding him that he was still damaged goods.

***

After she'd "broken in" to Garrett's place she knew it was time to go home. He had been giving off hot and cold signals all night and part of her truly got it. If her life was in flux, the way he was—but, really, wasn't it? She was trying to finally break free of the chrysalis that she'd placed herself in when her mom died.

And she wasn't in there anymore. She was doing things that scared her. Like hanging out with Garrett.

"How does a cop know how to do something like this?" she asked.

"I wasn't always a cop."

133

"You weren't?

"Nope. I was once a kid with too much money, parents who were willing to forgive pretty easily and some friends that let's just say could be called questionable."

"I'm dying to hear more. I'll let you pour me a drink and tell me all about it."

He gave her a sidelong look, which told her nothing. Did he wish she'd just gone back home? She had no idea. And to be honest, she wasn't going to worry over it. For too long she'd been living her life by rules that weren't her own. Doing things that pleased everyone else or at least what she'd thought would please others. Tonight and from now on she was doing things that she wanted.

Garrett was a big boy and if he didn't want her here she had no doubt that he'd tell her to hit the road.

"Okay. But all I've got is beer and some scotch."

Beer she'd had, but scotch was something she hadn't tried on its own. Her girlfriends drank pretty cocktails and wine was truly her drink of choice. But she was checking things off the bucket list—or rather the never-tried-before list. "Scotch it is," she said.

He poured two fingers of scotch into two large tumblers and led the way to his den, where she'd spent the night on his couch. She sat on one end of the couch and took a sip of the whiskey and almost choked.

Dear God! It burned. Her eyes watered and she glanced over to find Garrett watching her. She tried for a smile, but when he laughed she guessed the smile had failed.

"Not a big scotch drinker?"

"Um..." Her voice sounded raw. "No. This was my first time."

She put the glass on the coffee table as he took a sip and leaned back.

"So your life of crime," she said.

"I was sixteen and Pete had been away at college for one semester and was wowing everyone by making the dean's list and Mom and Dad were putting the pressure on me to live up to Pete."

"That's the downside to siblings. I always thought it would be cool to have one, but there was no one I had to live up to," she said. Except maybe her mom's expectations.

"Yeah. So while they were making the trip to see him at UC Berkley I found a new group of friends. I partied with them and when getting high wasn't enough we started breaking into places just for the thrill...I never took anything, so in my mind that made it okay. But we got busted, and everything sort of changed for me. The cop who took us in looked at me in such a way that I felt really small and petty."

She crossed her arms over her chest to keep from reaching out to him. His story had taken him back in time and he'd retreated from her. She wondered where he'd gone.

"Anyway, he said I had been given a gift that half the guys he knew would kill for. I had parents that loved me, money for a good education, and I was acting like a jerk. Throwing it all away. Then he left me in a holding cell until morning."

"Why were you kept in jail?"

"When I called my dad he and the officer decided that a night incarcerated would do me good."

"Was he right?"

"Yeah. I mean after that night I knew two things...one that I never wanted to be locked up again. And two, I needed to have my own moral code. Not one that was dictated by my friends or what people thought was cool."

She nodded thoughtfully. He'd changed that night. Found a solid core of strength in himself and she was a little bit jealous because she was still searching for that. Still reaching for it and coming up with pieces but not the entire thing.

"I'm amazed one night could change your life that much," she said at last.

"I'm not. One night is all it takes. I bet if you looked at your life you'd see that one night has changed it," he said.

She started to shake her head, but then stopped. The one

night she'd spent with him had convinced her that she wanted real changes in her life. Had cemented her desire to be a different woman than the one she had been.

"Has it happened more than once to you?" she asked.

"Hell."

"I guess that's a yes," she said.

"Um, yeah. The night that my partner died changed my life again. It's funny that one night breaking the law and one night enforcing it would bookend my career as a cop."

"Is your career over?" she asked.

"This civil suit isn't making it any easier to keep going," he admitted. "I have no idea what will happen next."

"So that's why you keep trying to back away from me," she said.

She needed to know. Her gut drew her to him. There was something about him...sex appeal and that smile of his, which she didn't see often enough. But more than that was the bubbly feeling in her stomach. How even though she knew she should go home she was sitting in his house, talking to him. She wanted to believe it was the beginning of love, but wasn't sure.

What she did know was she didn't want to leave. Didn't want him to leave.

"So what's next?"

"For the case...I'm meeting with our family attorney on Monday. For you and me?"

"Yeah," she said.

"I can't let you go," he said. "I know it would be better to wait until this is resolved. Until my life is sorted, but I also know that there is always going to be something lurking and waiting to change my life."

"So..."

"So, let's take it slow and easy. Okay?"

She nodded. It wasn't what she wanted to hear. But then she wasn't looking for forever....or was she? She didn't want to admit it, but she thought the disappointment in her gut meant that she had been.

136

Chapter 14

Monday night he was back at Hayley's house. Sandy was curled up on the couch between them. For a tiny dog she liked to make her presence known.

"How did Sandy do at the shop?"

"She was great. I kept her in my office and everyone who works for us came in to visit her. I think it's going to work. Iona even suggested maybe we could use her on the blog."

"Interesting," he said.

She chewed her lip and looked away from him. He was coming to realize this complex woman needed more than just some romancing and chitchat. He wanted to give her things she never thought to ask for.

"What else is on the bucket list?" he asked as he stretched out on his couch with their legs resting on the ottoman. His first day back at work had been odd and he was pretending that he didn't mind the fact that many of his coworkers were all treating him differently.

"Travel," she said around a handful of popcorn that she'd micro-waved and then tossed in a bowl with some caramel sauce to make caramel popcorn. It was delicious. Just like her smile.

Sandy stirred and climbed on Hayley's lap. Hayley pet her dog.

"Where to? I've got to admit I'm a homebody. Happy to stay

137

right here. I mean we've sort of got it all in Manhattan," he said.

"You're right, we do have it all. But I want to go places I've only read about. Exotic islands like Bali or maybe Dubai," she said. "Somewhere that feels foreign. I've been to a lot of places in the US and they all kind of feel the same."

"I know what you mean. It used to be that you could only get things regionally, but now those small chains have either expanded and are national or are gone."

"I shouldn't have said that. My dad's company bought up a lot of regional favorites and put them in his frozen dinners. I mean, without that I wouldn't have the money to travel."

He took a handful of popcorn and tipped his head back, tossing a piece up in the air and catching it.

She laughed. "Is that your party trick?"

"One of them."

"One? How many do you have?"

"You'll have to wait and find out. So all the places you mentioned are warm. Does winter have anything to do with this need to get away?" he asked.

She nodded. "Definitely. That and all the press that Iona sends me on. She's the pretty one, she should be out promoting The Candied Apple."

"She's not the only one who is pretty," Garrett said.

"You know what I mean. I'm okay, but I don't look like Io. And I hate having to talk about myself, which is in essence what I'm doing every time I have to talk about the store."

He stretched his arm along the back of the couch and put his hand on her shoulder. He understood what she was saying. Iona had more of what he'd call classic beauty. But there was something that shone from deep inside of Hayley and each time he was with her, he found she grew more beautiful to him.

He made a mental note to show her that. "I have to agree with Iona that you're the best one to promote the shop. It's all you."

She took another small handful of popcorn but just played with

138

the kernels in her hand. Her hands were a little red from where she'd burned herself that day at work making a soft caramel filling. He took her hand in his and rubbed his thumb over the mark.

"I had hoped that not everyone would notice that. Every time I read a review that says the place is a little too sweet or kitschy for their tastes I sort of want to curl up. I mean that's part of who I am. I'm not just throwing the stuff into the truffles unless I like it."

"Tell me who these people are and I'll go and arrest them," he said.

"No, you wouldn't. That doesn't fit with your moral code. In a country where free speech exists that's their right. If you arrested them it would put you in a gray area. Plus people would say you were crazy."

He looked at her. He was crazy. Crazy for her. The candymaker with the sexy-ass clothes and the sweet eyes. She was a mixed-up jumble of so many different things that he craved in his life and he had no idea how or if he could make this last.

He wasn't about to bring her down and talk about his day, but he didn't love working cold cases as much as he'd hoped. And if he couldn't make that work, what else could he do?

Be a security guard at his family's corporate headquarters? He'd rather stay in cold cases than do that.

"What about your bucket list?" she asked. "I don't think you really have one."

"You would be correct. I have always gone after what I wanted when I wanted it."

"Have you?" she asked.

"Yes. You're here with me now, aren't you?"

"How can you be sure this isn't all my doing?" she asked him as she put the popcorn bowl on the table and straddled his lap.

"I'm sure," he said, putting his hands on her waist and moving his head back so their eyes met.

She leaned forward, he lifted his face toward hers expecting a kiss but instead she dipped her head to the right and bit the lobe

139

of his ear. "You are too cocky."

"You like it," he said, shifting his hips under hers and getting himself comfortable.

"I do."

She didn't play games with him and right now, when everyone else was being too PC, she was exactly what he needed. Hell, he had needed her before she'd walked into his life. He just hadn't realized it.

"Why did it take me so long to meet you?"

"Fate," she said.

"Fate."

Or a bullet from Paco with his name on it. He pushed all those thoughts to the back of his mind and made love to Hayley on the couch. He held her in his arms afterward until she had to leave to go home.

He walked her next door and as he entered his own brownstone again it felt cold and lonely. Two things it had never been before.

***

Sandy had been a great hit in the back of the candy kitchen. Her assistants Laura, Melanie, and Peter were all enamored with the small dog. Sandy had been sweet as could be and then retreated to her pillow in Hayley's office in the back while they worked.

Her new Garrett-inspired truffle had become a top seller and in the week leading up to Valentine's Day, Hayley had challenged her staff and customers alike to come up with a flavor inspired by someone they loved.

"These are the top ten flavors we voted on," Hayley said as Iona and Cici came into the kitchen after she'd texted them both to get down here.

"Did mine make the cut?" Iona asked.

"Um...the ouzo flavor was okay, but not as good as some of our other suggestions."

"Don't tell my mother that when you come for brunch on Sunday or she might not let you eat."

"I hadn't planned to mention it," Hayley admitted.

"I'd like to narrow it down to six and then put them in that special box we had designed. Cici, have you gotten an invoice from them?"

"We did and I paid it. I think we should receive the boxes tomorrow."

"Great. So now we just need to figure out which six to put in there," Hayley said.

"I've labelled the trays, all you have to do is check off six boxes on your little card and then I will tally the results."

Laura, Melanie, and Pete had helped make the fillings for the truffles, but Hayley had made the outer shells and assembled them herself. So no one knew which flavors had been suggested except her.

"This is kind of exciting," Iona said. "I wonder if we should put it out to our regular customers this afternoon."

Hayley suspected Iona was thinking with her marketing hat on, which was great, but there was no way they could make all these truffles this afternoon and give them away.

"Whose budget would that come out of?" Cici asked. "Marketing?"

"Um...never mind. I already am in danger of going over this year with the big Easter event I have planned."

"That's what I thought," Cici said.

Hayley's staff were the first ones to sample and finish their ballots and they went back to working on the rest of the truffles that had to be made for the day.

Cici closed her eyes after she took a bite out of each one, which made Hayley smile. Her friend was being very serious in her decision-making process.

Iona, on the other hand, had taken half a bite out of each of hers and made some notes on her card.

"Cici, hurry up," Iona said. "I want to know which ones won."

"Don't rush me. We are really close on the margins for this idea. I want to make sure that I don't pick one that won't sell," Cici said.

"Let's go out front and have a cocoa while she's deciding. Can you take a break?" Iona asked.

Hayley glanced over at Laura, who nodded that she had it under control. She loved the way her kitchen looked, the countertops were all stainless steel on one side and marble on the other. The floor was tiled and the walls were done in a design that she'd seen in a picture of a villa in Tuscany. The earthy tones suited chocolate-making. On one wall hung brass molds that they used to shape their famous candy chocolates.

She admitted she'd been inspired by the movie *Chocolat* when designing it and had wanted it to feel homey and comfortable. She spent a lot of time working in this kitchen, so that had been a key concern.

She stopped by her office to give Sandy a treat and noticed that she moved it to her bed and then curled back up on it. Hayley followed Iona out to the shop floor and the café area. They were doing a brisk business and she felt a rush of pride at how her little idea had taken off.

"We're doing good aren't we?" she asked Iona as they sat down at a table toward the back. She was holding the cards that everyone, except Cici, had filled out in one hand.

"Yes, we are." Iona signaled that they wanted two cocoas and put her elbows on the table, tucking a strand of hair behind her ear. "So how's things with Hot Cop?"

"Okay. I really am not sure if we are in a relationship or just in some sort of highly sexual partnership," Hayley said.

Iona shook her head. "I'm trying to figure out if that's bad."

"I don't know. I mean changing from my routine was my original goal, but I'm coming to understand that I really didn't want to change too much of my life. Having Garrett around is interesting. But I like quiet nights and coming to work and thinking about candy."

"So...what's different now?"

"I think about him a lot of the time. And I am spending an inordinate amount of time worrying about what I'm wearing and wondering when I'll see him again. I don't like it. Instead of feeling thirty I feel sixteen, you know."

Iona laughed in a kind way and put her hand on Hayley's and squeezed it. "I do know. That's love. My mother says it's the great equalizer. It hits the strong and the weak and makes us both strong and weak. But it can never be controlled."

"I don't think I love him," Hayley said. Did she? Love was something that she really wasn't sure about. She cared for her dad and had been conflicted about her mom. She wasn't saying she didn't love her parents, just that the affection she had for them was complicated.

Just like Garrett.

"He's been dealing with a bunch of stuff from his job and I'm kind of just hanging back and taking what time he can give me. But that's not really me. I'm not passive normally. But I don't want to scare him off."

Cici drew a chair up as she rejoined them. "Who are you trying not to scare off? Garrett?"

"Yeah. Did you bring your card?" Hayley asked.

"Yes," Cici said, handing it to her. "We should all go out this Friday. You can invite Garrett. That way we can meet him and see if he's worth all the energy you are spending on him."

Hayley had to smile at the way Cici said it. Her friend saw life like a balance sheet and she kept her own life balanced between red and black, something that Hayley admitted sounded nice right now.

"Okay. I will ask him. Where should we go?"

"Olympus," Iona said. "The new deejay is hot and I've been trying to catch his attention."

"I'll let you know if Garrett can go," Hayley said. She had no idea if he could go dancing or if he even liked to.

"Either way, I think the three of us should go. We haven't been out since your birthday."

And look what had happened on that night.

***

Poker night. It was the first night he'd spent apart from Hayley since they'd started dating. If you could call sitting at each other's houses every night talking, watching TV, and making love dating... which he did.

Hayley was changing him in ways he hadn't been aware of until now. As much as he looked forward to the monthly poker game, he wished he could have spent the night with Hayley watching her favorite reality singing television show. There was something about her that brought him comfort and made him forget for a little while about Hector, Paco, and that night.

There was a knock on his door and he opened it expecting to see his friends, but instead it was Mr. Kalatkis.

"Hello, Garrett. I was wondering if you could come and help me. Tony is out on a delivery and we're supposed to get snow and I need help getting everything inside the shop."

"Let me grab my coat, Mr. Kalatkis, and I'll be right down there."

"Thank you."

Garrett grabbed his coat and his cell phone, dialing Hayley's number as he locked up.

"Did you already lose all your money?"

"Ha. Not yet. The game hasn't even started. But I have to run to the Kalatkises' to help. How do you feel about playing hostess to my friends until I get back?"

There was a little silence on the line and he heard the jingling of Sandy's collar as he assumed Hayley got up.

"Sure. Should I just break in?" she asked.

"I'm standing outside your place with my keys," he said.

She opened the door a few seconds later and he tossed her

144

his keys as he disconnected the call and pocketed his cell phone.

"I'll be back shortly."

"Okay," she said. "Can I bring Sandy with me?"

"I don't see why not," he said. "I don't want to keep Mr. Kalatkis waiting, are you sure about this?"

"Of course. Go and help them."

She scooped her little dog up and jogged down the steps on the cold February night. He caught her close and gave her a hard kiss on the mouth before turning and walking away. He wanted her. He wasn't sure how she'd become so important to him, but pretending she wasn't was a lie he no longer told himself.

A part of him hadn't been sure he deserved to find this kind of happiness. And there were nights when he still woke up wondering why he had lived and Hector hadn't. But he knew there was no way to go back and change it.

He entered the Kalatkises' grocery store and found it busy with the usual after-work crowd.

Mrs. Kalatkis waved at him as he made his way to the back with his first load of produce from the front of the store. Mr. Kalatkis followed behind him. They worked together until everything was inside.

He turned to leave when he saw that Mrs. Kalatkis had put down two cups of espresso. Mr. Kalatkis reached for one and handed it to Garrett. He realized that before his injury he wouldn't have had time for this.

"Angela made some baklava for you to take home too. Enough to share," Mr. Kalatkis said.

"Thanks," he said. He had the feeling the Kalatkises were trying to keep him and Hayley together. He wasn't sure how he felt about it, but he finished his espresso and took the baklava with him as he left.

When he returned to his house, he wondered how his friends and Hayley would be getting along. He entered the foyer, put the baklava on the table and heard the sounds of music and laughter coming from his game room. He walked down the hall realizing that his knee ached a little.

A nice, long soak in the bath with Hayley would be nice, he thought.

"So they ask for volunteers to go first," Ramirez said. He was wearing a faded NYPD shirt and held a glass of red wine in one hand. "Garrett looks at the rest of us and says F—it, I guess I'm the only real man here. And he goes first."

Hayley smiled. "What happened then, Javier?"

Javier? Ramirez always went by his last name, in fact, if they hadn't been through the police academy together Garrett wouldn't have known his first name. He glanced at his friend and wondered if he was crushing on Hayley. He couldn't blame the guy, but it was his tough luck that Hayley was his.

"Well, let's just say being tased has nothing to do with being a man and hurts like hell. But once Garrett did it everyone started volunteering. He's good like that," Ramirez said. "You can always count on him to run in first."

"Interesting," she said, glancing up as if she felt him watching her. "Would you say he has more balls than brains?"

"Definitely," Hoop said.

"Hey, I don't think that's true," Garrett said walking into the room.

Hayley had put all the chips in bowls and lit a candle. He'd never seen poker night like this before. "Since when do you boys drink wine?"

"Since the lady offered," Maxwell said. "Some of us have more brains..."

He punched his friend in the shoulder and walked over to Hayley, leaning down to kiss her. "Thanks for taking care of my friends."

"I didn't mind it. I guess I'll be going. It was nice to meet you all. Hoop, I will see you on Friday."

"Why will you see him on Friday?" Garrett asked.

"Because we are going out with my friends. Javier and Clay have to work," she said.

Nice. They were all on a first-name basis. Damn him if he wasn't jealous of his friends. The guys who'd had his back and that he knew better than his brother. He needed to shake this off.

"Cool," he said. "Boys, why don't you deal while I walk Hayley to the door?"

He led her out into the hallway.

"Why are we going out on Friday?"

"Because we haven't been out on a real date and Iona and Cici were dying to go out," she said.

"And?"

"I want to see us in a normal date setting. See what we are like," she said.

"Fair enough."

He walked her and Sandy back over to her house, took the kiss he'd been wanting all evening and then went back home. The guys teased him about his new girlfriend and he joked and made light of it, but he knew that Hayley was more than girlfriend, that somehow she'd become his touchstone.

Chapter 15

He hated wearing a suit and realized that he associated the suit and tie with his dad and the pressure to fit in. He tugged on his tie as he got off the elevator. His father was waiting for him in the lobby of Lionel Fairchild's offices. For as long as he could remember Lionel had been representing his family in all personal matters.

When he'd eventually gotten out of jail it had been Lionel who'd come to bring him home. He was his dad's best friend and like a second father to Garrett—or a really cool uncle, because with Lionel there was none of the pressure that he got from his dad.

"Dad, I wasn't expecting you to be here."

"I'm only here as an observer because your mom and I are worried about you, son."

For years Alan had been worrying about him and Garrett freely admitted he'd done nothing to give his parents cause for concern. It was simply something they did.

"Well, you don't have to worry, Dad."

"Thanks," Alan said with a hint of a smile. "The press have your name, but so far they haven't linked you to our family or the business."

"What happens if they do?" Garrett asked. He didn't want that one night to have consequences for his family. He'd gotten onto the force to stay out of trouble.

His phone pinged with a text message and he pulled it out of his pocket. It was from Hayley.

Hope I didn't overstep the boundaries last night when I invited your friends out.

"Dad, I'm going to outside real quick to make a call," he said.
"Okay. Don't be too long."
"I won't.

He walked down the hall to the stairwell. He dialed Hayley's number and she answered it right away.

"Garrett?"

"Hey. I was going to text back, but this is the kind of thing that should be said, not written. I want us to be in a real relationship. I want to be the man you share your bucket list with and whose friends know you. But you have to understand that my life is a crazy mess right now. So when I pull back it's not you—"

"Don't say that. We are both trying to swim and keep our heads above the water, but it's hard. Life is just like that. My dad always says it's the struggle that reminds him he's alive and until now I didn't realize what he meant. I thought I knew it because opening my own shop was hard, but this thing with you is a challenge and...not to sound sappy, but sweet. I like it. I keep cautioning myself to go slow and then I text you something or invite your friends to go out with us."

He wanted that. Truly he did. But he also felt trapped. Not so much by Hayley as by his own conscience. He was struggling with the fact that he was in the midst of this exciting new relationship with her while two men were dead. He couldn't understand for the life of him why he'd survived. He knew there had to be a reason. Didn't there?

There should be.

He leaned back against the cold cement wall and tipped his head toward the ceiling. Maybe this civil suit would help to resolve something in his head. Give him the means to make amends or free him once and for all from the guilt.

"Garrett?"

"Yeah?"

"Just making sure you were still there."

"I am. I can't talk for much longer, though. I have an appointment with my attorney."

"Okay. I hope it goes well. Let me know if there is anything I can do."

"I will," he said and then disconnected the call. He almost wished she hadn't texted him. He needed to concentrate on the case--on being his sharpest instead of thinking about Hayley and the fact that he'd dreamt of being in her arms last night. But it had been too late to call her after the guys had left.

And after being ribbed all night long about his "girlfriend" he hadn't reached out to Hayley to prove something to himself.

That he was an idiot.

What man turns away from a woman like her?

But he knew the answer. Felt it deep in his wounded soul. It didn't matter how much she soothed him, she also reminded him of how vulnerable he was. Of the good thing he wanted, but had never gone after.

"Son?" Alan asked, opening the door to the stairwell.

"Coming," he said.

His dad looked like he always had. A man who knew where he was going and what he wanted out of life. And Garrett knew it would have been so much easier to get along with his father if just one time he seemed fallible. Human.

All the things that Garrett knew himself to be but had never seen in his dad.

"Lionel asked if you'd like me to be a part of the meeting," his dad asked.

Garrett thought it over for a moment and then nodded. He needed someone who could give him good advice. Someone who knew the right choices to make. Because Garrett had never been perfect and his father had always seemed to be.

"Sure. But just for me to talk things over with. I don't want you making any decisions, Dad."

"I know. You're an adult. I'm just here for moral support," Alan said.

Moral support. God knew he needed it right now when his strong moral code felt weak. When he was questioning his own actions and wondering if he'd done the right thing.

He'd never questioned himself before this and he hated that feeling. Garrett was used to knowing he was living his life on his own terms. But now he was sitting in a leather guest chair in an attorney's office with his father beside him.

Despite the time that had passed, he felt seventeen again and like he hadn't learned anything. The only real difference was that this time he understood how much he had to lose. Not just his career but also his chance at a future with Hayley.

And that thought was the one that made him realize he could pretend all he liked that he wasn't sure what he wanted, but the truth was he wanted her. Period.

***

The next morning was crisp, clear, and cold as she locked her door and headed up the block. Sandy trotted along beside her, checking out the street as they walked. But when she got to the corner and Mr. and Mrs. Kalatkis's grocery store she stopped. The front window had been smashed and it looked like the store had been robbed.

She texted her assistant Laura to say she was going to be late to work. She picked up Sandy so the little dog didn't step in any of the debris and went inside, where Mrs. Kalatkis was sweeping up the mess left.

"Mrs. Kalatkis, are you alright?" Hayley asked as she came up next to the older woman. She set Sandy down.

Mrs. Kalatkis leaned on her broom as she looked up at Hayley. She seemed more angry than upset. "I'm fine. Which is more than I can say for whoever did this when we find them."

"What happened?"

"Someone broke in last night, Hayley," Mrs. Kalatkis said slowly.

"I figured that out. I guess I meant what do you know?" Hayley said, bending down to start picking up the bigger pieces of the boxes that had been smashed.

"The cops think that after the thief broke in and realized there was no money left in the cash register he got angry and started busting up the place."

"Is there nothing missing?"

"Some liquor and cigarettes, but otherwise no."

Senseless. What made people act that way? As the thought entered her head she realized it was something her mom would have said. Maybe she wasn't as different from her mother as she'd always thought.

"I'll help you clean this up. Have you called someone to replace the glass?"

"Yes. The insurance people don't want us to do too much until our agent gets down here and takes some pictures. I'm just picking up the worst of it. We could probably use your help later," Mrs. Kalatkis said.

"Okay. Here's my cell number. Text me when you can start cleaning up and I'll come back and help."

"Thank you," Mrs. Kalatkis said, tucking Hayley's business card into her pocket. "You don't need to do that."

"I wouldn't be able to live with my conscience if I didn't. You are like family, Mrs. Kalatkis."

Mrs. Kalatkis put her broom down and gave Hayley a hug. "I'm so mad."

"Me too," Hayley said. She glanced around the little shop that she thought of as part of their community. She knew it was more than a place to pick up milk or juice. It made her feel like she was home. In a way that the cold mansion in the Hamptons never had.

"Did they hit any other places?"

"No. The Chinese restaurant across the street is fine and the flower shop was also untouched. Just our place."

Bastards.

Mr. Kalatkis came in from the back with a police officer that Hayley thought looked familiar. Maybe he had been at Garrett's for poker? She couldn't remember.

"Can you believe this, Hayley?" Mr. Kalatkis asked.

"I can't. I'm going to come back later when it's okay to clean up. Do you need anything?" she asked him.

"Thank you," Mr. Kalatkis said. "We're fine."

Hayley nodded and then left the store, Sandy walking along beside her. The smells of the morning were heavier than usual; the rotting trash and garbage scent that lingered in the early morning, and Hayley knew that was because she had glimpsed the reality of her city.

She might live in Manhattan, but most of the time it felt small and like her own little neighborhood. Today, reality had shown her that the big City was right there.

Laura was waiting in the kitchen when she arrived at work. "Everything okay?"

"Yes. There was a break-in on my street and I stopped to make sure everything was okay."

"There was a break-in in my building last month. I swear I didn't sleep a wink after that. I'm still keeping my Louisville Slugger next to the bed."

"I pity the fool who tries to break into your place," Hayley said with a lightness she didn't feel. She got Sandy settled in her office and came back to start making the candy for the day.

No wonder Garrett felt called to be a cop and be out on the streets. She wondered how he was going to feel about the Kalatkises being robbed. In a way she bet he'd feel like she did, violated.

153

"What do I need to make today?"

"Just our regular truffles. We are packaging them in an eight- and twelve-candy heart-shaped box for Valentine's Day," Hayley said.

Hayley shoved the thoughts of Mr. and Mrs. Kalatkis to the back of her mind and got to work. The kitchen was always the place where she lost herself and she did it now. She went to the whiteboard and wrote the quantities that were needed. She had two junior assistants, who would be in later. One of them worked on the ganache fillings and the other on the different types of tempered chocolate for the outer shells.

She also put a notice on the board that they were making the truffles from the competition for Valentine's Day, so that the sales associates and café workers would be able to share it with their customers.

She went out into the shop and paused in the doorway, looking around it. It was clean, the refrigerated cases, where they stored the truffles once they were made, buzzed slightly. She'd feel so scared and angry if someone broke in here and did to her shop what had been done to the Kalatkises' grocery store.

Her hands shook a little as she got the stool and went to the big slate board and listed out their specials for the day and an invitation for their customers to submit their truffle ideas.

She did a good job of pretending that nothing had changed, but she realized that her mom's death wasn't the only ending that would occur in her life. What if the Kalatkises decided to move out of the city? What if someone broke in here and she lost her shop?

She sat down on the stool as the truth she'd been hiding from suddenly jumped out. What if she let herself care about Garrett and he walked away?

***

Clay texted to say he was in the neighborhood and did Garrett want to grab breakfast before he headed into work?

Garrett said yes and met his friend at the corner, shocked to see that Clay was working a break-in at the Kalatkises' store. He did what he could to help, but they were still waiting for the insurance agent to arrive and nothing could be touched.

"Do you have a security system?" Garrett asked Mr. Kalatkis as Clay finished a call he was on.

"No. We never needed one," Mr. Kalatkis said.

"You do now," Garrett said. During his convalescence he'd spent some time on the internet researching different security systems, in case he'd had to take his dad and brother up on their job offer. "I will get what you need and install it."

"Thanks. This has been a morning of loss, but we've also had a chance to see how good our neighbors are. Hayley and the Jeffersons have already been here. And everyone is so willing to help. It means a lot to us."

"You mean a lot to everyone here," Garrett said. He wasn't surprised to hear that others on the block wanted to help. This little store was their hub of activity. Kids bought candy and ice cream there. Moms stopped and chatted after walking their kids to the park.

"I guess we do. So what kind of security measures do you think? Tony wanted to get a gun, but—"

"Definitely not," Garrett said. "You don't need that. I'll put in some cameras and motion detectors and we'll get bars for the windows."

"Bars? Angela really didn't want bars," Mr. Kalatkis said.

"I know. But they are a nice passive security measure," Garrett said.

"I'll think about it. Do you think the thief will come back? They already know we don't keep money in here."

Garrett wasn't sure. He didn't know why the Kalatkises' store had been targeted to begin with. He would ask Clay about crime in the area and try to figure it out.

"Who knows? But why take chances?"

"True," Mr. Kalatkis said. The insurance agent arrived and Clay and Garrett left to get breakfast.

Garrett wanted to go back and help the Kalatkises, but he had to be at work. "Do you think the break-in was random?"

"Seems like it. I heard you mention putting in security cameras. That will be a help. We just don't know why the thief picked that place. And there wasn't much evidence."

"I bet it's someone who lives nearby."

"Maybe. We haven't had any other break-ins. Could it be a kid they wouldn't sell liquor to?" Clay asked.

"I will ask when I go back tonight. You think it's someone they know?" Garrett asked as he finished his breakfast burrito. He ordered two to go as well as two coffees.

"It's a possibility. And let's face it, right now, it could be anyone."

Clay left when Garrett's order arrived and he took a few minutes to walk back to the Kalatkises and give them the food. They were both grateful since the insurance agent had a bunch of forms for them to fill out.

When he got to the station the captain called him into his office.

"The civil suit seems to have been dropped, so you're cleared to keep working in cold cases. Have you talked to your doctor? Is there any news on when you can pass the physical to get back to work?"

News of the civil suit being dropped was good. Garrett wondered why his attorney hadn't called with the news himself. "When did you hear about the suit?"

"Ten minutes ago. Don't you know what happened?"

"No, what?"

"Seems that an out-of-court settlement was reached."

Garrett didn't like the sound of that. "With whom?"

"I don't know. Figured you'd know."

Fuck.

He had an idea but he didn't like it. "My leg is still on the mend.

156

I should be able to attempt the physical in about three weeks."

Garrett left the captain's office and went down to the basement where the cold-case office was. His "partner", Ern, was fifty-five and had four children and six grandkids. But he wasn't at his desk when Garrett got down there. He dialed his attorney's number and was put through after a few minutes on hold.

"Garrett, great! I was going to call you in a few minutes. I'm sure you heard the news that Paco's family accepted the settlement your father authorized me to make."

"Lionel, I thought that was going to be a last resort," Garrett said.

"It was. But as soon as the press found out about your family, your father was adamant that we make the offer and get this out of the news. Are you still okay with that?"

"Yes. But I would have preferred getting the news from you rather than my boss," Garrett said. He wasn't okay with it. It went totally against the grain to take responsibility for Paco's death when...had he been within his rights to kill him? He'd been wrestling with it and still wasn't sure if he had been.

But that didn't mean he'd wanted to pay off Paco's family. "I tried calling this morning and then got pulled into a meeting. I'm going to do a press release and then hopefully this will all die down.

"Fine."

"I think this is the best solution."

Of course he did. Lionel and Paco's family attorney would get a cut of the money that his father had put up. His father wouldn't get linked to the killing in the press. Garrett could put the incident behind him. Garrett was sure his father was thinking that he'd fixed everything.

But he hadn't. This just made him realize that his father had no clue about him.

He was tempted to call his father, but instead he dialed Hayley's number.

She answered her phone on the second ring.

"Hey. It's been a crazy morning. Did you hear about the

Kalatkises' shop?"

Her voice soothed the anger that had been brewing inside of him. And he chatted with her about the Kalatkises, pretending that nothing had changed, but knowing that he wasn't going to be able to keep ignoring his family. He was going to have to confront his father and also figure out the future.

Hayley couldn't talk for long and when they hung up he realized she'd done what he needed her to. She was like a balm for him. He wasn't sure that he should let himself depend this deeply on her.

Chapter 16

Pete was dodging his calls, which meant that he knew what Dad had done. Garrett had a choice when he got off work: go and confront his parents or head back home to help out the Kalatkises. Hayley texted him to say she was on her way over there and he texted back he'd be there soon.

It wasn't his nature to avoid confrontation. Especially one that was long overdue. He took a cab to his parents' house in Brooklyn. Traffic was heavy and he was aggravated by the time he got there, so he walked to the end of the block and sat on one of the benches that overlooked the park.

He needed to be calm. All of his training as a police officer came back. He went back to the house where he and Pete had grown up and rang the doorbell. He heard it echo through the house and the sound of Butch – his parents' beagle – barking before the door opened. His mom stood there wiping her hands on a dishtowel.

"Garrett, honey, I didn't know you were stopping by tonight."

He gave his mom a kiss and then stepped inside, closing the door behind him. "I think Dad did."

"I wasn't sure," his father said from the end of the hallway. "I've only just gotten home."

"We need to talk," Garrett said.

"I just poured your dad a Martini. Can I get you one?" his

159

mom asked.

He shook his head. "No thank you."

"Let's go in the den," his father said.

"Alan, what is going on?"

"Dad paid off the Rivera family. He settled my civil case without talking to me," Garrett said. He suspected his mom had been in the dark too.

"Alan, how could you? We said—"

"I had no choice. You agreed we needed to do everything to help Garrett heal and move on. He couldn't do that with the case hanging over him."

"I'll let you boys talk it out. Are you staying for dinner, Garrett?"

"No, Mom. I'm sorry, but I have to get home," he said.

She nodded before turning and walking away. His father didn't say a word, just went into the den. The room was lined from floor to ceiling with bookcases. There was a heavy Persian carpet and the desk that sat near the window had been there since before Garrett was born. He and Pete had signed their names underneath it on the wood during a long-ago summer when it had been raining for several days and they'd been trapped inside.

Sitting down on one of the leather guest chairs, he felt the tension in his knee and fought not to let that small pain show. He had been given every privilege growing up. He knew that, but he saw now the one thing he craved – acceptance for his choices from his father – would never be his.

"I asked you not to get involved," Garrett said. "When you offered me your attorney I took it because Lionel knows me and understands what's important to me."

His father stood behind his desk, apparently looking out the window, but Garret knew his father was keeping him in his view as well.

"I know. I wanted to stay out of it, but when I saw that they'd connected you to us it was hard."

Garrett understood that. "I wouldn't have let the company get dragged into it. I know how important that is—"

"It's not more important than you," his father said. "And they were upping their settlement request. As soon as they learned you were more than just a cop they called Lionel and let him know they had retained a new attorney.

"He still had their original offer on his desk and it didn't expire until midnight. He tried to call you, couldn't get in touch, and then called me. Settling before their new attorney took over was the only way to mitigate the amount."

Garrett leaned back in the chair. It was hard to argue with that. His dad had been simply looking out for him. "I hate this."

His father turned to face him. In his eyes he saw emotions he couldn't read. But he didn't think he saw disappointment. God, he hoped he didn't.

"I know. I do too. If you were the negligent playboy cop the suit alleged I wouldn't have gotten involved. But, son, you are one of the most honorable men I know. I couldn't let the case continue and allow their greed to sully your name and reputation."

He thought that the Rivera family would have had their work cut out proving that he was a bad cop or that he had acted with malice. But his father had done what he always did, acted to protect their family.

"I guess I should say thank you," Garrett said.

"You could. But in your shoes I would be mad too. Lionel called me after he talked to you. It was only the fact that we had gone to that initial meeting together that he felt he could call me. Otherwise—"

"I'd be fighting a big-time attorney who knew how to do a smear campaign, right?"

"Yes," his father said.

"Then, thank you," he said. Leaning forward, Garrett ran his hands through his hair. He was tired of dealing with the aftermath of one incident.

"One night shouldn't change so many things," Garrett said.

161

"No, it shouldn't. But oftentimes all it takes is one incident."

He looked at his dad. Usually he only saw him as a parent, but there was something in his tone that forced Garrett to look at his dad as a man.

"Did something happen to you?" Garrett asked his dad. He'd never really thought about how his parents had met. He'd heard the stories of the college debate team, but beyond that…well they'd seemed old and who wanted to think about parents falling in love? He never had until now.

"The night I met your mom," he said. "I knew I'd found the woman I wanted to spend the rest of my life with."

"How'd you know, Dad?" he asked. "How were you sure?"

His father turned back to the window, looking out at the small side yard. And Garrett wondered if he was going to respond at all.

Finally, he turned back around. "I was never sure, I just knew that the thought of not spending my life with her scared me."

Garrett remembered those words later that night as he watched Hayley laughing with Mrs. Kalatkis as she restocked shelves in the grocery store. She made him so aware of everything. But he didn't know if it was the lifelong mate kind or something else.

***

Hayley could tell something had happened to Garrett by the way he kept his distance from her as they both worked to help the Kalatkises get their shop cleaned up. They had new windows installed and bars put up, despite the fact that Mrs. Kalatkis had objected to it.

Hayley had brought a basket of candies and some cookies she'd baked while waiting for Garrett to show up. She'd hoped he'd join her for dinner before they came down here. But he hadn't.

And now he was avoiding her. She had enough experience of being dumped by guys to know what that felt like. Was he trying to dump her or was it just that civil case against him?

She wasn't sure what was going on with him. But she wasn't going to just let it be.

They weren't a couple...she knew that because they hadn't been on a single date. They'd slept together and poured out little intimate details of their lives, but hadn't been out together yet.

Did that matter? Wasn't it easier sometimes to share things with strangers precisely because they were strangers?

She'd dated tons of guys who were still strangers after months of basketball games, concerts, and expensive dinners. She wasn't sure that a date was the key to getting to know someone.

But she did know she wasn't a fan of being shut out by Garrett. They'd been playing an odd little ping-pong game, where one of them advanced and then retreated and Hayley realized she was getting past the point of game-playing.

She'd changed and if he hadn't, she needed to know before she let things go any further.

Finally when the locksmiths were almost done fitting the new doors and locks on the store, she felt like she'd done all she could to help the Kalatkises get their shop fixed up. They were going to take a few days off while Garrett worked on getting some security equipment installed. Their kids had insisted on the break. Plus it would take time to get the shop fully restocked.

But they were planning a big re-opening in two weeks' time.

Garret was talking to the cop who'd been there this morning when she'd stopped by. And soon he left and Garrett was alone.

"Walk me home?" she asked.

"I don't think there is anything dangerous out there," he said.

The real danger, she realized, was letting herself care for this man. That he was still not sure what he wanted in his own life and kept shoving her a little further away from him.

"Fine."

She had already said goodbye to everyone, so she turned away from Garrett and walked out of the shop, buttoning up her coat as she walked. It was snowing again and she tried to pretend that was an interesting fact as she walked up the street toward her brownstone.

Why did she even bother with men? But then she remembered the way Garrett looked in those faded jeans that fit him just right and groaned.

"Hayley!"

She refused to stop or turn. He couldn't be a jerk and then expect her to just take it. Or maybe he did. Better to find that out now before she let herself fall any deeper for him. Right now he was just a guy she liked. A guy she'd slept with. He wasn't someone she cared about.

Liar.

"Dammit, Hayley," Garrett said as he caught up with her. He put his hand on her shoulder and forced her to stop.

She shrugged his touch off and took a step back, looking up at the street lamp and watching the snowflakes falling around them.

"Dammit yourself. I don't know what is going on with you, but I'm not about to let you be rude—"

"I'm sorry."

"What?"

"You heard me. I haven't had the best day. I am worried about Mr. and Mrs. Kalatkis and I don't know what to do about the way I feel for you," he said.

"That's a laundry list of things," she said. And it sounded like a list that he'd made to keep from admitting what was really going on. She knew that her timing wasn't great.

He sighed. "I know. Want to come inside and I'll make you something to drink and we can talk?"

"Fine. But let's go to my place." He never had anything in his house except take-out containers and beer.

"Okay," he said.

He didn't say anything else as they walked up the block, but he did pull her to a stop as they approached her brownstone, to keep her from being hit by a snowball from one of the Jefferson twins.

164

The six-year-olds were laughing as they lobbed snow at each other.

"Sorry, Miss Dunham," Andy said. "Did we get you?"

"Nope, you missed," she said with a smile. Kids! She wanted them, so why was she messing around with someone like Garrett? "Have fun, boys."

She paused on the top step before unlocking her door. There was snow all around them and she heard the tinkling laughter of the boys as they pelted each other with snow. She'd never been in a snowball fight.

"Brings back some good memories for me," Garrett said.

"Really? I've never done that," she admitted. She imagined some of her friends had snowball fights, but she never had. She'd gone sledding with them and made snow angels, but snowballs… no way would her mom have approved.

"Never?" he asked.

"Nope."

"When I was a kid Pete and I used to try to sneak outside to make snowballs before each other," Garrett said. There was joy in his voice, something she rarely heard in it. Garrett had had a good upbringing. He was lucky. Not that she was the poor little rich girl talking, but Hayley could tell having a brother had been a good thing for him.

"I bet that was fun. Being an only child, I never had that," she said. "Mom didn't approve of throwing snow. And Dad was always gone."

"Want to have a snowball fight now?" he asked, wriggling his eyebrows at her.

She wondered if she did. It was something different. A thing her mom hadn't approved of. Why hadn't she done this before? "Yes. But let's do it in the backyard."

"You're on."

She unlocked the door and dumped her purse and keys on the table. Sandy raced over to her and Hayley bent down to pick the little dog up. She checked her water and feed bowl as they walked through the kitchen.

"Are there any rules I should know of?" Hayley asked.

She opened the back door and Sandy scampered out and then came right back inside, looking at the snow, which reached her belly.

"No face shots," Garrett said. "Otherwise all's fair."

"Sounds good," she said.

"I'll take that area and you have this one. Since you're new at this I'll give you a few minutes to make some snowballs."

Sandy followed them outside and kind of pranced around the yard as they both started to make snowballs. Hayley packed the snow together, her hands getting really cold as she did so.

She glanced over at Garrett, who had knelt in the snow and was concentrating on making a pile of snowballs. She took a quick breath and then lobbed it over at him. She caught him by surprise, hitting him on the shoulder.

"I guess the game is starting."

He tossed one at her and she turned just in time to get it in the middle of her back. They spent the next fifteen minutes playing outside and Hayley forgot how aggravated she'd been earlier. And it seemed to her that Garrett had too. She snuck up behind him with one hand behind her back.

"Had enough?"

"Sure," he said, tossing his last snowball on the ground.

She took the snow in her hand and pressed it against his neck before he could move. He yelped and caught her as she turned away.

They both lost their balance and fell to the ground. Garrett maneuvered them so he was on the bottom. And she realized that he always did that. They'd fallen enough for her to notice that he made sure she never got hurt.

***

166

The snow fight made it easy to believe that they didn't have any problems. That he hadn't had to chase her down the street to catch her, but he knew the truth was they did. Or rather he did.

He liked her, but he was starting to depend on her. She'd been the first one he'd thought of when he'd found out the case had been dropped. He had needed to talk to her after he'd had that conversation in Brooklyn with his dad. But needing someone – anyone really – this much scared him.

She put her hands on his chest and her legs had fallen between his, so when she levered herself up their groins pressed together. And he groaned.

How could he be getting turned on when he had a big layer of icy snow pressed against his back? His body needed to work on its priorities. Getting warm should come before getting laid.

But she felt good.

Hell, she always felt good.

Which was why even though common sense dictated he be anywhere but here, he was in her backyard lying in the snow.

"You made me mad," she said.

"I know."

"Why were you acting like that?" she asked.

"Can I tell you in the house?"

"Maybe."

Sandy noticed them both down at her level and came over, standing up on her back legs and looking at them expectantly.

"What do you think she wants?" Hayley asked.

"No clue. But then she's female, so that's to be expected."

Hayley turned her head, staring down at him and he knew he'd disappointed her again. But the truth was, he could only guess what she wanted and could only fake the fact that he might really know what that was for so long.

Before she realized that he was faking it.

"Really?"

"Yes." He put his hands on her hips and shifted her as he sat up. She wrapped her legs around him and he enjoyed the sensation of her sliding against him.

Dammit.

"I want to be all cool about things and pretend I get whatever it is that upset you, but tonight I've got a ton of crap in my head and I really just wanted to have a few minutes with you to enjoy myself, but for some reason needing you..."

She wrapped her arms around his torso and leaned her head against his shoulder. "It's hard, isn't it? I hate that one comment from you cut me. I've been feeling sort of loopy happy and then all of sudden you popped that bubble."

He wasn't sure what "loopy happy" meant to her, but it described the way he felt about her. How having her in his life made no sense and yet felt right. Maybe that was what was frightening him.

Sandy got tired of waiting for them to pay attention to her and put her paw on his chest like Hayley was doing. Garrett scooped the little dog up and let her get between them. She turned around, trying to find a comfortable position, which made Hayley laugh.

"If only we could be so easily pleased," she said. She used her hand on his shoulder to get to her feet and holding Sandy in one arm, she offered him her hand.

"Indeed."

He took her hand and got to his feet. He was cold as they made their way back into her house. His jeans were soaked.

"We haven't had date night yet," she said.

"Okay."

"Sorry. I was thinking—why don't we shower, change, and then we can have a picnic in front of my fireplace."

"A date?"

"Yes. I'm asking you out. You said you weren't ready to say goodbye to me yet."

"I'm still not," he admitted. "Okay. I'll be back in thirty minutes?"

168

"Perfect," she said.

He let himself out of her place and walked over to his. His house, when he entered it, looked different to him and as he showered and changed and then grabbed a bottle of wine he acknowledged that he was the one who was changing.

He'd always had a full life, but after his injury and the night that changed everything, he'd forgotten.

His focus had narrowed down to what he didn't have or couldn't do any longer and that was no way for a person to live.

Hayley had changed all that. With her innocent smile and wickedly sexy body, she'd woken him to the fact that he'd been existing, not living.

She'd done that.

He had said he wasn't ready to say goodbye to her. He still wasn't, but was staying with her. Letting her become more deeply entrenched in his life...was that a good idea?

He'd never believed a cop's life was too dangerous to invite a woman to share it. But Hector's death had changed all of that. He was out of the line of fire, so to speak, with his new assignment in cold cases, but he hated it.

He knew as soon as he was healthy enough he wanted to be back out there. Risking his life to keep the streets safe.

So did that make this time with Hayley a different kind of limbo? One where he could pretend to be building a future, even though it was one he didn't want.

He put the wine back on the counter and leaned against it.

He wanted the answer to be simple. He wanted to be able to just make Hayley his woman and not worry about what might happen, but the way he felt about her was anything but casual.

He still wanted to be a cop and the fact that Hayley was messing with that bothered him. He remembered what his dad said about knowing his mom was the woman he wanted to spend the rest of his life with and Garrett wondered if he could make the same choice his father had.

Other officers were cops and had families. And until recently he'd thought he could do it too. But he had a bum leg and God knew if he'd ever be one hundred percent with it again. Was it fair to let this go any further until he could accept the weakness in himself?

Chapter 17

Hayley had the fireplace roaring...not a mean feat given that it worked from a switch on the wall. It was one of those gas-log versions, so it put out some heat but was really there for ambiance.

She'd moved her coffee table and found her thick picnic blanket in the hall closet. She spread it out on the floor and Sandy, who'd been dogging her steps, decided that the blanket looked comfy and curled up in the center of it, making Hayley smile.

She put on her stereo, which was frankly outdated, but she liked it because she had one of those CD jukebox players. She had over a hundred CDs in there. Albums she'd never had the time or space to get moved over to her iPod.

Anita Baker – her mom's favorite – was the first one up and Hayley stopped in the hallway looking at the envelope from her mom.

She lifted it up and glanced at it in the light. She wanted to know what was in there. She didn't want to know just as much. Still torn.

She put the letter down as there was a knock at the door. She figured it was Garrett and when she opened the door she saw she was right.

The snow continued to fall and he had a light dusting of it on his hair and collar. He looked handsome and a little weary as he

171

stood there.

They were both so afraid to let anyone past their defenses. Had both loved and lost. She didn't mean romantically, she meant... well for her it had been her mom. And she was beginning to suspect for Garrett it had been his career.

"I brought a bottle of wine," he said, holding it up.

"Looks good. I started getting things ready in the living room. I had some puff pastry in the freezer so I doctored that up with some deli ham, artichoke hearts, and Dijon mustard."

"Sounds delicious," he said. "What can I do to help?

She led him into the kitchen.

"You can pour the wine," she said.

She got out the bottle opener and noticed he was staring at her slate board. She'd changed the message since he'd been here last.

"Just Breathe?"

"Yes. I've been stressed about the shop. Iona wants to expand and Cici thinks we could do with a place in lower Manhattan, but I'm not ready. I like my kitchen and my staff...I'm whining, sorry. You don't want to hear about my work," she said.

She finished putting everything on the plates. She'd made a salad of mixed lettuce, candied walnuts, dried cranberries, and crumbled blue cheese.

"I do want to hear about it. Let me carry that tray and you can get the wine glasses," he said.

She swapped with him and led the way into the living room. Sandy looked up from the blanket at Garrett and came over to greet him. Garrett set the tray on the ottoman to pet the dog.

As he did that Hayley pulled some pillows off the couch and set them on the blanket. The music had changed to some sexy southern blues. Stevie Ray Vaughn sang about "little sister" and she let the music wash over her. In a way Stevie Ray was a lot like remembering to breathe. Electric blues soothed her all the way to her soul.

Sandy settled back down and Garrett sat on the blanket next

to her. He put the tray between them, stacked a pillow to his left, and lounged across from Hayley.

"So you're thinking about expanding?" he asked.

She was grateful to have work to talk about. It made it a lot easier than trying to come up with something romancey to talk about. She'd never really been that good on dates. Mainly because she wanted them to be perfect, which usually left her awkward. Trying to say the right thing was a perfect recipe to ensure she said something weird.

"Yes. Well, we have been doing well financially. And our investors think expansion is a good idea, but I've argued that if we expand we lose the uniqueness of our brand. Like we were saying about how every place seems homogenized when you visit it. Any town, USA."

He nodded. "So you'd have to make the location unique. When I visited The Candied Apple what struck me the most about it was that I felt as if it had been there for years. It didn't feel slick and new."

That was what she wanted to hear. She'd worked hard to keep the bones of the building intact when they'd had it refitted two years ago. And that was part of why she was reluctant to try lower Manhattan. She wasn't as familiar with the area and didn't know how her shop--well it was Iona's and Cici's too—their shop would fit in.

"We have thought about looking for a place near the Pier. I think that would be interesting. But I spent months walking past our current location while I was working in a restaurant as a pastry chef."

"Why is that important?" he asked, taking a sip of his wine.

"I started envisioning it as my own place. I pictured the wrought-iron sign I'd have made to hang outside. I knew it would be mine before I bought it. And if we expand...it won't be just this vision of mine. It will become more of a corporation and I'm afraid of that."

Admitting it out loud made her feel lighter. She'd been carrying that around with her for a while now. She couldn't talk to Iona and Cici about it because they were her partners and she didn't want to hurt their feelings, but she knew that she didn't want to give up the control she had right now.

"I don't know what to tell you," Garrett said. "If it were me, I'd make a design for the store and then let someone else go and make it happen."

"Would you?" she asked. "That sounds so sensible, but I can't see you just letting go of anything."

He gave a wry shake of his head. "No. It does sound sensible, and you're right, I wouldn't."

"I noticed."

"Did you?"

"Yes. That was why I wanted you to walk me home," she said, carefully weaving her way back to the questions she wanted to ask him. "But you didn't want to, why?"

***

He wasn't sure how to answer her question, so instead took a big bite of the pastry dish she'd prepared. The flavors blended together well. Hell, he would have loved boiled shoe if it meant he could chew and not talk. The main problem was that with Hayley he wanted to tell her everything. And leaving himself naked with her was great if it was physical, but emotionally...that was the last thing he wanted. He knew he was going to have to say something. She was only going to put up with so much backpedalling before she shoved him out of her life.

Would that be a bad thing?

She shook him to his core. Made everything in his messed-up life seem secondary. He wanted to believe that he knew himself well enough to handle these feelings. To maybe think they were real, but it was that self-knowledge that made him doubt it.

His life had been shattered with that exchange of bullets. Each day since Hector had died and Garrett had killed Paco had been harder. Not easier.

His leg was healing, the nightmarish remembrances of the shoot-out were even starting to dull, but he knew that his life was nowhere near back on track. And Hayley gave him something else to focus on.

She made him feel a little less alone.

Frankly, he'd be happy to talk about her shop, as she called her popular food store, all night long, if that meant he could continue to ignore the facts and doubts that were rattling around in his head.

But as the flames danced around behind her and she stared at him expectantly, he knew he was going to have swallow his bite of food and give her some sort of explanation.

"I was...I mean, I have no idea, Hayley. I really can't tell you anything more than I said on the street. I don't want to lose you, but every time you get closer I want to push back."

She crossed her arms over her chest, arching one eyebrow at him. "Bullshit."

"What?"

"You heard me. You're a cop. You're a man who would have been broken by that shoot-out if you gave in to doubts. And yet you haven't been. So I'm going to ask again, what's the deal?"

The deal.

The deal? He wasn't ready to feel. He knew this because he didn't understand it himself. He wasn't ready to feel this much for a woman because right now he had no fucking clue who he was and where he was going.

Yet into the mix comes this woman.

The one person to make him feel alive in a long time and he had no idea how to handle her. He hoped like hell that what he felt for her was real, but it seemed to him she was the kind of woman who came along once in a lifetime. Yet at the same time he was afraid he felt that way because he desperately needed something – someone – to cling to.

Some part of his messed-up life that would seem good and on the right path.

"You piss me off."

"Because I won't let you pacify me with excuses?" she asked.

"Yes."

"Sorry, but I like you, Garrett. More than any of the other men I've dated lately. And I can't afford to let myself fall for you if you are just dicking around with me."

He sat up. Well there it was.

"Why can't you afford it?"

"You mean other than the fact that I'm not a masochist?"

"Yeah, other than that," he said. Damn if her frankness wasn't a turn-on. Every time he thought he had her figured out she did something else that made him realize he hadn't even come close.

"My mom died when she was thirty-eight," Hayley said. "She was diagnosed with the cancer at thirty-five. I have regular check-ups with my doctor, but she can't give me a guarantee that I won't get it too. So that means there's a chance that I might only have eight years left. I don't want to waste them."

Wasted years.

He didn't want that either. But as she'd said, this was their first date. Except he knew it wasn't. She wasn't the intimate stranger she had been. She mattered to him. He wanted to make promises about being with her and making those years worthwhile, but he wasn't sure he could keep them. She wanted a man who could be her man.

But Garrett was still trying to figure out who he was if he was grounded at his desk and had a weak leg. Maybe that wasn't a big deal, but for him it was.

"Fair enough. I like you, Hayley," he said. "I wouldn't be here if I didn't. But I just had my entire future plans shaken up. I have no idea what I'm going to do next."

He got up on his knees. "But I do know that I don't want to

walk away from you. You're the only thing I have right now that makes me smile. Makes me feel like I have more choices. I can't explain it better than that."

She leaned toward him. "Was it that hard to say?"

"Yes," he said with a growl. She kept shoving at him, making him feel alive.

"Good. You are punishing yourself," she said.

"How do you figure?" he asked.

She pushed against his chest, but he didn't let her budge him.

He hadn't felt like he'd been punishing himself, so he wanted to know why she thought he was.

"I'm not sure if it's because Hector died or because you killed Paco, but I can see it in your eyes. You have guilt. You feel like you shouldn't have the dreams of your future that you once had. I think that's why you aren't sure about me."

He sat back on his heels. He didn't like that. She had to be wrong. Was he just torturing himself because of guilt?

"Well, you're wrong," he said.

"Fine," she said. "But until you figure that piece out, you aren't going to be able to move on. With me or your job."

***

She hadn't meant to get that real. But she was tired of running and hiding from the truth. Even from herself. He had to know that she wasn't going to keep tiptoeing around.

She owed it to herself.

And Garrett owed it them as a couple. He had been the one to pursue her. She was happy to let him be her little sexy thrill, but he'd kissed her in the pantry of The Candied Apple that night and changed everything.

Everything.

She had made the choice to go after him and then the way he made her feel had made her want to hide out again.

177

She was always aware of the clock ticking in the back of her mind. She wanted the same things most women did. A family. Kids of her own. But she also wanted to cram as much success into her life as she could.

She'd worked hard to get where she was and now she was stuck... stuck. That's right, she'd given up family for years and now that she was thirty it was clear how fast time went by. She wanted it all. But she didn't know if she'd ever get it.

"I'm sorry if that sounded harsh."

"It did, but I deserved it. It's so hard to get out of my own head these days. I keep trying to remind myself that I'm alive, but you kind of hit the nail on the head when you said I was guilty. I am. Why me? Why didn't I die that night?"

So they could meet? She wanted to believe that. It felt like fate had a hand in putting them in each other's path, but she knew she couldn't be his saviour.

The music changed and Beastie Boys "Intergalactic Planetary" came on.

He gave a startled laugh.

"This is some crazy playlist," he said.

"It's my old CD jukebox. I have all of my mom's CDs in there with mine. Sometimes it's nice to hear old music."

"So whose CD is this one?"

"Mom's. She loved the Beastie Boys. I do too. It was one of the things we agreed on."

She smiled to herself and gave her mom a little thank you. It didn't hurt to see her mom in everyday things.

"What happened at the grocery store? Did I do something to crowd you?"

"No. Not at all. I have had a crazy day and when I saw you tonight I realized how much I needed you...it scared me."

Fair enough.

"Want to tell me about it? I was relieved to hear the civil suit had been dropped."

Ever since they'd had to sneak into his house and dodge the reporters she'd been worried about him.

"You were the first person I wanted to share it with."

"Really?"

"Yes. Tonight I was just dealing with the reality of my life and feeling a little sorry for myself. No man wants to tell the woman he's starting to fall for something like that."

Starting to fall for?

He was admitting little bits of how he felt, but still trying to protect himself. Who could blame him? She was doing the same thing. Both of them tiptoeing around the emotions.

And why not? They were both old enough to know that sleeping with someone didn't mean love. It would be easier if this was simply an affair, but for her it had changed when she'd climbed his fence.

"Okay. So where do we go from here?" she asked. He'd moved around on the blanket so that his back was propped against the couch and he held her cuddled against his side. She looked up at him when he didn't answer and saw he was staring into the fire.

She looked at it too. There were no answers. Sort of like when she stared at the envelope from her mom. She wasn't going to know until she took some action. She didn't want to leave this decision of where to go next to Garrett. She had to own it. Own her choices.

Sandy must have gotten warm by the fire and got up and went into the kitchen.

"I want to keep seeing you. I'd like to date and see if this continues to grow or if we both shut it down," she said at last. "What about you?"

He squeezed her tight to his side, tipped her chin back with his finger under it and looked down into her eyes. In the shadowy room, lit only by the dancing flames of the fire, it was hard to read his expression but his intent was obvious.

"I want that too."

He lowered his head and kissed her. She kissed him back, the embrace felt the promise she'd been afraid to ask for and as they made love in front of the fireplace she realized that she was living even those moments when she'd felt like she was hiding.

She'd been moving toward this moment and this man. And no matter what else happened, she couldn't regret it. Garrett made her feel like she was alive and at the apex of her feminine power. Especially when she rolled on top of him and took him into her body.

Her days of being passive were gone. She took Garrett. Took her orgasm and then gave him his. She rode him hard and when they both collapsed in each other's arms afterward, she wrapped her arms and leg over him, held him to her.

She had claimed him.

No matter what happened from this point forward she was no longer pretending that he meant nothing to her. She had admitted it to herself.

Garrett Mulligan was hers.

She leaned up so she could look down into his face and see his expression. "You're mine now."

He nodded. "And you're mine."

She didn't know what the future held and that was okay because no one had it all figured out. But having him by her side was enough.

For now.

Chapter 18

Going out on a date was something different for them. Sure, they'd had drinks at Rockefeller Centre, but that had been accidental, even their fireside picnic had been impromptu. This was a real date.

Garrett needed it. He was tired. His new job was full of cases and new possibilities, but as he'd told Hayley when they'd walked in Central Park, he looked at the world in black and white and some of these cases weren't that simple.

But for tonight he wanted to be like every other couple in Manhattan. It was time to hit the clubs and remember they were young and full of life. He needed that and he suspected that Hayley did too.

Hayley walked into the living room, where he was waiting for her and his breath caught in his throat. She was dressed in a silver A-line dress that ended at the tops of her thighs. It left her arms bare and she'd put a stack of bangle bracelets on one arm.

She had some sort of sparkly thing in her hair holding her bangs back from her face. The eye-liner she wore made her look different. Pretty and intriguing, but different.

"You look...beautiful," he said.

She gave him a little curtsy. "Thank you. You look nice too. I think we have about ten minutes before the car is supposed to pick us up. Is your friend meeting us here?"

"Yes," Garrett said. "He's off the subway and should be here in a minute."

"How do you know that?"

"He texted me while you were getting ready."

"That's good. Iona and her brother are already there. We just have to give the bouncer her name," Hayley said. "This is going to be so much fun."

He hoped so. They needed some fun. While he enjoyed the time he'd spent with Hayley, their lives had been full of intensity lately. Of course he was back on the force and the civil suit had been dropped, but he was still trying to sort out his career.

There was a knock on the door and Hayley grabbed her handbag—a cute little clutch that had her monogram on it. "I'm going to skip the coat since we are just dashing from the house to the car and then the car to the club."

"If you're sure. I have mine in case you get cold later," he said.

As he did that, he was reminded of his parents and how his dad always gave his mom his coat when she got cold. The feelings he had for Hayley scared him most of the time, but tonight it felt right that he should take care of her. If she'd let him, then he wanted to.

What did that mean? Was he finally going to have to admit that she was the kind of woman he'd always sort of hoped he'd find? Or was it going to be safer to just continue to ignore it?

He reached around her to open the door, ignoring the questions he put to himself. Tonight was light and fun.

Hoop stood there with a light dusting of snow on his head.

"Come in," Hayley said. "I think I need that coat after all. The driver should be here soon. But if you want a drink, Garrett knows where everything is."

Hoop waved at Hayley as she disappeared back upstairs. He closed the door behind his friend.

"Thanks for inviting me along tonight," Hoop said. "We haven't been out with women in a long time."

"Don't say it like that. We're not desperate," Garrett said. But the truth was they'd all been busy working the last few years. Not like in their twenties, when they'd worked and partied hard. Maybe it was their age, but life had settled into getting ahead instead of going out.

"Maybe you aren't. But I wouldn't mind having a woman like that in my life."

"Why don't you?"

Hoop shrugged. "I'm busy at work. There are long hours and... that sounds like excuses, doesn't it?"

"Only you can say. I will tell you if it weren't for my accident I wouldn't have met Hayley. Maybe there is something to be said for slowing down a little."

Hoop nodded.

"Who's slowing down?" Hayley asked as she came back down the stairs. "I just got a text from the driver saying that he's stuck in traffic. Cici is going to walk over, since her place is only half a block away, so that the driver doesn't have to stop there."

"Want a drink while we are waiting?" Garrett asked, as Hayley was busy texting on her phone.

"Yes. I'll have a glass of that Sauvignon Blanc we opened last night."

"Got any beer?" Hoop asked.

"We do, but it's all girly. Blue Moon or Corona."

"I'm a girl," Hayley said with a smile. "He just thinks it's girly because we have to put a wedge of fruit in it."

"That does sound girly. I better stick to wine," Hoop said.

"I have some tequila if you want to do shots, but it's old. I bought it to make some margarita-filled truffles for Cinco de Mayo last year."

"Wine's fine."

They all moved into the kitchen and Garrett liked the way that Hoop and Hayley got along. It was as if different areas of his life were merging together. Like Pete had said about finding the right woman. She made his life complete.

He felt a bolt of panic at that thought. He needed his life to be okay without her. There were no guarantees and he didn't want to depend on her this much. It made the back of his throat feel tight and he was the first to admit that it scared him. Way more than he wanted to admit. She poured them all a glass of wine.

"To good friends and good times," Hoop said, lifting his glass for a toast.

Garrett clinked his glass and took a deep swallow, hoping that he didn't ruin this. But knowing that the out-of-control feeling was deep inside of him didn't bode well.

***

Olympus was an upscale club with a private area on the second floor that overlooked the masses of sweating bodies on the lower level. They were seated in one of the private areas since Theo knew the owners. Hayley took a sip of her wine. Even in the club she wasn't much of a mixed-drink person. Her friends sometimes teased her about it, but tonight it seemed like everyone was just trying to forget about reality.

Lord knew she was. Garrett and she had fallen into something that was sort of like dating, but more like walking on eggs. Since the night they'd talked about bucket lists, he'd pulled back.

It seemed telling that she had a list and he always went and did what he wanted.

She wasn't sure what he'd meant by that. And though he'd made love to her afterward, she hadn't felt that same soul-shattering closeness she had the first time.

Maybe it was her.

She was tired from working so hard at The Candied Apple trying to get ready for Valentine's Day. She took another sip of her wine and felt that wonderful feeling of being slightly buzzed.

The new Pitbull song came on and Cici yelled and hopped up.

"I love this song," Cici said. "Let's dance."

184

She grabbed Hayley and Iona's hands and Hayley grabbed Garrett's. He got to his feet, followed by Hoop, as they all made their way downstairs. The beat of the song pulsed through Hayley and she moved her hips along with the beat.

Cici stopped on the stairs to turn and sing the chorus to her and Iona. A wave of pure joy went through Hayley.

The worries she had about her future with Garrett and if the shop would keep growing financially were pushed to the back of her mind. They really didn't seem important as she found a spot on the packed dance floor next to her best friends and Garrett.

He wasn't a professional dancer, but he knew how to move to the beat and kept hold of her hand. Someone shoved her closer to Garrett and she fell into his chest.

He tilted a little, wrapping both arms around her until he had his balance again. She kissed his chin. Every day he seemed physically stronger to her. She knew he worked out a lot and that he was trying to get back into shape so he could meet the physical requirements to make it back on the street as a detective.

"Your balance is getting a lot better," she said. "When we first met you would have fallen over."

He shook his head. "Maybe I did that so I'd know what you felt like pressed against me."

He was joking. She saw it in his eyes. It was the first time that she'd seen that kind of lightness in his body language when he was talking about his injury. She thought he was finally starting to accept it. To understand that his knee was going to heal and he was going to move into the next phase of his life.

With her?

She wanted that. She danced closer to him, brushing against his body as the music changed from Pitbull to Usher. Cici was in her groove and Hoop seemed bemused as he stood next to her, sort of swaying to the music, but really just looking out of place.

Love is strange, she thought.

It was clear to her that Hoop liked her friend, but seeing the two of them together they looked as if they'd never fit together. How did she and Garrett look?

She had the feeling they were just as odd a couple as Cici and Hoop seemed. Garrett, with his solid view of his future and his moral code.

Her still rebelling against her dead mother.

Damn.

She needed more wine. Her thoughts were going down a path that she didn't need to follow. She pulled Garrett behind her as she left the dance floor.

"Are you okay?"

"I need more wine or a distraction," she said.

"Why?"

"I don't want to say," she admitted, looking into those dark-chocolate eyes of his.

She wanted to be the woman she hoped she presented on the outside. One who knew what she wanted and went after it. One who was whole and not fixated on and driven by her past.

But tonight she realized she'd been lying to herself. She hadn't changed at all since her birthday. She'd just been hiding behind this sexy man and the way he kissed her. Pretending that something real was happening here.

Garrett stepped into the shadowy hallway under the stairs and pulled her into his arms. The music was slightly muted here but still loud enough that she could feel the bass line pulsing through her body.

He looked down at her and she saw the questions in his eyes, but she really, REALLY didn't want to talk tonight. So she put her hands on his hips, leaning up into his body, and kissed him.

She felt the moment of surprise in him before he leaned in around her and took control of the kiss. He tasted of the bourbon he'd been drinking earlier and of something elusive that was simply Garrett. He put his hands on the wall behind her so that only her hands on his hips and their mouths were touching.

186

Yet she felt surrounded by him. Felt safe and secure in his embrace. That wildness that had been building into a storm inside of her started to ebb and then his tongue brushed over hers and a different storm started.

This one was fiery and hot. Had nothing to do with the past and mistakes and though she hoped she wasn't lying to herself again, this embrace felt like the future. It felt like the kind of storm she could let go and follow.

Garrett lifted his head. "Distracted enough?"

She licked her lips, tasting Garrett one more time, and rolled her head against the cement wall.

"For now."

***

Hayley was different tonight. So full of energy and life that he wanted to get closer to her and see if it would rub off on him. He couldn't put his finger on it, but when he'd kissed her, he'd felt it. Her embrace felt wild, as if she were on the verge of running.

Had she decided she'd had enough of him?

Granted, their "relationship" hadn't really had a chance to get off the ground. He was spending a lot of his energy on trying to keep up the appearance that he was nonchalant about all of the different bits of his life that were going to shit.

The job chiefly.

He leaned in closer to her. Hayley was the one thing he had right now that seemed good. That seemed worth pursuing. When he was with her he didn't feel as if Paco had stolen his life from him.

So unfair.

He'd taken Paco's life, not the other way around.

"Damn."

"What?" she asked.

"I think I need a distraction."

"Drink or sex?" she asked, her eyes were electric and that

wildness he'd tasted in her kiss was back.

"Sex."

He'd never been a big fan of drinking away his problems. He'd seen the path that led a man down and it wasn't pretty.

She wrapped her hand around his wrist. "I know you're not a big fan of bucket lists, but this is on my 'dirty-girls' one."

She opened a door marked private and led him down the hall. She stopped and looked up at him.

"This might work if you make it quick."

"Um..."

He wanted to. Hell, his cock was getting harder by the second, but this was breaking about three different laws.

She gave him a long, sensual look from under her eyelashes and he knew that if he didn't do something quick he was going to ruin the moment for her and possibly lose her forever.

He glanced around and saw a private bathroom. He led the way down there. Luckily it was empty and clean.

She followed him inside, giggling a little as he closed the door and locked it.

"What are you going to do with me now, Officer?"

"I'm afraid I'm going to have to frisk you," he said.

She pouted at him. Then put her hands out to her side. "If you must."

He realized then that he really liked Hayley. And if he wasn't careful he could easily fall in love with her. He knew she wanted to playact and he was willing to oblige her.

Hell, he was breaking the law for her.

He skimmed his hands down her sides and she reached for his crotch, but he brushed her hands away.

"Keep your hands to yourself, ma'am."

"Sorry, Officer."

He bent to a crouch carefully and put his hands around her left ankle. The heels she had on were at least two inches and her calves were well formed. He'd never really taken the time to study her legs before, but she had nice ones.

He brought his hands up one leg to her thigh, skimming her inner thigh and letting his finger brush against her center. She moaned a little and spread her legs a little wider.

He went on to her other leg, putting his hands around her thigh and running them down to her ankle again.

Then he stood up, careful to give his knee time to adjust to his weight, but he wasn't having any real problems with his leg tonight.

He took her wrists in his hands and lifted them up to the wall behind her head. "Keep your hands there while I finish frisking you."

"Yes, Officer."

Her voice was huskier than he'd heard it since that night in his kitchen. And he was already so close to losing it, he wasn't sure how much longer he could continue to play her game. He brought his hands slowly down each of her arms, caressing the bare skin. He got to her torso and fanned his fingers out so that his thumbs brushed over her breasts and nipples as he kept moving downward toward her waist.

Her nipples hardened and he brought his hands back up, rubbing his thumbs over them as his lips came down on hers. She thrust her tongue deep into his mouth and he kept the slow, languid movement of his thumbs against her nipples until she shifted, lifting one leg off the ground and wrapping it around his hips.

He thrust forward into the cradle of her thighs. His cock was hard and he wanted to be inside of her now.

He reached between them, unzipping his pants and freeing his erection.

He reached into his pocket and took out the condom he'd put in there earlier. He lifted his head and ripped open the packet and quickly put the condom on.

He brought his mouth back down on Hayley's as he reached beneath her skirt and pulled her panties down her legs. He tucked them into his back pocket before putting his hands on her hips and pushing himself into her body.

She gasped his name as he drove himself home. He thrust into her again and again. She tore her mouth from his and whispered demanding, sexual things to him, which just whipped him into a frenzy.

He felt his orgasm coming hard and fast and reached between their bodies to brush his fingers over her clit. He felt her tighten around him and then he pumped into her again and his own release washed over him. He kept pumping until he was empty. He held her to him with one arm wrapped around her body and leaned to the left, bracing himself against the wall. She hugged him close and rested her head on his chest as his pulse slowed. He looked down at her and knew that there was no way this was ever going to be normal. What he felt for her was different and exciting and wild.

And he had no idea how to control it.

Chapter 19

They fell into a routine of sorts over the next week. Winter dumped a lot of snow on them and they played in it. In a way Hayley felt like she was making up for all the years she'd been so focused on work and hadn't really lived.

Without her really planning on it, Garrett was living with her. She was busy at the shop and found that she spent most of her time there, working later hours than before.

She couldn't say for sure that it was because Garrett was spending the nights at her house. But she knew that a part of her was afraid to let herself get too deeply attached.

The questions that had been in her head about love and if she could truly know that she was in love had gotten bigger. And as Valentine's Day approached, Iona had scheduled a class for almost every night, offering couples a bottle of champagne when they attended.

It was really popular and Pete and Crystal were coming to the class on Valentine's Day. Hayley's world was expanding. Before it was her and her friends and the candy shop. Now she had a dog and was still volunteering at the shelter. She had learned to play poker with the guys and had been to taco night at Garrett's parents' house in Brooklyn.

The boxed truffles were selling like mad and there was a decision between herself, Cici, and Iona that they would continue the custom boxes even after Valentine's Day.

Though the next holiday that Iona was keen to use to promote the store was Mother's Day and that brought up all sorts of issues for Hayley.

She said goodbye to the last of her students and went downstairs as Carolyn was finishing up closing the downstairs registers. The shop was quiet as the last of the customers had left and everything was spotless. Carolyn was the assistant manager of the retail operation.

"Do you need me to go with you to the bank to make the deposit?"

"Yes. I let Casey go early because you were still here. Is that okay?" Carolyn asked.

She nodded. Maybe it was her mentality from the early days of owning her business, but having to pay an extra person to "hang around" didn't seem smart to her. "Let me grab my coat and then I'll be ready to go."

"I want to leave a note for the opening," Carolyn said.

Hayley went into the kitchens to her office and donned her coat. As she buttoned it, her cell phone pinged and she glanced down to see it was a text from Garrett.

Want some company on your walk home?

Hayley smiled as she typed. *Sure. I have to go make the deposit at the bank up the block.*

A second later her phone pinged again. *Sandy and I are waiting outside.*

Hayley went back to the main shop, where Carolyn was ready. "Some guy is waiting outside. Should I call the cops?"

"No. That's my...boyfriend," she said. Boyfriend. It sounded so high school, but really, what else was she going to call him? They were dating, sleeping together, sort of living together, but to call him her partner would be wrong. They were both being very careful to keep their lives separate. They talked about food, sports, but not about the important issues.

Garrett refused to talk about work or about his physical therapy, which, based on the amount of ice he'd been putting on his knee, she suspected he was pushing.

She didn't discuss the unopened letter from her mom or the fact that she hadn't committed to a date to go to California to make those desserts her dad had asked her to.

The complicated things they left alone. And she had thought that was okay until she saw him standing there under the lamplight with a light snow falling around his head. She stood there for a moment observing him. She felt like she knew him, yet at the same time that she never would.

He had on a pair of faded jeans and biker boots. She knew that the physical therapist had given him an insert for the left one to make his leg the same length as it used to be. His leather bomber jacket had seen better days and he had on a skullcap against the cold. He'd taken the time to put Sandy's snow coat on and the little dachshund was dancing around his legs in the snow.

"He's hot."

"He is," Hayley admitted. But he was so much more than the Hot Cop she'd first met. She felt that odd feeling again, wondered if it was love.

What if it was?

How would she know?

And could she let him in? Relax enough to get to the point where they weren't in this state of limbo. She knew she wasn't the only one who'd let them drift here. Garrett was supposed to take a physical tomorrow, which was probably why he was here waiting for her. He'd admitted that being alone with his workout equipment just raised his testosterone and made him ready to act.

"And brave. My boyfriend wouldn't be caught walking a tiny little dog like that."

Hayley glanced at Carolyn. Her boyfriend surely had some issues then. And she realized something about Garrett that she

193

hadn't realized might be an issue for him. He had a core of solid strength. It didn't matter that his knee gave him trouble sometimes or that he had a toy dog to walk, he still owned the street when he did it.

"Stuff like that doesn't bother him."

"I can see that," Carolyn said.

Hayley unlocked the front door and opened it for Carolyn and then locked it and set the alarm as they stepped outside.

"Evening Garrett. This is Carolyn. She's got to walk with us to the bank," Hayley said.

"Nice to meet you, Carolyn. Are you a chocolate-maker like Hayley?" Garrett asked. He handed Hayley a thermal mug and she lifted it up to take a sip.

It wasn't much, bringing her a warm drink on a cold night, but she appreciated it. When he glanced at her she blew him a kiss as a thank you.

He turned his attention back to Carolyn. Hayley wondered if this wasn't love. Having him do something little like this for her and having it mean more than she wanted to admit.

"Nope. Just an eater and seller," she said, with a tinkling laugh. "I used to work for a clothes retailer before I came here."

"Carolyn has been instrumental in getting us to have better processes for the shop. Frankly, I had no idea about some of the things she established, like store layout. There's a science behind how merchandise should be placed."

Garrett arched one eyebrow at her as Sandy stopped walking. "I think the diva has had enough of walking."

Garrett bent down to pick up Sandy as Carolyn started to explain how customers instinctively gravitated toward a certain flow through the shop. "That's why we put the café in the back. And once I got Hayley to let me have some t-shirts made we added them to the display right next to it."

"That was a good choice," Hayley said. "I guess people like taking home a little piece of the Apple, as the slogan says.

"I think they...."

Carolyn stopped talking as Sandy started barking like mad, clamoring to get out of Garrett's arms. Hayley glanced up to see a group of young men stepping out of the shadows.

She grabbed Carolyn's hand and drew her to a stop. Garrett passed her Sandy's leash and they just stood there.

"We will take the money," one of the men said.

"Not tonight," Garrett said.

The young man was Garrett's height, but Hayley worried about his leg. Would it hold up? Could he take on three guys and still walk away? Fear drove an icy lance down her spine and she realized that she needed to know that Garrett was safe. He was worth more to her than anyone else ever had been.

She loved him.

Love.

It had been dancing around her subconscious for too long. But there was no denying it as they faced down the muggers.

And the money in the bag, though substantial, wasn't worth his life. She took the bag from Carolyn.

"Garrett—no."

He gave her a cold, hard look, grabbed her hand and pushed her behind his back with Carolyn. "There is no way I'm giving them the money."

"What about now?" the leader said pulling a gun.

***

Garrett was beyond pissed. But he pushed his anger aside and used his training as a cop. Brute force wasn't really a tool that most cops used. It was their training with being in control that allowed Garrett to assess the situation. He ignored Hayley and would deal with her doubts about him later.

"Drop the gun," he ordered. All his doubts if he could still do the job faded. He was a cop, whether he sat behind a desk or not.

"Give me the bag or I'll shoot you," the kid said.

"Not happening," Garrett said. "Drop the gun and put your hands in the air."

"Yeah, right," the kid said.

"Come on, Joe, let's beat it," one of the other guys said.

"No. I'm not backing down," Joe said.

Garrett noticed the gun shaking in the kid's hand. He had a brief flashback to the last time he'd faced an armed assailant. Paco hadn't been nervous. Paco had killed before and would have killed again, just like this kid Joe was prepared to kill now. And it was in that moment, as the realization dawned, that Garrett moved. Taking the kid's wrist in his hand, twisting it up and back. The gun fired, the powder burning his arm as the bullet shot into the air.

"Run!" one of the other kids shouted.

"Pussies!" the kid holding the gun yelled.

Garrett wasn't distracted, just kept his grip on the kid. He was thin and wiry and desperate. Each of his moves had power behind it, but the kid was no match for all the working out that Garrett had done.

Sandy was yelping and one of the women screamed, but everything narrowed in Garrett's eyes and he focused only on the other man, who held the gun. The kid kept trying to point the barrel back at Garrett as he punched him hard in the gut. Garrett felt the impact and twisted, his knee screaming in pain as he punched the kid first in the throat and then in the face. The kid jerked backward and Garrett was able to twist the gun free and he reached behind him, tossing it on the ground near Hayley.

She bent toward it, almost touching.

"Hayley! Don't touch it. Just make sure no one else picks it up," Garrett said. The other two guys ran, but he held onto the kid, not letting him go.

"Call 911," he ordered Hayley and she just looked at him as she fumbled in her pocket for her phone.

The kid, realizing he was about to be arrested, punched Garrett hard in the gut and tried to rip his hand free, but Garrett held strong. He balanced on his good leg and used a sweeping kick to knock the kid's legs out from under him. As soon as he was on the ground, Garrett climbed on top of him and pulled his hands behind his back.

He was vaguely aware of Hayley talking in the background, but really he was focused on the kid. His knee ached and Garrett had the feeling that getting up wasn't going to be easy.

"What's your last name, Joe?" Garrett asked. The cement was cold and a few snowflakes drifted down.

"Fuck you."

"Interesting choice for your parents to make," Garrett said. "I'm Officer Mulligan. You heard of me?"

The kid went still underneath him. "Yeah, you're the cop who killed that kid."

"He wasn't a kid and Paco Rivera killed my partner first," Garrett said. "A gun changes everything. I'm sure you weren't thinking about that when you pulled it, but if you shot me you'd be running the rest of your life. Cop-killers don't walk, you hear me?"

The kid mumbled something, squirming and trying to get free. If back-up didn't get here soon, Garrett was going to have to find something to bind the guy's hands with.

"What did you say?"

"Yeah, I hear you," the kid said. "I don't need another lecture from a guy who's no better than me."

The patrol car pulled up with its lights flashing red and blue before Garrett could respond. Was he no better than this punk?

"Put your hands where I can see them," the lead officer said as he stepped out of the car.

Garrett put his hands above his head, but kept his good knee in the middle of Joe's back. His gut said the punk would bolt and Garrett wasn't taking any chances.

"He's a cop," Hayley said. "He stopped that man from mugging from us."

"Get to your feet, cop. You, on the ground, hands where I can see them."

Garrett maneuvered himself to his feet as the officers told them both to put their hands up. Garrett did as he was directed, as did Joe.

"My badge is in my pocket," Garrett said.

The officer nodded, while his partner pulled Joe from the ground and cuffed him. Garrett's aching ribs felt a little better when he noticed the dried blood on the kid's nose. All that working out had paid off.

He felt the officer pat him down, reaching into his back pocket and taking out his badge.

"Mulligan?"

"Yeah."

"I'm Derek Long and that's Harry Miller," Officer Long said. "What happened?"

"He pulled a gun, demanded money from the women and I relieved him of his weapon." Garrett nodded toward the kid. "And subdued him while waiting for back-up."

"I'll need to take your official statements," Long said.

"Can I go first?" Carolyn asked. "I'll miss the last train to Jersey if I don't."

"Yeah," Officer Long said, going over to Carolyn and talking to her.

Garrett leaned back against the storefront as his knee was throbbing and he wasn't too sure he could continue to allow it to hold his weight. Hayley came over to his side, with Sandy in her arms. She had tears in her eyes, but also anger.

"You're not up—"

"Don't."

She took his hand and dragged him away from the cops. But he stumbled. His knee buckled under him. She cursed and slid closer to him, wrapping her arm around his waist.

"I'm so mad at you," she said.

"Why, because you didn't think I could protect you?" he asked.

"Don't be an ass," she said, hugging him as tightly as she could with Sandy under her other arm.

Maybe she wasn't as mad as she'd said she was.

Was he being an ass? He was barely holding on to his temper where she was concerned. From the moment they'd met, he had thought she saw him one way and tonight he realized he was wrong.

"Your doubt isn't flattering."

"Neither is your stupidity. A bag of cash isn't worth your life."

"Or yours," he said. "You don't know what was in that kid's head. And I'm not trained to just let a crime take place."

She nodded.

"I know that."

"Hey, you two. I need to get your statements," the officer called.

Garrett forced himself to stand on his own and carefully walked over to the other cop. He was going to have to talk to the physical therapist about the wedge for his boot. While it gave his shorter leg extra length it was forcing his hip into a weird position that hurt his knee.

He gave his statement to the officer and then signed it. When he was done, he noticed that Hayley and Carolyn were both finished as well.

The mugger was in cuffs in the back of the car. The gun he'd been carrying had been used in a convenience-store robbery two nights ago where a clerk had been murdered.

"I read about you in the paper," the officer said.

"Yeah, I know," Garrett said. "Everyone has."

"I think you're a hero. If my partner and I were ever cornered like that..."

"It was a rough night," Garrett admitted. He didn't feel like a hero and doubted he ever would. He couldn't save Hector and Paco was dead. He called it a draw.

Much as he felt this night was going to be long. There was no easy way out of this. He'd come to see Hayley because tomorrow was supposed to be the day he took his physical and got back on the force.

But this night was making him realize that facing down armed assailants wasn't something he wanted to do again. Granted, he wouldn't have to do that every day at work, but tonight had made it crystal clear that he had a lot to lose. And more than that, he really wasn't sure of his own ability to pull the trigger again. He knew from what he'd read about Paco after the fact that he'd been a killer for years. That he'd murdered desk clerks and street thugs before.

The kid in the back of officer Long's car wasn't there yet. But he might be one day soon. And Garrett didn't fancy facing him again on the street.

But that wasn't his problem. Hayley was. Tonight had also made him very aware of the fact that he couldn't protect her the way he wanted to. Did that mean he couldn't be the man he wanted to be for her?

Chapter 20

Hayley didn't say word to him as they walked toward their brownstones. The cops had taken Joe away and Carolyn had texted Hayley to say she'd made her train. Sandy was happily sitting in Garrett's arms as they walked back. He held the little dog close, taking comfort from the way she just sat in his arms, seeming secure with him protecting her.

Something that Hayley hadn't been.

It stuck in his craw that for the first time he had a woman he wanted to give the world to and she didn't believe he could protect her. He'd always been the strong one, the one who charged in when others hadn't and now...well, now, Hayley wasn't sure he should be charging.

Truth? Neither was he.

The snow had stopped and trucks were out gritting the streets for the morning, but otherwise there was silence. Even Sandy was subdued. As soon as they got to their homes, Garrett knew he should say goodnight and leave her be. But he didn't want to.

Tonight had raised uncomfortable questions for him. Ones that he'd never thought to ask. He had believed that his reluctance to move forward from the events of the night Hector had died had stemmed from a combination of guilt and grief. But now he had to acknowledge that fear also played a part.

Though he hadn't frozen when Joe had pulled that gun on him, he had battled through a flashback and it was only the fact that he had to protect Hayley that had kept him grounded. He handed the dachshund to her and Hayley kissed the little dog on the tip of the nose before putting her on the ground.

She walked up the steps to her place, Sandy's tags jingling as she followed her mistress up the steps. Hayley put her key in the lock and then looked back at him. She had on her thick, red wool coat that ended at the top of her thighs and those spiky-heeled boots that she'd been wearing since he met her. Her skirt ended just below the hem of her coat and she'd put on a thick knit cap over her head so that only her bangs sweeping over her face were visible.

"Are you coming in?" she asked, bending to unleash Sandy, who went bounding into the brownstone, no doubt in search of her warm bed.

"Am I invited?" he asked. He wasn't sure if he was. He also wasn't too sure of what would happen if he did follow her inside. He felt edgy and like he'd used up the last of his control tonight. He'd kept it together when he'd faced down that punk and he wanted to analyze all the emotional junk that had stirred up inside of him.

He knew he had things he should have done before this. Like the fact that he'd never gone to visit Hector's widow and his kids. He thought about that as Hayley waited there for his answer.

He shrugged.

She put her hand on her hip. "Sometimes you really tick me off."

"Fair enough."

She did the same to him. He was ignoring the fact that she'd wanted him to give those punks the money. What did that mean? Didn't he want to know?

He did.

He was afraid of what she might say and how that might impact him, but he did want to know.

"Do you want me to come in?" he asked. He needed to be needed by her. Hoped she wanted him as much as he wanted her tonight because he craved her company. Didn't think he could handle a night alone. Not tonight anyway.

His knee was still throbbing and it was only pure machismo that had kept him on his feet this long.

"Yes, even though I'm still mad at you," she said.

"Fair enough," he said, climbing the stairs and walking into her home. It smelled of vanilla and cinnamon and all the things that grounded him. All the things that made him feel okay because they were Hayley.

She sighed as she closed the door and locked it. "Can you climb the stairs?"

He would, but he wasn't sure his knee could handle it. "Maybe."

"So that means no. Will you be okay for a few minutes while I run a warm bath for you?"

"No."

She looked at him, concern in her eyes. And it was enough for him that she was here with him.

"What's the matter?"

"I don't think I'm ever going to be okay again, Hayley. The mugging shone a big spotlight on problems I wasn't even aware were there. And I put you in danger,' he said. "You distract me, woman. I should have been paying attention to the street and not how short your skirt was and how good your legs looked in it."

"You like my legs?" she asked with a teasing lilt in her voice.

Running. She was running from him and from the emotional entanglements that might crop up from his confession. That was Hayley. As soon as things got too deep she pushed them back into the lovers-only ground.

"Never mind. I'll be fine," he said.

She walked over to him and put her hand on the wall behind him and looked not at him but at her hand on the paneled wall. "I'm mad at you because for a second, when he pointed that gun at you, I thought you might die. And though I've known loss, it was expected. I knew my mom was going to die and I was able to come to terms with it – well, as much as I could – before she died. But there was a very real chance I would see you killed—"

Her voice broke off and he heard the ragged inhalation of her breath and she kept moving her mouth, but no sound came out. "I don't ever want to feel like that again."

Her voice had dropped an octave and tears he wasn't sure she was aware of streamed down her face.

***

Hayley had never felt more unsure of anything in her life. Her worry for Garrett mingled with anger at a gut-deep level and she realized there was no way forward from this point. Facing off against the mugger, she'd seen the real Garrett, not the friendly guy she'd seen since they met.

The guy who'd been injured and was slowly recuperating was gone. In his place was this man. This warrior-cop, who wouldn't be content sitting behind a desk.

He'd intimated that at times, but she'd been too busy seeing him through her own lens to really admit that he wasn't the guy she'd made him into.

Yes, he was sexy as hell.

Yes, he made her stop hiding from life.

Yes, he'd made her realize that she could fall in love.

Love.

She hadn't really had a chance to figure out what that meant to her. And, to be honest, she wasn't a hundred percent sure she wanted to. This fear was driving her. Giving her something safer to concentrate on.

But she knew that love was tied to her fear and her anger. If she didn't love him she'd walk away. Right now. It would be much easier than having to face the fact that he could have been hurt.

Hell.

He could have been killed right in front of her and she wouldn't have been able to stop it.

He'd been wounded in the line of duty and he couldn't wait to get back to it.

Oh. God.

"Hayley, baby," he said, pulling her into his arms. She wrapped her arms around him and leaned her head on his chest. She knew that he was letting the wall support him. That his leg was shaking right now.

She heard the boom and clap of his heart. Knew that he was alive and she lifted her head, saw the questions in his eyes, but she closed her own.

She didn't want to think or talk.

She wanted him. She needed this moment, to remind them both they were alive.

She kissed him. Pouring all the fear and anger and the love. God, the need for him that swamped her. She tugged at the zipper of his bomber jacket and pushed it open, found that he wore a thermal Henley shirt underneath it and she slid her hands underneath it, running her fingers over his six-pack abs and over the light dusting of hair on his chest.

She tilted her head to the side and went up on her tiptoes to deepen the kiss. She thrust her tongue deep into his mouth, couldn't get enough of him.

He was alive.

Alive. They both were.

Adrenaline was flooding through her as she reached for his belt and struggled to undo it, so she left it and reached for his zipper, lowering it and pushing her hand into the opening of the fabric.

She palmed his erection, slid her hand up and down it. He groaned and then pulled his mouth from hers as his hands slid down her back and slipped up under her skirt.

He cupped her butt and pulled her more fully into him, but

he lost his balance and stumbled a little. Sliding down the wall at her feet.

Tears started flowing again and she ignored them. Bent to unzip her boots and toed them off and then she reached up under her skirt and removed her tights and panties.

Standing over him she realized that she was saying goodbye.

That loving him and living with the kind of life he had was never going to be something she could do.

"Hayley, I think we should—"

She crouched over him, putting her finger over his mouth.

"No talking. Not now. Do you want me?"

"Hell, I always want you," he admitted, reaching between them and undoing his belt and then freeing his erection.

He was hot and hard and she wanted him. She reached between them, stroked him up and down and he groaned.

"Always?"

"Yeah, about two minutes after we make love I want you again," he said, caressing her thighs. Stroking his hand up and down her legs making her shiver as she shifted closer to him. Straddling him but on his thighs.

She looked at him. Memorizing his features. Seeing the familiar flush of desire on his face and how it made his pupils dilated and his breath rasp in and out just a bit.

He smiled at her.

Her heart broke a little as she saw that vulnerable, sexy smile of his. The expression he only made when they were intimate like this.

She put her hands on either side of his face and leaned in close over him. Smelled the minty freshness of his breath as she rubbed her lips lightly over the stubble on his cheek before biting his lower lip and kissing him deeply again.

His hands moved up her thighs around to her butt, drawing her closer to him. But this was her show and though she shifted closer, she kept him from entering her body.

She wanted to take everything he had to give her.

The way he repeatedly did to her. Each time they'd made love she'd lost a little bit more of the shy woman who'd been hiding for the last ten years and become more of the Hayley she wanted to be.

He'd given her that.

Confidence in herself as a woman.

Acceptance of herself.

And she needed to make this time they were together the best of all of that.

But she was at war with that driving desire of his, and his knee might be weak but there wasn't anything wrong with his upper body strength as he pulled her closer.

She felt the ridge of his cock rubbing against her center. She rocked back and forth against his length. She was warm and wet. She had no idea how long she could make this last, but she needed it to.

He let go of her and brought his hands between them, unbuttoning her coat and shoving it down her shoulders. She shrugged out of it, lifting her head and looking down at him.

**

Garrett had felt this rush of adrenaline before after an incident, but never in such a sexual way. He had absolutely no idea what was going on with Hayley. Part of him – granted a very tiny part – thought that maybe they should talk.

But his cock was hard and he had a lap full of warm woman who wanted him. So his mind was overruled. He pushed her blouse up and reached behind her to undo her bra and when the fabric fell away from her breasts he lifted his hands and cupped them. She shifted on his lap, arching her back so that her breasts thrust into his grasp.

He palmed her nipples and then put one of his arms behind her back and brought her forward until he could catch her nipple in his mouth. He tongued it and then suckled her. Her hands

207

came to the sides of his head, holding him to her.

She rubbed her pussy over the length of his cock. She rocked against him and the fever of desire raged through him. He lifted his head and looked up at her. Saw her eyelashes spiky from the tears she'd cried earlier and he lifted his hand to touch her cheek.

She turned her head away and shifted on him until the tip of his erection was poised at her entrance.

She shifted up and then slowly brought herself down on him. He was deep inside of her when she braced her hands on the wall behind him, brought her mouth down on his and thrust her tongue deep.

He sucked on her tongue and pinched her nipple between his fingers, felt her pussy tighten on him. She felt so good wrapped around him. He held her tighter to him and thrust up into her.

He couldn't be inside of her and not move. He wanted to make this last or to maybe slow it down because there was fear underneath this.

First was the feeling of being alive. Of having come out of the incident the victor and proven himself to his woman and to himself. But he needed to reinforce that she was his woman. That nothing could take her away.

He twisted his hand in her hair as he thrust up into her, trying to sate the need in his soul to mark her as his. To ensure that Hayley belonged to him.

She moaned and rocked harder against him and he reached between them to find her clit and flick his thumb over it as she kept rocking on him.

Her breasts rubbed against his chest and the sounds she made in the back of her throat drove him crazy. He felt like he was going to explode and wanted to make sure she was with him. Needed to believe for this one moment that he was in sync with her and with the world.

Then everything would be okay.

Then that knot in his chest would relax and he'd know that

he'd survive.

She tore her mouth from his and looked into his eyes. He saw the passion in her eyes and something else.

He didn't have the ability to think of anything but fucking her at that moment and he drove himself deeper than before. Saw her eyes widen and felt her pussy tightening around him as his orgasm rushed through him.

He thrust up into her two more times, emptying himself completely into her body. She kept rocking against him and he felt that minute tightening of her around him as she continued to orgasm.

Then she fell forward against him. Collapsed on his chest. He wrapped his arms around her and held her to him. Stroked his hands up and down her back.

He closed his eyes and took some deep breaths. The scent of Hayley was all around him. Partially sex, but mostly home. The vanilla and cinnamon scent that had started to bring him comfort.

He loved her.

Hell.

How had that happened?

He'd always been so careful, but somehow when he hadn't been looking she'd found her way into his heart.

He held her closer to him, afraid now in a way that he'd never been before. He couldn't let her go.

He couldn't keep her.

How could he?

He wasn't sure if he could continue to be a cop. Or even what the future held for him. He was on the edge and he knew it.

Could he ask her to stand there with him? On the edge of the cliff that was the future and jump with him into the unknown? Tonight had brought two things into sharp focus—that he could easily go back on the street when his body was ready and that he wasn't sure he wanted to.

That night when he'd seen Hector gunned down and shot Paco

209

had changed him. He was no longer the man he'd been before that. And though protecting his community was important to him, he wasn't sure he was ready to go back out on the front line.

She pulled back, her grey eyes stormy as she looked down at him. He smiled up at her, but she shook her head. "Let me get that bath ready for you." She stood up and walked away and he knew that Hayley was on the edge too.

The danger of the night had somehow crept into this room and into their lives. He knew no matter what he'd been working toward with Hayley that nothing was the same anymore.

He tucked himself back into his underwear and zipped up his pants. He had to slowly maneuver himself to his feet. His knee ached but that pain was nothing to the ache in his soul. He'd thought of love as something that would make him stronger. He'd had no idea it would have the power to bring him to his knees or to make him ache like this.

He knew he wasn't going to quit the force. He needed to conquer his doubts that he could still be an effective cop. Hell, he would because he knew he'd rather face down twenty armed punks than walk into the bathroom of the woman he loved and face the uncertainty of the future.

Chapter 21

Hayley wasn't sure what she was going to do next. Making love to Garrett...for the first time she regretted it. She shouldn't have invited him in tonight.

She didn't feel strong enough to face him again. But she also knew that she wanted to keep him with her for as long as she could.

Conflicting desires, but the truth was she knew she wouldn't keep him. She hated how vulnerable she'd felt tonight. And the fear that still held her in its icy grip.

Yes he'd sort of won tonight. But he was broken. His knee was still recovering and she suspected in time it wouldn't bother him at all. But it would always bother her.

Not the knee, but the fact that he was going to risk his life again and again. That was what he'd been trying to tell her when they'd first got together. When he'd said he hoped he could get back on the force, he needed to be a cop. It was a part of him that even she couldn't touch.

Hell, she wasn't sure she understood it.

She made candy for a living and hid away in her kitchens happily experimenting with flavors and pretending she was being daring.

While he went out in the world and had real scary adventures.

"Hayley?"

She glanced up from where she was with her hands braced

against the bathroom counter and met his gaze in the mirror. "Sorry. I haven't started the bath yet."

"It's okay. I think we need to talk."

She nodded.

"How's your knee?" she asked.

"Okay. I went upstairs and washed up after very carefully pacing around the living room to loosen it up," he said.

She noticed he seemed subdued and all of the excess energy he'd had when they'd come into her brownstone was gone.

She felt drained as well.

More unsure of herself than she had in a long time. Not for the first time she wished her mom were still alive.

She wanted to be able to talk to her. Even if she just told her she was better off without Garrett, it would be nice to have another person's opinion on this. Not another person's, her mom's.

She felt the sting of tears again.

Damn. Was it almost time for her period? She was welling up too much tonight. Or maybe that was what facing down a gunman did to her.

She laughed as a crazy thought struck her.

"What?"

"Just thought this was another never-done-before thing...face a guy with a gun. Not exactly on my bucket list."

He gave her a wry smile that seemed sad to her. "Never let it be said that I don't deliver new experiences." She nodded.

"You do that and so much more."

"Why do I get a feeling that it might not be enough?" he asked.

She tipped her head to the side and studied him. There was no hiding anything under those lights. She shifted her weight, aware that she hadn't cleaned up. That she still had on no underwear and if she could just be quiet she might be able to cuddle in Garrett's arms tonight.

But now that the fever of lust had passed the anger she'd tamped down was back.

"Maybe because you take dumb risks," she said.

"Dumb? Risks, maybe, but dumb? I've been a cop for my entire adult life, Hayley. I think I know what I'm doing when I face off against a mugger," he said.

She crossed her arms over her chest. "Maybe you do. But you weren't a cop tonight. You were a boyfriend meeting his girl after work. You should have just let me give him the money. Then we wouldn't have both found ourselves staring down the barrel of his gun."

"Do you think I could do that? It doesn't matter if I'm on duty or not, I'm not about to let a mugger go. That's dumb."

"You're right. That is dumb. You had no weapon and a bum leg," she said, knowing that anger was making her say things she might not otherwise. "I know you think you're Superman because you work out more than a mixed-martial arts fighter, but you're broken, Garrett. There's a reason why the captain put you in cold cases and I think it's so you don't have to face down guys like Joe."

He advanced on her, got right in her face and she wondered if maybe she should have thought a little more before she decided to poke the tiger. But she couldn't have done anything different. He'd taken a chance tonight without even thinking how it would affect her.

He'd let his own feeling of machismo drive him and instead of being smart—

"The reason is that I haven't had an all-clear from my doctor. The captain believes in my skills and me. Something that you'd think my girlfriend would as well. But you can't do that, can you? You can't focus on anyone other than Hayley. Or maybe your shop."

She pushed him out of the way and walked out of the bathroom, down the short hallway into the living room. She flicked on the fireplace from the switch on the wall and then stood there.

"Did I get a little too close to the truth? Is that why you are running away?" he asked.

"Not at all. I admit it. There are some things that make me uncomfortable. One of them is letting anyone too close. And I am trying to figure out what's next."

"Fair enough. I am too. Tonight showed me some things about myself I didn't know were issues. Things that I haven't had to face before. But I'm glad I did."

"I know you are," she said. Finally she was able to say to him what had been in her heart for a while. "I think I might love you, Garrett. I've felt for a while now that you were more than just a guy to me. But loving you and trying to live with you might be more than I can handle.

"Coward."

His words hurt, but only a little. The fear she'd felt as she'd watched him tonight had already driven a spike into her heart. Made her realize that if she couldn't find a way to put distance between herself and Garrett she was never going to have a minute's peace again.

***

She loved him.

Or sort of thought she might. What was that all about?

Damn.

Love.

He leaned against the doorframe. Elation and anger filled him at the way she'd said it. As if their love wasn't worth fighting for or was something to be thrown away.

Garrett followed Hayley into the living room, but walking gingerly on his leg. She had a point when she'd said that he'd been dumb. Dumb to think that she was ready to handle a relationship with him.

Anyone who thought changing their clothes would change their life...was adorable. How could he really argue with her when he found himself agreeing with her?

But as he watched her standing in her living room, seeming unable to go forward, he wanted to go to her and wrap his arms around her. Tell her that everything would be okay. That this time she didn't have to face life on her own.

But he also knew that any promises he made would be hollow. He wanted to be back on the street. Tonight had shown him that his judgment hadn't been clouded by anger or fear. Because he'd been more afraid with Hayley by his side than he'd ever been before and still he'd kept his calm.

He was ready to be back on the force. Really on the force—not banished down to the basement on cold cases.

"You love me?"

She looked up at him. "I think so.

"You think so? What does that even mean?" he asked. Either she loved him or not. There was no in-between. Or, at least, there wasn't for him. He had realized when she'd straddled him on the floor that there was no going back to before. No pretending that she didn't own him—body, heart, and soul.

"I told you love is complicated for me. I'm not sure what it's supposed to feel like."

"It's supposed to make you stronger," he said. Not weak. Not like she made him feel right now. So unsure and like if she didn't say she loved him he might never be whole again. If he knew that, why didn't she?

"Well, I don't feel strong. I feel angry and scared. And not just because of what happened with the mugger. But I'm also not sure what I'd do if you weren't here by my side."

She turned to face him. "That makes me feel weak. Really weak and not at all like the woman I've always been. Since my mom died I've been on my own."

"You have your dad and your friends. That's not really on your own." Surely she had room for him in her life. When had convincing Hayley to love him become his number-one priority? What if he couldn't?

He ignored that.

"That's different. My dad and I...we have that survivor thing going for us."

"Um...you have the dad-and-daughter thing too."

"That's just it," she said. "It hasn't felt like dad and daughter since Mom died. Oh, I'm making a mess of this and dragging up things that don't matter. What we had...it was fun, but it wasn't real. Even the emotions I feel."

He didn't know how to respond to that. What she was running from he had no idea, but she was determined to do it on her own. He had been a loner for most of his life. But he wasn't afraid to let the people who mattered in his life close. Something that it seemed Hayley was incapable of doing.

"Maybe you don't really love me," he said at last. "When you first said it I thought, yes! Finally I've found someone to spend my life with—"

"But you don't know how long the rest of your life will be, do you?" she interrupted. "You take crazy chances and just because you walked away tonight doesn't mean you will the next time."

She had a point. But if he'd learned anything during that one night that had changed him, it was that no one knew. There were no guarantees for the future. No promises that you'd have forever.

"We just have to grab onto each other for as long as we have. You said yourself you might only have eight more years. I might have that or more. The thing is, Hayley, I want to spend those years with you. There, I said it. No hiding or hedging, I love you. I don't sort of love you or maybe might, I do."

"Bravo for you. You're braver than I am, but then we've both known that from the start. I'm not going to let myself fall in love with someone who..."

She tightened her arms around her body. "It's too late, isn't it? There is no letting myself fall for you, I already have and instead of being smart and finding myself a nice safe guy who works in an office I fell for you."

"That's not a bad thing," he said, walking over to her. "I fell for you too."

"You did, didn't you?" she asked.

He nodded and slowly crossed the room to her side. He pulled her arms away from her chest and wrapped her in a big bear hug. He held her closer than he had before, so afraid she might slip away from him.

"Okay. You're right, we can do this. You'll have your job in cold cases and I'll have my candy shop."

Cold cases?

No, tonight had proven to him that he needed to be back on the street. He wasn't going to be content to sit behind a desk for another day. He knew it now.

"I'm not staying in cold cases," he said.

"Why not? Why would you take a chance when we could be safe and happy together?"

"We wouldn't be happy. I don't like working in that basement on cases that haven't been solved. I like the action. I'm going to be back as soon as my body will allow."

She pulled away from him. "Okay, if that's your choice."

"My choice?"

"Yes. I'm sorry, Garrett, but it's me or your job."

***

Hayley pushed herself out of Garrett's arms and took a step back. Why would he risk his life? He knew how hard it was for her to tell him she loved him. He knew how much she'd lost. Or maybe he didn't.

"You know, I haven't felt this close to anyone my entire adult life, Garrett. Admitting I love you to myself and out loud was a huge step for me."

"I know."

"I thought that you'd understand how much I need stability. I

217

want to start a family and build my life with you."

"We can do that. I'm not saying it won't be difficult. Being on the force means weird hours sometimes and if I'm working a case then I might be gone longer, but I will always come back to you."

"You don't know that," she said. "I'm sure your partner thought he'd come home the night he died."

"Hector definitely believed that," Garrett said, there was a note in his voice that she couldn't place. "I'm sure his wife expected him to as well."

"He was married?"

"Yes and had two sons," Garrett said.

Hayley just stared at him. That poor woman and those kids. She knew first hand what it was like to live without one of your parents. "How old are his sons?"

"Four and six."

Hayley bit her lower lip. That wasn't right. "I can't do that, Garrett."

There were a lot of promises she'd made herself, but one of them was that she'd have a better marriage than her parents if she ever decided to get married. She wanted the kind of family she'd always dreamed of. She wanted that for herself and for her kids. It was the one thing that Garrett couldn't give her.

Well, he could, but he wasn't willing to.

"Okay. So where do we go from here?" he asked.

"I think you have to go. And we should probably not see each other anymore."

"Dammit, Hayley. Every day on the force isn't a dangerous one. I had been a cop for over ten years before I was in a situation like the one that killed Hector."

She nodded. "I hope it's ten more years at least before you face one again. But I can't...I just can't deal with it. I know that if I were stronger maybe I could, but I already have a hole in my life where my mom should be. I don't want one where my husband should be."

He gave her a hard look and she had a feeling she knew what Joe had felt when Garrett had advanced on him earlier this evening. But he didn't scare her. Yes, he was fierce and he owned the room. Even injured he exuded confidence and moved like a man who knew his place in the world. Something she still wasn't confident she did.

Was that why she was picking on him? Had she seen that he was so strong and she knew that she never would be? She was the type of person who would give a thief what he wanted just so he'd go away. Garrett wasn't.

And somewhere in between that she had to figure out if she loved him enough to bridge the gap. Was love strong enough? Was she?

"You called me a coward, but you're the one who is running scared. I'm not sure why, but you have been very careful not to let anything or anyone into your life. You say you have a gaping hole where your mom should be, but she gave you a bridge in the form of those letters she wrote to you—a letter you won't even open. I'm not sure that there is a gap so much as not a need. You like being an island, pretending that you are better than everyone else."

"I'm not better than everyone else," she said. She knew that more than most. And an island? Not even close. She had so many anchors holding her in place that she never took a move on her own. She thought every day of what her mom would think of her. She worried about Cici and Iona and whether she saw Garrett again or not—she knew she'd be worried sick about him every day.

But to live with it. To wake in the morning and see his smiling chocolate-brown eyes and then have him go off to a job where he risked his life.

Well, hell, that wasn't for her. She was the needy one. She needed the security of a man who she could believe would be there. Not a man like her father, who was always jetting off to another work location. She wanted someone who would be home when she got home.

219

She wanted that man to be Garrett. But he didn't want to walk away from the life he'd built for himself. From the man he always believed himself to be. And what did it say about her that she wanted him to change?

Damn that Paco.

If he'd never shot Garrett that night she'd never have met him. Then her life would have continued to bump along and she wouldn't have this feeling inside like she was dying.

"No, you're not better than everyone else, neither am I. Hayley, we're both just human. Two people who found something in each other that they've never found with anyone else. I think that's worth risk. I want you to take it with me." He held his hand out to her and she wanted to take it. Didn't understand why she couldn't just reach out and take his hand. Say yes, she'd do whatever he wanted. But she couldn't. She put her hands behind her back to ensure she didn't.

His face tightened and he dropped his hand. She had never felt so alone before. Not even when her mom had died. Because she'd always hoped she'd find someone to share her life with. Always believed she'd blossom into the woman she always wanted to be.

Until this moment it had been a possibility, but she didn't believe it anymore.

"I can't not go back to being a cop," he said. "I have to prove to myself that I'm still the man I always was. This leg of mine isn't something that I'm willing to let dictate the rest of my life. That punk that shot me—"

"What if another punk shoots you, Garrett? What then? How is that going to prove you're still the man you think you are?"

"I have to do it," he said. "I'm not quitting my job because you're afraid. I have to prove to myself that I can."

"I guess that's your choice. Goodbye then."

He pivoted and she saw his knee buckle, but he caught his balance and walked away from her. He picked up his bomber jacket, put it on, and strode out the door without looking back.

The closing of her front door had a finality to it that suited what she felt in her soul. She'd made her choice, but really there had been no options. She'd been honest with him and with herself. She wasn't the kind of woman who could live with the fear of losing the one man she'd loved.

She went and locked the door and then turned and sank down on the floor, pulled her legs to her chest, and put her head on them. She didn't cry. She felt numb.

Numb.

It had been so long since she'd experienced the myriad emotions that being with Garrett had stirred in her and she hoped she never experienced them again.

She'd been so anxious to shed her cocoon and get out in the real world, but she hadn't realized it would hurt this much. That caring was a double-edged sword.

She lifted her head as Sandy trotted over to her and licked her on the arm. She petted the small dog and then got to her feet. Her eyes found the envelope from her mom and she reached for it. She had to read it.

Hiding away all these years hadn't helped her at all. Instead it had made her feel like she was behind the bell curve and not at all ready for life or love.

Chapter 22

Candles glittered on every surface and she sank deeper into the bathtub. Her little dog sat on a pillow in the corner of the room and Ed Sheeran was singing about lying lovers. She adjusted the bath pillow behind her head and sank lower in the tub.

Every time she risked her heart, this was what happened. She ended up alone. She wondered if it was because she tried too hard. She wanted it too much.

She knew she wanted a family to replace the one in her imagination. The one that wasn't real. So she believed men when they told her pretty lies.

Except she had to admit that Garrett had never really lied to her. He'd told her the truth from the beginning.

He hadn't made any promises and she knew that. She wanted to have that bad-girl affair, force her life out of the rut she'd been in for too long and she'd had it.

She learned stuff about herself that if she were being totally honest she almost wished she hadn't. She didn't want to know that she wasn't as happy being independent as she'd always believed.

She hated to admit that she missed him. That even though she knew their break-up was for the best, she wished he'd walk through that door and scoop her up out of the tub...but he couldn't. His leg wouldn't allow it.

And that small weakness for him was at the heart of all of his discontentment. She knew that. She also acknowledged that he'd lashed out at her simply because she was a convenient target.

But she didn't want to be. Love in her mind wasn't about abusing the person who was closest. Love should be about support and taking care of each other. Something that Garrett would never allow her to do.

It didn't matter what actions she took, he had yet to forgive himself for being human.

He had seen himself as morally superior. The kind of man who made the right choices. She knew that from their talk in the park. He had always been a good guy and a sexy man.

Sex.

She knew her attraction to him had made it that much easier to fall for him. She'd never met a man before who'd been so obsessed with her body. She glanced down at her figure underneath the thin veil of bubbles. This average body had been his playground.

He'd made her feel so alive, so full of feminine power and she missed that.

She felt the burn of tears in her eyes and then the warmth as one rolled down her cheek. She didn't want to be crying alone in her tub. She was a woman of action, except at this moment she wasn't.

She couldn't do anything other than sit here and miss him. This was what she hadn't counted on. Because the euphoria of falling in love with Garrett had made her ignore the truth of the two of them.

They were very different people and it had seemed for a very short time that those differences would make them a stronger couple, but she had to acknowledge now that she'd been wrong.

Big mistake.

She'd had no idea she could hurt like this. She reached for the letter she'd brought in with her. The one from her mom, which had been taunting her as it sat unread on different tables in her house.

She hadn't wanted to be reminded of the past and the dreams her mom had for her that Hayley knew she'd never be able to live up to. But tonight, feeling very low and knowing that she never wanted to be in this place emotionally again she opened it.

Her mom had always opened envelopes delicately, a skill Hayley had never mastered. So the paper flap was ragged as she pulled out the letter. It was scented with Chanel, which had been her mom's signature fragrance and for a moment she tipped her head back and let the scent wash over her.

Felt her mom's arms around her in a hug that Hayley admitted she desperately needed. She wanted someone who would tell her everything would be okay. But her dad wouldn't ever do that, her mom was gone, and she and Garrett had torn the bond between them to pieces. There was no one.

She shook her head, trying to dispel the depressing thought that it might be her and Sandy for the rest of her life.

She unfolded the monogrammed stationery sheet and saw her mother's pretty cursive handwriting through the haze of tears. She wiped her eyes with the back of her hand and focused on the paper.

Dear Hayley;

Thirty! Oh, my. When I turned thirty you were nine, nearly ten, and so full of yourself. I knew then that your spirit was always going to be fierce and it scared me. I never knew how to relate to you.

I hope that your life is truly on a great path. This is hard for me. I want so much for you. And I know that in the last few years we haven't exactly seen eye to eye and remembering you as you were when I was thirty has reminded me that I thought you could rule the world.

I bet that's what you are doing. I hope you owned your twen-ties and know that you are going to continue to grow in beauty and strength.

Remember, whenever you need me I'm here. Maybe just in spirit,

but I will always be watching over you.
  Love,
  Mom

Hayley closed her eyes, felt that hug she desperately wanted, and then folded over the page. Her mom hadn't told her anything that Hayley hadn't already felt, but for some reason she felt acceptance from her mother.

The thing she'd never really felt before this moment.

She put the letter on the side of the tub and got out. She toweled herself dry before putting on her robe and walking into the bedroom.

She was fierce. Something she'd forgotten.

She didn't give up and walk away.

So did she want Garrett? Was he a man she was willing to fight for?

***

Hayley went on with her life. February came and went and she pretended she didn't miss Garrett, but the truth was she thought of him each morning when she got up at four-thirty.

Sandy sometimes ran over to Garrett's fence when she went outside like she was asking for him. Hayley ignored the little dog and went back inside the house. When it snowed she remembered him and the fight they'd had in her back yard and how she hadn't had that much fun in the longest time.

When she walked past the Kalatkises' grocery shop she remembered how they'd both helped them after the break-in. The shop had reopened and was doing a great business. But Hayley couldn't bring herself to go in there. She was afraid they might ask about her and Garrett and, really, what could she say?

Cici was acting odd too. Avoiding her and Iona, but this morning they had a meeting to discuss the financials from

Valentine's Day and there would be no dodging them then.

Actually she hoped that Cici had a fun secret or maybe something new in her life. Anything that would distract Hayley from the few glimpses she'd caught of Garrett as he'd gone on with his life.

Hell, it was only fair that he do that, she'd done it, hadn't she?

Well, she'd gone back to her old way of living.

And she existed.

If falling in love had been unexpected, falling out of love was hard.

She kept reminding herself that she wasn't sure she'd fallen for him, but her heart was convinced otherwise. And to be honest, her head was starting to agree. She'd spent the entire previous evening, which she'd had off, sitting in her front room looking out at the street through a crack in her wooden blinds—watching for Garrett.

She'd drunk in the look of him as he'd walked up the street with his bomber jacket on and the collar turned up against the cold. If he'd hesitated in front of her brownstone or even looked her way, she would have gone to him, but he hadn't.

He walked straight past.

Like they were nothing.

Strangers.

And she guessed that was only right. They were strangers now. She knew it; she just didn't want to believe it. Maybe she would be able to soon.

She sat at one of the tables upstairs in the classroom area, waiting for Iona and Cici. It had been awkward to see Garrett's brother Pete and his fiancée on Valentine's Day, but they both had been friendly and hadn't really talked to her that much.

Which had been fine with her.

She wondered if Pete even knew that they'd broken up?

Garrett wasn't really someone to talk about his relationships. She'd learned that much during their time together. And he seemed closer to his cop buddies and Hoop than to his family.

"Hey, girl. I'm surprised you're here early," Iona said as she came in. She had dyed the ends of her jet-black hair bright scarlet for Valentine's Day and decided she'd keep it for now. It was exotic and daring, just like Iona.

"I came in to try out some new flavors," she admitted. She was tired of making her Garrett-inspired truffle, but hadn't been inspired lately.

"Anything?"

"Not really."

"What's up with you?" Iona asked. "Something hasn't been right for a while. What's going on?"

She took a deep breath. What was she going to say? She'd had one other relationship that had sort of come close to heartbreak and that had been more disappointment in herself. And even then, she hadn't been able to talk about it. She hated it when she failed at anything.

"I'm not seeing Garrett anymore."

"Why not?"

"It's complicated."

"Men always are. Does it have anything to do with the night you were mugged? You've been off since then. Laura said Garrett was the hero that night. He took out the mugger—"

"Yeah, he was great. That's not the problem. Do you know that he rushed him unarmed? We didn't have that much money. We should have just given him the money," she said. She was still mad about that. If that stupid punk hadn't come along and tried to mug her she might still be with Garrett.

"So it was something that happened that night, but not the mugging," Iona said. "Want to talk about it?"

Hayley put her head on the table. "No. Yes. Hell, I don't know."

"That means yes. I'm going to go and get us both a hot chocolate and then you are going to spill all."

Hayley looked up at her friend.

"Iona, I'm afraid to love him. I told him if he went back to being a cop I wouldn't be with him."

"You didn't."

"Yes. I did. I've already lost my mom, I can't...I know it's selfish, isn't it? But I can't change the way I feel."

Iona wrinkled her nose. "We can figure this out if you want him back."

"Even if I did, I doubt he'd take me back. How could I prove that I'd changed my mind? Ugh. I haven't changed it at all. I don't want to spend every hour he's at work worrying about him."

Iona leaned her hip against the table next to Hayley and crossed her arms over her chest. "Are you really not worrying about him now?"

Oh, hell no. Really? She was scared each time he left for work. She had no idea if he was back on the streets working a case or still in the basement. She watched or listened for him every night because she wanted to be sure he made it home.

She wasn't getting over him. She was falling deeper for him and he was gone. *Gone.*

***

Garrett knew there was no real reason for him to walk up Fifth and past The Candied Apple, yet he did it every evening when he got off work. He got off the subway two stops early just to indulge in this pointless effort.

He rarely caught a glimpse of Hayley. She was in the back making candy or possibly upstairs teaching one of the candy classes. He should sign up for one.

Fuck.

No, he shouldn't sign up for one. He wasn't into self-harm. So why did he insist on torturing himself by doing this?

Because just seeing her shop and knowing that she was in there made him feel good. The same way he sometimes went out into his backyard when he heard Sandy barking—just to hear Hayley's voice as she called the dog back inside.

It was a sickness—this obsession with a woman who couldn't, and wouldn't, love him as he was.

His knee still wasn't at one hundred percent, but it was much better than it had been the night when everything had gone to shit. He had a brace he wore now and he felt stable with his leg. He'd even been given a new partner and was due to start a new case tomorrow.

The same drug area that Paco had been working. There was a new dealer in the area and they were going after him. In a way he was frustrated that so much had changed, but in that area crime hadn't. He was determined this time to get not just the street dealer but the supplier and take care of it once and for all.

Maybe then...

What?

He'd retire? He knew he wouldn't. He was never going to walk away from being a detective on the force. He couldn't. He'd thought about it for a while. That night he'd walked out of Hayley's brownstone it had been the only thing he could think of, but once he'd woken up, he knew he wouldn't be able to live with himself if he quit because she was afraid.

That wasn't a good reason to change his life.

He'd gone to see Hector's wife, Paloma, and their sons. Spent the afternoon talking with them and remembering why being a cop was important. Not just to him but to Hector and to his boys. He was Uncle Gar to them and they looked up to him. Garrett knew he owed it to himself and to Hector's memory to make sure that his friend and partner didn't die in vain.

He couldn't do that working cold cases. No matter what Hayley thought. And he wondered how she'd feel if he asked her to stop working at her shop. But that wasn't a valid argument. He understood her fear.

He had it himself as the day got closer that he'd be back on the streets. Thanks to the mugging he knew he wouldn't freeze when someone turned a gun on him. But he still wasn't sure if he could take a shot. How would he feel with a weapon in his hands?

"Garrett?"

He glanced up to see Iona Summerlin, Hayley's business partner, standing in front of The Candied Apple.

"Hi, Iona."

"So, how's it going? Are you here to see Hayley?" Iona asked. She had a digital SLR camera in her hand and slipped the camera strap over her neck as she walked toward him.

A cloud of her expensive perfume enveloped him and he was struck again by how different she was from Hayley. Hayley smelled like home. A home he'd never had before and wondered if he'd ever find again without her.

"No, I'm not. Just walking home," he said.

"This is a little out of the way, isn't it? I thought you said you worked in lower Manhattan."

He shrugged. He didn't have to explain himself to her.

"I do. What are you doing?"

"Working on some marketing. Now that I've gotten Hayley to sign off on the new store I want to see what elements should go with us."

"That's a good idea."

"Thanks," she said, with a grin. "That's why I get the big bucks."

Iona was a beautiful woman but friendly and open. He couldn't help but wonder if it would have been easier if he'd fallen for someone like her. But he hadn't. He wouldn't have. He didn't want expensive perfume or a woman he could read easily. He liked the mystery of Hayley. The challenge of her.

He liked her.

He wanted her back, but had no ideas on how to get her back because he'd have to give up the very core of himself in order to do it.

"Well, good luck with your new venture," he said. He shouldn't be hanging around outside her place in case Hayley came out.

He glanced at the shop.

"She's not here."

"She's not?" he asked. "Where is she?"

"California. She's gone out there to oversee the development of a new specialty line of desserts for Dunham Dinners," Iona said.

Something with her dad. That was good. She needed to do that. He missed her now that he knew she was gone. "Is someone keeping Sandy?"

"I can't help but wonder why you care?" Iona asked. "You did walk out, right?"

Yes, he did. "She pushed me out, there's a difference but you're right, why does it matter?"

He started to walk away.

"I think it would matter a lot if you loved her."

Bull's eye.

"You'd be right," he said over his shoulder and kept walking. He had to figure out what he wanted. He knew it involved Hayley, but she couldn't push him into leaving his career. There had to be a way around the boulder she'd put in their path.

He'd been hiding out for a while now, seeming to forget that he didn't back down easily.

He wanted her. He was going to get her back. And she was going to like it. He'd make sure of it.

Chapter 23

Traveling with her father on Dunham Dinners' private jet on her way back to New York was enjoyable. They'd left Los Angeles at five in the morning and she should be back home by early evening. She was tired from the long days they'd spent in the test kitchens coming up with desserts that could be prepared, frozen, and then cooked at home and still taste good.

"All these years I had no idea you could cook," Hayley said.

"There's a lot you don't know about me, kiddo. You see me as your dad not as a person," he said.

She imagined they were all like that. The letter from her mom had reminded her that there had been more to her life than being a mom.

"I know you're more than my father," she said.

"Good. After your mom died, I felt...empty and working long hours was the only way I could get to sleep at night. Our bed felt too big. The house didn't seem right without her. You were in college and there I was all alone."

She'd never thought of how it had been for him after her mom died. "I'm sorry, Dad. I never noticed how hard it was for you. I thought you were happy to be back to work."

"I thought that's what you wanted me to be. But those years before your mom died and I worked shorter hours changed me.

Almost as much as losing your mom. I think I fell in love with her again then."

She crossed her legs and undid the seat belt as the G6 reached its cruising altitude. They didn't use a flight attendant when it was just her and her dad, so the only other people on the plane were the pilot and co-pilot up front.

"Did you? What made you fall in love with Mom?" Hayley asked.

She knew she loved Garrett. Could feel it in the way she missed him and how, no matter what she was doing, she would see his face all around her.

"Good question," he said with a wink. "I'm not really sure I can define it. Your mom had great legs."

"Yes, she did. She was a beauty queen at your college, right?" she asked.

She'd never felt like talking about her mom. Well, to be honest, she'd never thought her father would want to talk, but she knew now that he did. The both of them had been hiding away in their grief. And she was sad she hadn't thought to do this before then.

She hadn't realized how much of her life she'd shut off when she'd decided to go it alone.

Garrett had been right, she thought. Her father told the story of her mom winning his fraternity's bikini contest, but all Hayley heard was the tone of his voice. How she could tell from the way he was talking about her mom that she had made him happy.

Did she do that for Garrett? Did she sound like this when she talked about him?

"Dad, did Mom ever ask you to stop traveling so much for work?"

"She didn't like it, that's for sure, but there was no choice. As you know, I was the only Dunham left and I didn't want to see the company die out. And it's all I know. I don't think I'd take too well to working for someone else, so I had to keep doing it."

"Do you wish I'd followed you into the business?" she asked.

"Some days, but it's different now. We have our shareholders and one day you will take my place on the board or you'll decide to sell out the shares," he said. "It will be your choice."

"Why didn't you do that?"

"Because when you're young, you make choices based on what you want the future to be. When you get old like me you start realizing that all those plans you made weren't set in stone."

"Like Mom dying."

"Just like that. I was working hard for our future and yours, but you have your own shop – your own dream – and she's not with me. So who knows? Why are you asking me all these questions?"

She took a deep breath. "There's a guy."

"Okay. Is he serious?"

"Yes. Or rather he was. Dad, he's a cop," she said.

"So, what's the problem?" he asked.

She told him everything from the beginning—how she'd wanted to change who she was and how Garrett had helped her to realize that she was comfortable in her own skin. As she talked she realized that she couldn't keep asking him to change, not when she wouldn't.

"I asked him to quit his job. That mugger scared me, but what scared me more was that I realized how much I loved him and how easily it could be taken away."

Her dad turned his big, padded leather chair toward her and leaned to put his hands on her chair. "You can't keep him alive, Hayley. Nothing you do is going to guarantee that. Your mom was a housewife and she died. We can't control the fates of people we love."

"You're right. Daddy, I know this with my head. But my heart wants to do everything to keep him safe. Why wouldn't he just give that mugger the money?"

"It sounds like that's not the man he is. And if I know you once you get past this confusion you'll admit you wouldn't want him any other way."

"You're probably right. I can't make myself fall out of love with him."

"I'm not surprised," her father said. "I've been trying to do that for the last twelve years with your mom and it hasn't worked yet."

"Knowing what you do about how your relationship would end, do you wish you'd never fallen in love with her?" she asked.

It was the question that kind of played at the back of her mind.

"No. Not at all. I wouldn't trade the years we had together or you for anything. What's that saying 'better to have loved and lost'...?"

"Well I'm losing right now, Dad, and it doesn't feel so great."

"That's because you've got your mom's stubbornness. Go to him, tell him you want him back, then you'll see what I mean."

She thought about her father's words for the rest of the flight and when they landed in New York she made up her mind. First thing tomorrow she was going to find Garrett and talk to him. Tell him that she loved him. All of him, even his dangerous job, and she wanted him by her side.

***

Taco night with his family and he didn't want to go. He remembered the last time he'd come. He'd brought Hayley with him. It had felt right to him and he hadn't thought too much about it, but he'd felt like they fit in together with his family.

He'd liked it.

He got off the train and stopped at the corner shop to buy flowers for his mom and then continued walking to his parents' house. His new partner was good. And he was settling into his job, enjoying the investigation, but the more he thought about it the more he realized that the job couldn't compete with Hayley.

It had been over a week since he'd run into Iona outside of The Candied Apple. He had no idea if Hayley was back from California or not, but given that he hadn't heard Sandy in the back yard he thought she must still be on the West Coast.

He missed her.

It was silly because he didn't have to miss her. If he wasn't so stubborn, maybe. But he knew she'd been wrong too. He couldn't just quit his job. He didn't want to. And being on the force and working anywhere else...well that didn't suit him.

He let himself into the house and heard the sound of Santana playing. His mom loved the guitarist and always had one of his albums playing on the speakers in the kitchen on taco night.

He walked in and saw Crystal and his mom cutting up vegetables. He kissed his mom on the cheek and handed her the flowers. "I'll do the olives while you put those in water."

"I've got the olives. Go help Pete with the two-beer margaritas," his mom said. "Where is Hayley?"

"She's not with me."

"I can see that," Mom said. "Is she working tonight or not with you anymore?"

"Anymore," he said.

"Do you want to talk about it?" his mom asked.

Crystal put her knife down. "I'll leave you two alone."

"Don't, Crystal. I don't really want to talk about it, Mom," Garrett said. "I'll go help Pete with the drinks."

"Okay, but if you change your mind, I'm here," she said.

He noticed that she'd put her own knife down and had taken a half step toward him. She wanted to hug him like she had when he was little. He knew. So he went over and hugged her. "I know you're here, Mom. Thank you for that."

He walked out of the kitchen before he started spilling his guts like a prissy girl. Part of him said that maybe his mom would have an idea of what he should do. She was a girl, after all, but another part of him knew that once he started talking to her she wouldn't back down. And this felt like something he needed to figure out for himself.

"So you broke up with Hayley?" Pete asked as he entered the passageway between the kitchen and dining room. They had a dry bar there with two electrical outlets for a blender and mini fridge.

"Yeah, you were eavesdropping?"

"Yup," Pete said not ashamed at all. "I thought something was up on Valentine's Day when Crystal and I were at The Candied Apple. Hayley wasn't cold, but she wasn't chatty with us either."

"How'd she look?" Garrett asked, before he could think better of it.

"Truth?"

"Yeah."

"She looked tired. She smiled, but it seemed forced when she did it," Pete said.

Garrett opened two cans of limeade and dumped them into the pitcher while his brother poured in two Dos Equis. Garrett reached for the tequila and two shot glasses. He poured one for Pete and one for himself.

He lifted his glass toward his brother and downed it in one swallow. Pete did the same. Then Garrett filled the limeade container with the tequila and poured it into the cocktail pitcher.

"So what happened?" Pete asked as he poured them both another shot. "Let's go into the living room."

He followed his brother down the hall with his shot glass in one hand and the bottle of tequila in the other.

"I don't know," he said, honestly. "I mean I know what happened, but I've replayed it in my head a million times and can't figure out where I went wrong.

"Tell me about it. I'm older and wiser," Pete said with a grin.

"The wiser part is debatable. But you do seem to have figured out women."

"Ha, that's what you think. I'm always one step away from screwing up everything," Pete said.

"Really? How do you not screw up?"

"I remember that Crystal's more important than all the other shit. I mean I don't let her walk all over me, but she's important. I love her. Tell me what happened with Hayley."

Garrett sat down in his dad's recliner and put it back. He rocked back in the chair and looked up at the ceiling. "I faced off against a mugger, got the guy, but she wanted me to let him have the cash and let him go. Can you believe that?"

"Hell yes. Why didn't you?" Pete asked. "If Hayley was with you then you weren't on the clock."

"I'm a cop twenty-four-seven, Pete," Garrett said, regretting talking to his brother about this.

"It's a job," Pete said.

"It's my job. Why are you busting my balls over this? You wouldn't have given some mugger Crystal's purse—and don't even deny it."

Pete shook his head. "I wouldn't have. You're right. Sorry, it's just you're my kid brother and I hate that you put yourself in danger."

"That's what Hayley said. She said it was the job or her," Garrett said. "And I thought the job would be enough, but it's been three weeks, Pete and it's not. I miss her."

"Well, you have always had a chip on your shoulder about being a cop. You act like the rest of us don't get it, and you have something to prove. I'd say that getting shot in the line of duty proved it. But not to you."

Garrett leaned back, thinking on his brother's words as the front door opened and his dad came home. Pete gave him a hard look. "Maybe it's time you grew up for real and understood that."

Pete got up to greet their dad and Garrett did as well. He had already made up his mind to win Hayley back and if that meant finding a different job...well, he'd see about it. But he couldn't just walk away from being a cop for her. He'd always resent her if he did. He had to move on for himself.

By the end of the night he'd had too many margaritas and took a cab back to his street. When he got out of the cab, he knew he wanted Hayley more than he wanted anything else. He waved off his brother and Crystal and walked toward his door until the cab pulled away.

Then because he'd had a lot to drink and it was late at night, he got a really great idea. He'd break into Hayley's house and tell her how much he loved her and needed her.

***

Iona was not a pet person. Her words, not Hayley's, so Cici had volunteered to take Sandy for the week that she was in California. Her apartment was in Queens and Hayley's dad had his car service take her to get her little dog.

She knocked on Cici's door and heard Sandy's barking in response and a moment later her friend answered.

She looked frazzled, skinnier than usual in her tights and tunic sweater. "Hey. I didn't know what time to expect you."

Hayley walked into the apartment and bent to pet Sandy.

"Sorry about that. Hey, are you okay? You keep dashing in and out of the shop, so we haven't had time to chat," Hayley said. But this time she wasn't going to be put off.

"Yeah. I'm fine. Made another bad man decision and now I'm living with the consequences."

"What consequences?" Hayley asked straightening up and staring at her friend.

"I'm pregnant."

"What?" she asked.

Cici just gave her a hard stare.

"Okay, who's the father?"

"A guy I met at home over Valentine's," Cici said. Her family lived in Connecticut, so only a train ride away. "We went to a bar with my family and I ended up in bed with him. The next morning he told me he was engaged to someone in L.A. and just looking for a holiday hook-up," Cici said.

Hayley put her arm around her friend's shoulders. "Why didn't you say anything before this?"

"Um...I was embarrassed. This is a low, even for me," Cici said, "And you had that thing with Garrett."

"I know," Hayley said. "But that doesn't mean I'm not here for you. I'm sorry if I've been all about me."

Cici shook her head. "You weren't. I kept hoping I'd be wrong, but three at-home pregnancy tests and a trip to my gym don't lie."

"No, they don't. What are we going to do?" she asked. "Do you need me to go to your appointments with you? Have you told Iona?"

"I'd love it if you'd go with me to the appointments. I haven't told Io yet. She's been dating that deejay and he's high-profile, so she's busy going to events and all that. I didn't want to interfere."

"Um...we're friends, Cici, we want to know these things. What do you need? Are you okay by yourself?" Hayley asked.

"Yes, I'm fine. I'm sort of glad you broke up with Garrett."

"Why?" Hayley asked. She was hoping to get back together with him. In fact, she'd made up her mind to try to win him back. Try to find a way to live with his job.

"Because his friend Hoop keeps calling me and I'm too embarrassed to call him back. Maybe now that you two aren't dating he'll stop."

"Maybe you should call him back and tell him what happened. If he keeps calling he must like you."

She shrugged and Hayley had the feeling that Cici wasn't going to call Hoop back. She yawned, a little tired from flying all day, but made dinner for her friend and stayed at her place until it was almost ten when she called a cab to take her home.

When the cab pulled up to her brownstone she noticed that Garrett was breaking into her place. She grabbed Sandy under her arm, her carry-on suitcase with her other hand, and paid the driver as she got out.

"Busted!" she yelled.

"Um...what?"

"You're busted, buddy," she said, putting Sandy down and

240

walking up the steps to her front door.

"I am. I was trying to break in because it seemed like a romantic gesture," he said.

He had a loopy smile on his face and she could tell he'd had a little too much to drink.

"Where have you been tonight?" she asked.

"Taco night. Don't you want to hear about my romantic gesture?" he asked.

She reached around him and opened the door. Sandy dashed in, her leash trailing behind her. Hayley put her overnight bag down in the foyer and then turned back to Garrett, who was watching her.

"Tell me about your romantic gesture," she invited.

"Well, I wanted to remind you of the night we met because that's when I think I started to fall in love with you," he said.

She walked into her house and he followed her, closing the door behind them and leaning back against it.

"It does. But how is it romantic?"

"It's romantic because I love you. And I want you back," he said.

"I think that's the booze talking," she said.

"I'm not that drunk. In fact most of my buzz has worn off," he said. He straightened from the door and walked toward her. "I'm not sure I can stop being a cop, but you were right when you said I had to prove something to myself."

"I know. I was wrong to say it was the job or me. I don't know what I'd do if you said I had to give up The Candied Apple," she said. "I've missed you, Garrett."

"I've missed you too. Will you give me one more chance? Give our love another chance?" he asked.

She didn't have to think about it at all.

"Yes," she said. "I was planning to come to your place tomorrow and ask you the same thing. I know it's not going to be easy, but I want to give you a chance. I want to give us a chance."

He pulled her into his arms and lowered his head, kissing her passionately on the lips. She wrapped her arms around him and kissed him back just as deeply.

His romantic gesture showed her how deeply he loved her, recreating the first night they met. She wanted to continue it and pulled him off balance so that they fell toward the floor. As always, Garrett rolled to his side and made sure he landed underneath her.

"How'd that happen?" she asked.

"By design, I imagine," he said. "I was planning to leave you with just a kiss."

"Liar," she said.

"You're right. I want to take you to bed. I've missed having you in my arms."

"Me too."

Epilogue

"Hayley, I'm home," Garrett called as he let himself into his brownstone more than three months later. Finding their footing together as a couple wasn't as hard as either of them had expected.

He'd kept his job on the force working with his new partner Cannon Stiller and he had made an arrest today on the same corner where Hector had been killed. And this time Garrett was pretty sure they'd gotten the head of the drug ring.

"In here," Hayley called back.

Of course she was in the kitchen, since it was taco night, and instead of going to Brooklyn they were having his family, her dad and their friends over. Cici had moved into Hayley's brownstone at Hayley's insistence so she'd be closer to The Candied Apple and also so that they'd be closer to her.

She was sort of on her own with the pregnancy thing. Cici was still keeping mum about her pregnancy, something that Hayley had explained to him but that he still didn't understand completely. Finally Hayley had looked at him and said it was a female thing.

The second candy shop had opened and in a stroke of genius marketing Iona had suggested calling it Apples & Oranges, since the new store was featuring not only Hayley's signature truffles but also some baked goods now. The women had hired a renowned pastry chef Henri Charles Vernoux.

"Hello, gorgeous," he said, coming into the kitchen and kissing her. The best part of his day was knowing he'd come home to Hayley.

"Hey, handsome. Did you get your bad guy today?" she asked.

He bent to pet Sandy, who was standing on her back legs and looking up at him expectantly.

Hayley asked him that every day. They'd talked about how he'd needed to go back and finish the job that he and Hector had started. To catch the drug lord who'd ordered the hit on them and killed his partner. He knew Hayley was hoping that once he did that he'd find some peace about what had happened. But he'd done that when she'd moved in with him. That night had changed so much in his life and he'd thought it was the end of his future, but instead it was just the beginning.

"We did," he said. "You should see the news of the arrest announced later tonight. The DA is pulling together all the evidence to bring charges against him."

"That's great news," she said as she finished chopping up the tomatoes and turned to him.

Her hair was still in that short pixie cut and she had on a mini-skirt that ended at the top of her thighs and showed off her legs. He came back over to her, wrapping his arms around her from behind.

"How long until everyone gets here?"

"Not long enough," she admitted.

He hugged her close and realized that he was happier now than he'd ever been in his life, looking straight ahead he saw her slate chalkboard and today's message.

Live the life you love.

He was doing exactly that—with the woman he loved.